THE MEN DO NOT EAT
WINGS

THE MEN DO NOT EAT WINGS

A Novel

S. W. OMAMO

Richardson-Omamo Books

Manufactured in the Republic of Kenya
First Edition Published in June 2004
Second Edition Published in July 2023

New Growth International, Ltd.
P. O. Box 48044, Nairobi, Kenya

Second Edition: July 2023
10 9 8 7 6 5 4 3 2

For the men in my life

In memory of three of them:
Friends, Ken Abura and Peter Mboya
My father, Dr. William Odongo Omamo

There are so many of us – so many lives that come and go without being told, without being recorded. We know so few of our own stories. I don't mean the big stories told about us every day on the BBC World Service for Africa. I mean the small ones... like mine.

I

WAITING AND WAILING

"Is that it?" asked the younger man.

It had to come to this – the story. It was quite a simple story, actually. But it was also a very old one, its grip gnarly and layered – layered with generations of people. So the story was always reproducing itself. Always renewing itself. Staying alive. Continuing to breathe. But occasionally, someone living inside the story would see the whole thing. And that person would try to cut some branches off the old story, allowing new shoots to emerge and grow. And so it came to this.

"Is that what it means, dad?" continued the younger man.

"No, that isn't," said the young woman. "I mean it is, but then it's more … deeper… I think."

"Is that it dad?" asked the younger man again, ignoring his sister. "Dad? Are you still there?"

"I am here," replied the older man, their father. "I need to use the WC. You two carry on. I am coming."

Have faith in God but trust only yourself. The Old Man used to say this to him a lot. There were people around the Old Man all the time. Looking after him. Protecting him. Making money for him. But not one of them did he trust. Not one.

"I should have done the same. I should have listened!" he hissed, slapping his palm against his thigh. "I should have listened!"

He had climbed out of many ditches in his time. But this one... this one was deep and dark. There was shit everywhere. And blood.

"If there is a way out, I cannot see it. Dear God, help me see it. Help me find it."

It reminded him of the time Agnes caught him with that woman who was doing that thing to him. He was moaning like a donkey. He never understood how he got himself into that one. But even that did not end the marriage. Agnes. That woman had been full of problems from the very beginning. She thought she could manage without him. But of course she couldn't. Otherwise she would have left altogether. But she was still there. They just never saw each other anymore. Even when Lorraine died, they managed to avoid each other at the funeral.

Oh, Lorraine. She had understood him better than all the rest – her mother, her brothers, her sister. That useless man she had married had killed her – driven her to drink. What do you do when your daughter leaves your home, marries a fool who breaks her heart, and then drinks herself to death, right before your eyes? What do you do?

How the years had passed. So many years. And here he was, still in charge, but alone. Nobody to talk to. No friends. No real ones. Just hangers on. Never seeing the children. Just hearing about the things they were doing, using his name. They had so little common sense. They irritated him.

He was always irritated. He was always tired. But he could not rest. He had to keep moving. He had heard his bones creaking the other day. Not the joints. The bones. And more and more he could feel his liver moving around, expanding and contracting, as if breathing.

He was old.

But he had to keep moving, moving, moving. Always moving. Presenting a moving target.

Something had been bothering him last night. What was it? Oh yes. Security was behaving poorly, as if annoyed about something. Perhaps the constant movement was getting to him.

"I do not like him anymore," he muttered. "He's too slow these days. Probably sleeps too much."

He reached for the phone. Blue button, then star.

"Staff. Prepare a letter for Security... Yes... It does not matter. Maybe Ambassador to Australia or Canada. Consult with Protocol and Doc. No... leave Doc out of this one. I need him for something else. Who is next in line for Security? You should know! I want to talk to Yitzhak right away. Tell him to come this morning. You handle Security with Protocol. Immediately."

Yes, Security had to go immediately. Yitzhak was back from Tel Aviv. He would have some suggestions for a replacement from the group in training. Staff and Protocol were still fine... for a while. They were fighting each other again. Useful for now. But these characters, all of them were so pathetic. He could see that they thought he was past it. They thought they knew more than he did about things. But had they ever stood before even one crowd and asked for a vote? Had they? Bloody idiots! The people believed in him, not them. He had been doing this for fifty years. Fifty years! Only Doc got it... this business. But he was a hard one to understand, that one. Ungrateful. Knew he was needed, especially now... after... that thing. Bloody, bloody hell! How did he get himself into that one? Bloody hell!

His back was getting stiff. He stood up and walked to the window that faced the back lawn, where official luncheons were held during the dry months. He looked up at the calendar. He could never remember the day or date anymore without calendars, so they were all over State House. Friday. February 12, 1999. The rains had come early in parts of the country, but Nairobi was still dry, the skies clear. He took out his reading glasses, put them on, and glanced down at his watch. 0624. He had been up since 0400. As usual. He liked the look of the grounds this early in the morning. In the orange dawn light, the gigantic trees planted in the 1960s by the Old Man made long shadows on the dew-covered grass. He stood like that for many minutes, watching the shadows shorten, the orange fade. The sun rises quickly in Nairobi.

Doc was waiting outside. He had been there since 0530. He had come for an answer.

The President was stalling, trying to buy some time. This was the third time. The other two had been easier. They had ended things. This one felt like the start of something that would not be easy to control.

"OK," he said to himself. "It has to be." Yellow button, then star.

"Tell Dr. Siromene to come in."

He walked over to the new painting and chuckled to himself. The Norwegian Ambassador had liked it.

"That is an interesting red, Your Excellency," the Ambassador had intoned. "I have never seen one quite like it before. Very... em... deep."

"Yes, it is a special blend. If you come back in a few months, you will see that it is even deeper," the President had replied, allowing himself to look pleased.

"I am a painter myself... amateur, of course... in my free time.

I would very much like to buy some of that red. Where might I find it?"

"Unfortunately, the artist tells me that it is not readily available. But if I hear of some, I will let you know."

"Thank you very much, Your Excellency. I would appreciate that. It is quite extraordinary."

What a moron. If only he knew.

He walked across the room to his desk and sat down behind it.

Dr. Siromene knocked once and entered. Unlike the others, he never waited to be called in.

"Good morning, sir," said Dr. Alfred Siromene, stopping his advance at the edge of the long, plush rectangular Afghan that dominated the President's private study. The desk stood at the other end of the carpet. The President nodded his greeting and motioned toward the sofa immediately in front of the desk. Siromene advanced further, sat down, and waited, watching the man whose towering height, awkward gait, beady eyes, and graying close-cropped hair atop a small head had earned him "The Stork" as a nickname.

The Stork did not move. Siromene waited. They seldom spoke directly to each other. Staff and Protocol were the usual conduits. Only at times like this was direct communication necessary. There had to be no misunderstanding.

Dr. Alfred Siromene, fifty-seven years of age, six feet four inches tall, one-hundred-and-six kilos in weight. Long but proportional. A regular exerciser. Well-kept. Well-dressed. The only person in State House whose height approached the Stork's. Official salaried position: State House Physician. Unofficial position: special advisor to the President on domestic, regional, and international affairs, concentrating on large-scale business ventures. Immediate goal: enormous wealth. Long-term ambition: the Presidency.

Siromene had stopped thinking of himself as principally a medical doctor on the day in 1984 when he and other members of the

Kenya Ear, Nose, and Throat Association went to State House seeking seed money to launch a flying doctors service. They had found the President in an agitated mood. Students at the University of Nairobi had gone on the rampage the night before in protest over rotten food in the cafeteria. They had stoned shop windows and cars on Koinange Street and University Way. It was the third such outburst that year. The President wanted the General Service Unit to use more force this time. But key figures in the Cabinet were urging restraint, arguing that the students should be treated like adults and allowed to voice their grievances in peace.

While clearly preoccupied with other matters, the President had been impressed with the ENT Association's presentation and pledged five hundred thousand shillings from his office – half the amount they needed. The meeting ended abruptly with the news that the students were on the loose again. A large group was heading up University Way toward State House, apparently planning to seek audience with the Stork.

"These students!" the President had cried out, slamming his hand on the table in exasperation. "They are trying my patience!" He had dismissed the doctors hurriedly and risen to leave. During the meeting, Siromene had positioned himself as near as he could to the President, waiting for an opportunity to single himself out. Sensing his chance, Siromene had sidled up beside the departing President, just close enough to be heard mumbling under his breath, "These Kikuyus and Luos with sons and daughters at the university are just confusing the issue."

That was all it took.

The President whirled around and stared at Siromene, who had met the gaze straight on. Each saw the same thing in the other's eyes.

History.

Destiny.

"Car!" the President barked at his Chief of Protocol. "Come!" he commanded Siromene.

That was the day the President began to hold meetings – the real ones – in his cars... on the road. "Look," Siromene would say many times in the years to follow. "Who says that policy has to be made sitting down at a table in a building? Roosevelt, Witte, Rosen, Kamura, and Takahira were on a boat in 1905 when they negotiated peace between the Russians and Japanese, and so were Bush and Scowcroft in 1991 when they decided to bomb Iraq."

During that twenty-minute drive around Kileleshwa and Kilimani, the President and Siromene decided not only how to deal with the students that day, but also how to handle the Cabinet from that point forward. The dreaded General Service Unit was ordered to disperse the students immediately, using dogs, teargas, batons, and, if necessary, bullets. For the Cabinet, three changes were signaled. First, the Cabinet would no longer be consulted on security issues; it would be informed after the fact. Second, the delicate but influential political alliance between the large Kikuyu and Luo tribes had to be obliterated once and for all. Simultaneously, minority tribes like theirs had to be united. Third, from that day forward, students who took to the streets were to be referred to as "rioters." The phrase "student demonstration" was to disappear altogether from Government communications.

At the emergency Cabinet meeting called that afternoon to deliberate on the student problem, the President had opened with, "We must not confuse the issue."

History.

Destiny.

"He knows everything," Siromene began when the President had risen from his chair, slowly rounded the table, and sat down in the armchair across the carpet from him.

"Hmm," grunted the President in reply.

"He says he has damaged the system... changed the codes. We can make him talk. But, sir, even if he talks, we cannot afford to let him go. He knows too much. How should we proceed?"

"Hmm."

"Sir?" Siromene wanted him to say it. He waited.

"Do it!" snapped the President. "Finish him. Now leave please."

Siromene left, smarting slightly at the curt dismissal. But he had what he wanted – a direct order from the President to eliminate that stupid Luo farmer. He further consoled himself by focusing on the bigger picture into which this all fit.

History.

Destiny.

The President waited for the door to close behind Siromene before letting his face drop into his hands. How had he let himself get into this one? He stood up and walked over to the painting. At least there would be another one of these soon. Small consolation, but consolation all the same.

Siromene went directly to his secondary office in the basement. His primary office – the one next to Protocol's – would not do for this. He found Geoffrey waiting for him outside his door. He did not know the man's other names. He did not want to know. All he knew was that this Geoffrey fellow never failed to complete a job.

They shook hands quickly. As always, Siromene was surprised by Geoffrey's dazzling smile. The man was unnervingly handsome. He always looked cool and dry, even on the many occasions they had met in sweltering Mombasa. He was very dark, a little over six feet tall, wide-shouldered, narrowwaisted, full-mouthed. But as always, his lively and observant dark brown eyes were not touched by his smile.

"We are to proceed," Siromene informed Geoffrey as they entered the office.

"OK," replied Geoffrey, smiling a little. "The amount will be as usual."

"OK." Two hundred thousand dollars in cash.

"Where is the gentleman?"

"He will be taken to Nakuru today. The DC has been briefed."

"No. Not Nakuru. Not that DC. He is too eager. Take the gentleman to Londiani. The DO there is better."

Siromene began to protest but stopped himself. He did not care where it happened.

"Fine. He should be there by..." he checked his watch. "He should be there by six this evening."

"OK. I will be finished with him by midnight. I will let you know in the usual way. Please note that that all arrangements must be completed properly. I did not like what happened last time."

Siromene's courier had failed to wear a black shirt as instructed and had been shot dead. No questions asked. The money had therefore not been "delivered." Siromene knew that Geoffrey had taken the money from the dead man. But fearing for his own life, Siromene had made a second payment as demanded.

"Make sure he suffers," said Siromene, looking Geoffrey directly in the eyes for emphasis. "He must feel pain."

"OK."

"Do not forget the spear and flag. Remember also to send text messages to his wife from his phone tonight, tomorrow, and on Sunday. At least seven."

"Yes."

"And be sure to fill the flask and seal it immediately, and then shake it well for thirty seconds. And put the flask into the ice chest right away."

Geoffrey nodded his understanding of this last piece of information and left quickly, leaving his client already beginning to engage with an appointment book.

As Siromene looked over his plans for the day, he saw that he would need to base himself upstairs in his primary office for the rest of the morning. At 0700, he would be with the Coast MPs prior to their 0715 audience with the President. They were driving a hard bargain. They had lost credibility in the eyes of many Kenyans because of the part they played during the last tribal clashes, but in return for what they saw as too few rewards from State House. This time they wanted more up-front. He glanced at his watch. 0640. That gave him about ten minutes for breakfast, if he hurried. He picked up the appointment book and read it on his way to the dining room. The President would probably give the Coast MPs ten of the fifteen minutes allotted to them. So he would have five minutes to make phone calls before the next group – the troublesome Kambas. Those Kambas! If only the Party did not need them so badly. They made a lot of unnecessary and annoying noise in between elections, but, to their credit, they always delivered on election day. OK. Thirty minutes for them. That would take him to 0800. Breakfast – the daily business breakfast hosted by the President, who, as usual, would not eat anything, but just ask questions, listen, and watch. Siromene would be doing the same. Bacon, eggs, toast, and juice loosened tongues and lowered defenses almost as effectively as did beer and whiskey. The day's breakfast guests were members of the moribund Council of Economic Advisors. They wanted to revive it. What made those people think anyone needed them? Should be interesting anyway. Between 0900 and 1200 there would be one after another foreign dignitary, ending with the US Ambassador, who wanted forty-five minutes, fifteen more than usual. That meant it would probably include a personal matter. Probably the teenage son again. Siromene had heard that the boy had been involved in something odd with a beach boy in Malindi over the Christmas holidays. The Nation and Standard were going to publish what they knew, which was not very much, but still enough to embarrass the

Ambassador and the US. The Ambassador wanted the President's help in quashing the story. Why these people brought such tiny matters to the President was beyond him. There was a very simple solution. Find the journalists and pay them to take a holiday somewhere far away. Or, if necessary, use someone like Geoffrey. These Ambassadors sometimes behaved like small children. The afternoon was free. Maybe he'd fly Laura and that other one to Mombasa for a late lunch and massage? What was the other one's name? Doreen? Dorcas? But he had to be back in Nairobi by 1900 for the Rotary Club dinner. He was the guest speaker. A massage would certainly get him in the right frame of the mind to let the Indians and Kikuyus know who was really running the country. But it would be too tight. No. He'd have lunch with Christopher, and then go to Athi River to check on the flower farm. Maybe Christopher would come. The boy was 24 but still drifting. The mother was still pampering him. He would have to find a way to put an end to that. It was very worrying... Anyway, he would have to be through with the Rotary Club by 2100. The consultants from Washington had been in town since Wednesday. They had been calling continuously, begging for a meeting. Their firm was one of the bidders for the contract to restructure Customs and Immigration. Eleven million dollars over 3 years. He had met them in December. Old men, all of them. They'd already given their best years to the US and were now going around Africa collecting huge fees for mediocre work. But he preferred them to the irresponsible young boys and girls the other companies had sent – the ones who saw Kenya as some kind of playground. He would tell them eight percent up-front, or nothing. And then at 2230 he needed to see the Commissioner of Lands to make sure the man acted promptly to finalize procedures for the President's upcoming land reallocations in Mombasa and Nakuru. For Siromene, there would be twenty-five acres of prime land in Nyali. Excellent.

While Siromene was staring into his appointment book plotting his day, Geoffrey was being driven down Dennis Pritt Road in a shiny black Range Rover. He told the driver, Nicholas, to stop at Caledonia shopping center. One of his women lived in a flat behind the petrol station. He always needed sex, a cold shower, and cocaine before a big job. He was back within forty-five minutes.

"To South C. I need BJ, Spike, and Pele," Geoffrey instructed Nicholas as he climbed back into the car. Nicholas could read the signs. The rapid speech. The sniffing. The sunglasses. He was about to be released for the day. Pele would drive the boss wherever he was going.

*   *   *

For Pele, driving the Range Rover was always the highlight of the jobs. The longer the drive, the better. Limuru, Naivasha, Gilgil, and Nakuru flew by in quick order as they headed west out of Nairobi. They would soon be there.

Once, in 1993 or so, they had driven all the way to Goma. What a trip! The shocks had been finished by the time they got back to Nairobi, but it had been worth it. That was the only time they had seen Geoffrey afraid. It was in Uganda, at a checkpoint outside Kinoni, a small town near Mbarara. One of the police officers had stared at Geoffrey for a long time and ordered him out of the car.

"What is your name?" the policeman had asked.

"Geoffrey."

"Do not be stupid to me!" snarled the policeman. "I want to know all of your names!"

"Smalley. Geoffrey Adrian Smalley."

"What is your country of origin?"

"I am a US citizen. Here is my passport."

"I did not ask for your passport. What is your country of origin? Where were you born?"

"I am a US citizen, officer."

"You are a Black American?"

"I am a US citizen, officer."

"So in America there are people who look like Obote, eh? Eh? Why do you resemble our deposed disgraced ex-president Dr. Milton Obote? Why are your eyes like his? Why, Mr. Smalley Geoffrey? Is he your brother? Your cousin? Your father?"

Silence. Beads of sweat forming on Geoffrey's forehead. Widening wet patches under his armpits.

"No answer from you, Smalley Geoffrey? Anyway, no problem. Clinton is our friend, yes?. Ha, ha! You can go."

As Geoffrey climbed back in, Pele, BJ, and Spike looked at each other knowingly. They had long suspected that Geoffrey was Ugandan. But each knew better that to bring it up. When cornered, Geoffrey was vicious and ruthless.

But they were wrong. Geoffrey was as much a Kenyan as were the three of them. He had recognized the policeman right away. Twenty years before, during his years as a member of Idi Amin 's Special Defense Unit, he and the man had come face to face in a banana field, near Bugiri in eastern Uganda. Each had lost contact with his colleagues. Each was wielding a blood-stained machete. But one, Geoffrey, was the hunter, the other the hunted. Geoffrey – at the time he went by the name Mussolini – was disoriented. He had spent only three days in Bugiri, and even then, only in the area immediately surrounding the SDU camp. He was certain he could find his way back to the camp. But at that moment nothing around him looked familiar. His uncertainty must have shown on his face because the man lunged at him. Mussolini jumped to one side, preparing to counter. But the man darted past and into the banana field, already moving at close to full speed. Mussolini did not give chase, deciding instead to try to make his way back to the camp. "If I ever see that man again, I will kill him," he vowed to himself.

Pele, BJ, and Spike did not understand the chuckles that Geoffrey let out periodically during the rest of the trip to Goma. Nor did they understand why, on the return leg, he kept them waiting by the roadside for three hours while he drove into Kinoni on some "personal business." When he returned he had a smile on his face, a cut on his left hand, but not a word for any of them, all the way back to Nairobi.

Limuru, Naivasha, Gilgil, and Nakuru flew by. Rongai. Mau Summit. They pulled into the Londiani District Officer's compound at two o'clock. They had four hours of daylight left to prepare.

* * *

Gilbert Kuria Kimani, the District Officer, Londiani, was fifty-three years old. He would be retired in two years. He had no illusions about life on a civil servant's pension. Poverty. Hell. He had six children, all still in school. He needed money. This was the fourth job he had done with Geoffrey. In the previous three, he had played smaller roles but done well enough to be given a lead supporting position this time. Fifteen thousand dollars. Nine hundred and fifty thousand shillings. Twelve times his net annual salary. It would bring his total earnings from Geoffrey to slightly over two million shillings. Enough to start a business that would educate his children and other dependents, and keep his wife happy.

DO Kimani knew the routine. They needed him plus one more person, bringing the team to six. One person for each limb, one to do the work, and Geoffrey to give the instructions and ask the questions. But first they needed a secluded spot. The fellow was probably going to scream. They usually did. Kimani had the perfect spot. It was an abandoned shed on a former white settler farm. It had been well-built and was still in fairly good condition. It measured about five meters by five meters. He had hammered plywood sheets onto the window frames. There were four kerosene lamps for light. The area surrounding the shed had been gazetted as a forest reserve. There had been little encroachment by squatters. It was very isolated. The Range Rover took one hour to cover the two kilometers from his office to the shed. There was no road to speak of.

"This will do very well," said Geoffrey nodding his head rapidly in approval. "Good. Water?"

"There is one full drum outside, sir. I can bring more."

"No, one is enough. Table and chairs?"

"They are coming, sir."

"How? Who is bringing them?"

"My colleague, sir. No need for worry, sir. He is under my instructions."

"OK. Let us go and eat. We will need energy."

They returned to find the police van bearing Luka Sollo parked outside the DO's office.

Sakawa would later recall that he was irritated when he heard the news. The day had begun well, though. It was a Monday. Monday, February 15, 1999. He and Maaike had made love late into the previous night, yet he had awoken early, and without any of the usual pleasant but impairing side effects. He had caught both the KBC and BBC radio newscasts, taken a quick jog through the neighborhood, and returned to find Maaike in the shower. He had joined her, emerging only when the water began to run cold. Breakfast had been one of soft looks between them and kind words for the children – Malcolm, Jimmy, and Anita. Sakawa had arrived at his office in the Department of Economics at the University of Nairobi in a very good mood. His mid-morning lecture in International Trade had been just right – compact but clear. The students had asked the kinds of piercing questions that showed that he was reaching them, and which, for a moment, helped him forget the steadily sliding working conditions at the university.

But back in his office, Sakawa's mood began to sour at the memory of a recent visit home to see his parents. He had disagreed with his father. Looking back, Sakawa could not put his finger on the exact source of the disagreement. In fact, they had not even raised their voices at one another. But there had been no mistaking the clash of viewpoints. It had begun when he announced that his thirty-seventh birthday was coming up.

"Thirty-seven, eh?" his father had said. It was just the two of them.

They were sitting in the verandah, looking out on the small orange grove. The orange blossoms were in full flush, their sweet smell wafting in on them. "Thirty-seven is a good age. By then, you know which direction your life has taken."

Sakawa was silent, waiting for more. But his father did not continue.

"What do you mean?" asked Sakawa in the end, fighting to keep his voice flat. He hated it when his father left things hanging like that.

"Eh? Oh, I just mean that by thirty-seven, most people have made most of the big choices in their lives. That's all. Don't you agree?"

"I'm not sure," replied Sakawa, still fighting with his voice. "I reckon I still have time to explore."

"OK," said his father, falling silent again, picking up a newspaper he had already read. Ending the conversation.

Sakawa had returned to Nairobi in the sort of huff that usually lasted for several days. This one had been with him on and off for well over a week.

"He thinks I'm moving too slowly," mused Sakawa as he returned his lecture notes to their home folder in the filing cabinet. "He's probably comparing my life with his. But I'm not him. And this isn't 1969. It's 1999. Things are different now." His brooding was interrupted by the sound of the phone ringing.

"Dr. Sollo?"

It was one of the university's switchboard operators.

"Speaking," he answered.

"Hold on for your caller," she said.

"Hello," he said, as the call was put through, "Dr. Saks Sollo here."

"Hello, Sakawa."

It was his mother.

"Hello, Mama. I was not expecting it to be you."

She seldom called in the middle of the day. Something must be wrong, Saks thought to himself. She sounded odd, too. Stuffed up. Maybe she had a cold.

"How are you?" he asked tentatively.

"I am fine," she replied, also rather tentatively, it seemed to him. "Has your sister rung you yet?"

"Maybe she tried. I have been in and out of my office since about nine o'clock. What's wrong? Has something happened to Soru?" Saks asked, beginning to feel hot and sweaty as he did whenever he was nervous.

"No, Soru is fine. I spoke with her earlier. She was going to try to reach you, too." Pause. "Sakawa, I have some sad news for you." His heart lurched. "You must come home today. It is your father. He has been killed."

"What do you mean?! When? How? Was it a car accident? Which one of the drivers was with him?"

It was not possible. How could his father be dead? Killed?!

"I cannot say over the phone. I will explain when you arrive. Organize things with the university and come this evening. Soru will also be flying up."

He remembered thinking that his mother sounded a little too calm, until she said, "Everything will be alright, Sakawa. God is with us."

Unlike his, her faith in God was strongest at the times when His goodness and mercy were least in evidence.

Saks had taken the one-hour flight from Nairobi to Kisumu many times, typically on his way home to Panderi Farm, the family sugar cane estate in Songhor, some fifty kilometers east of Kisumu. He much preferred to travel home by car. Despite the terrible condition of the road and inevitable near misses, the drive was always pleasant and engaging. He especially loved the section beyond Nakuru, where the road heads diagonally across the Rift Valley. Right before it reaches the western escarpment, the road cuts back sharply to the southwest and continues that way up the steep escarpment and on to the high plateau. Midway across the plateau, just past Kericho, it slices back northwest again, down into the Lake Victoria basin, and then northward in the direction of the Nandi Hills, which separate the eastern lip of the Lake basin and the western wall of the Valley. Saks most liked the long climb up to the plateau, the vegetation growing greener and lusher with each passing kilometer, the temperature falling almost as quickly. The first sight of the bright green tea plantations near Kericho seldom failed to soothe him. He always looked forward to the first sighting of the Lake, which on clear days was visible from the western edge of the plateau. Once or twice he had been able to pick out the faint outline of Panderi, near the southern tail of the Nandi Hills. With the rapid descent into the lake basin, the vegetation quickly changed back, becoming sparser and browner again, the temperature rising once more.

But that day he flew. He was in no state of mind to picture the changing landscape below. All he could think about was his father's being dead.

"Dead as a doorknob."

The phrase that kept reverberating uncontrollably in his head.

"Baba is as dead as a doorknob." He could not drive it out.

"That's not a very nice thing to say, Saks," protested his sister, Soru, who was seated next to him.

"I know," he replied. "It just keeps coming. I can't stop it. Sorry."

Their parents' driver, Jairus, was waiting for them at Kisumu Airport. Neither Saks nor Soru said a word during the journey from the airport until they reached the Chemelil roundabout, where Jairus turned southeast in the direction of Muhoroni instead of continuing to the northeast toward Songhor and Panderi.

"Why are you going this way?" Saks asked him sharply.

"We are going to the DO's office," Jairus replied very quietly. Saks had hurt his feelings. But Saks did not care that day.

"Why are we going to see the District Officer?" Soru demanded.

"Mama Madi is waiting for us there," replied Jairus, concentrating on the road ahead.

They left him alone. Jairus was merely following instructions. He was also one of the family employees who knew that if he brought up their late brother's name like he had done in referring to their mother as "Mama Madi," Saks and Soru would leave him alone.

Madiany – or Madi as everyone had called him – was their elder brother. He had died in a car accident almost twenty years before, not too far from Chemelil. Saks was with him when it happened. It was late on a Friday night. They had been out with friends in Kisumu. Instead of taking the safe but badly pot-holed Kibos route –which Saks would have preferred – Madi had insisted that they use the longer, smoother, but much more dangerous road past Ahero and Awasi. Madi drove. As always, he drove much too fast for that road, that late at night. But they almost made it home. Just outside Chemelil, near the railway depot, they were traveling at about eighty kilometers an hour when they slammed into the back of a stationary truck that neither of them saw until the last second. They were both trapped in the car. The truck driver later claimed that he and his assistant had not been there at the time. That the truck had broken down. That they had gone off in search of a repair team. At that hour, there were few other travelers on the road. No other vehicle came along for a long time. Neither Madi nor Saks seemed to be too badly hurt. But in fact Madi was bleeding heavily from his leg. He lived for no more than about thirty minutes after the crash. And he died suddenly. One minute they were talking, encouraging each other to hang on, the next Madi began to shiver violently, then he let out a half-gag, half-snort and fell silent. Saks was alone with him in the car like that for at least another hour.

They heard their mother long before they saw her. She was waiting for them. Waiting and wailing. Sakawa had forgotten the sound of that wail. How awful and heart-wrenching it was. He had last heard it when his mother came to see him in the hospital ward after the accident, and then went to the next building over to view Madi's body in the morgue. It made him cry then, too. He and Soru, who was also sobbing, held hands tightly as they stepped out of the car and approached their mother.

Their mother was standing next to her car, which was parked a few meters from the DO's office. Some of their aunts were with her, also wailing. Silently, grim-faced, off to the side, stood two of their uncles: Boro Tindi, their father's elder brother, the Member of Parliament for Kisumu East, and Mala Okoth, their father's youngest brother, a foreman at Chemelil Sugar Factory. Two other men they did not recognize were also there.

In marked contrast to her calm demeanor on the phone, their mother was simply beside herself with emotion. To her, if you were going to express grief, there was only one way to do it, and that was to wail, to let your feelings show, in detail. So right there, outside the DO's office, standing next to their aunts and uncles, surrounded by what seemed like a battalion of Administration Police officers, through their mother's wails, from her wailing, Saks and Soru began to piece together what had happened to their father.

"Luka, son of Ang'awa, grandson of Osewe, descendant of Silual, my beloved husband, my friend, you left the house last week and never returned! You left, left and never returned! I waited, but you never returned! You sent me many text messages, but when you did not ring me, I knew something was wrong. When you did not ring me, I knew something was wrong. When the DC came to my door this morning, before I had even bathed, I knew you were dead!

When the DC came to my door this morning, I knew you were dead! He brought me here and took me there and I saw what they did to you! I saw, I saw with my own eyes what they did to you! I saw something that I never thought I would see! They wanted to take you away, but I told them not to touch you until your children were here to see what they did to you! Oh, Rhoda Sollo, daughter of Ochoko Nyawere, you know this is God's will, but your heart is breaking!"

Rhoda went on like that for some time. Nobody tried to stop her. It was better that she let it out. But it made Saks and Soru cry even more. The other women joined in, adding their own lamentations to hers. After a while, the uniformed District Officer emerged from his office. He was a young man, thirty-five perhaps, with light skin, shiny hair, and sharp features that told he was from northeastern Kenya. But he was young only in body. His face, eyes, and mannerisms were those of an older man: arrogant, weary, impatient, authoritative. Those of a man who had seen that sort of thing many times before. The women stopped wailing as he approached.

"Sorry, Mama, sorry," he said to Rhoda. "It is a terrible thing. Mr. Sollo was a good man."

And then, with barely a decent pause, he added, "Would you come with me please?"

He had on his respectful face, which helped soften the abruptness of his manner and firmness of his tone. He shook hands with Saks and Soru but without warmth, conveying nothing by way of comfort or understanding. Rhoda did not say anything.

"Where are we going?" Saks asked. "Where are you taking us?"

"To show you where Mr. Sollo was found," replied the DO. "Follow me in your car."

That was a command.

It was silent in Rhoda's car. She sat in the back with Boro and Soru. Saks sat up-front with Mala, who was driving. Boro told the other men to follow in another car. Rhoda asked the other women to return to Panderi to prepare for visitors who were sure to begin arriving soon.

The spot was only two kilometers from the DO's office, but the road was so badly potholed that they took well over thirty minutes to reach it. They found the DO's boss, the District Commissioner, waiting for them, along with several police officers of differing rank. There were also some silent characters from the Central Intelligence Department and the Special Security Unit in the Office of the President. In all, there were about thirty people there, plus two search dogs.

Saks and Soru had arrived at the DO's office a little after six o'clock. It was now past seven and already quite dark. The team of investigators had come prepared with four bright lights which had now been connected, creating a pool of light with darkness gathering just beyond.

"Oh, Luka my friend, what did they do to you?" moaned Rhoda from time to time. It was hard for any of them to imagine what sort of person would do something like that to another human being. Saks noticed that there was no blood anywhere, just body parts. He concluded that the murder had taken place somewhere else.

Or maybe something worse had happened.

When he, Madi, and Soru were children, they liked to help the farmhands slaughter livestock to be eaten by the family and friends. The doomed animal's feet would be tied together, two by two. Its head would be forced down and held there, neck arched back, eyes bulging in terror. Then its throat would be slashed open. Blood would spurt out, sometimes onto the grass, sometimes into a waiting bowl where it would be mixed with bile for blood-meal. All the while, the animal would be shaking uncontrollably. That image – the shaking, shaking, shaking – would not leave Saks's mind as he stood in the artificial light watching the police officers pick up the scattered pieces of his father, and reconstruct him bit by bit in a cheap, dirty, well-used wooden coffin.

What did they want with his blood, he asked himself. Who were these terrible people?

Luka's hands were never found. Had it not been for their search dogs, the police might never have found his smashed-in head either. And it would have rotted out in the open, on its own, not underground with his torso, arms, legs, and feet, which were also severed and found in different parts of the thicket. Brutal killers, these. Brutal but meticulous in a twisted way. Luka's severed parts appeared to have been carefully arranged in a stretched-out, spread-eagled outline of a human body. It took many minutes of heavy sawing and digging before the police were able to remove the jagged-edged spear that had been thrust through Luka's torso, deep into the damp soil. They took that away, too, as evidence, along with the strange red triangular flag tied to its end – no doubt a signal of some kind from the killers, but one that nobody seemed to understand at the time.

"We have arrested the killer, Mrs. Sollo."

Someone was talking to Rhoda. They were back at the DO's office. It was the District Commissioner speaking. The DO, wearing his fawning face, was at his boss's side.

"Mama, we have arrested the killer," the DC repeated to Rhoda, who seemed not to have heard him the first time.

"Who?!" This from Saks. He knew he sounded crazy but did not care enough to try to control it. "Who have you arrested?"

"His name is Semoe Barsone," replied the DC.

"Barsone?" asked Rhoda, clearly surprised. "Barsone the squatter?"

"Yes, that one."

Rhoda shook her head but did not say anything further.

"Why have you arrested him?" This from an agitated Soru. Both she and Saks wanted to pursue this further and were puzzled and irritated by their mother's reaction.

"As I said, we believe he killed Mr. Sollo... your father." Then to Rhoda the DC continued, "As you know, Mr. Barsone was a squatter on your farm. You and Mr. Sollo had asked him to leave severally but he refused. We have received a report that two nights past at a hotel in Muhoroni he said he would kill Mr. Sollo. We believe that he did as he threatened."

Even as Saks and Soru were struggling to absorb this information – their parents had never mentioned this Barsone – Rhoda stood up to leave. "Uncle Boro, Uncle Mala, Sakawa, Soru let us go home please," she said.

"But Mama, the DC is still telling us about this Barsone man," Saks protested.

"Yes, Mama, we really should find out more," agreed Soru.

"We have heard enough," said Rhoda. "Let us go." She took each of her children by the hand and led them firmly away.

Back in the car, Saks and Soru forgot for a moment the horror of their father's butchered corpse, so annoyed were they with their mother. She was treating them like young children.

"Mama, why didn't you let the DC tell us about this Barsone man?" asked Saks, almost shouting. "Don't you think the identity of Baba's killer is important?"

"No," came the response. She seemed to be only half-listening to him.

"Why not?!" stormed Soru.

Rhoda had other priorities.

"Sakawa and Soru, you know better than to raise your voices when speaking to your mother! This is not the time to discuss such things. Let us bury your father first before we talk about people like Barsone. There is too much we need to do."

6

Rhoda was right. They would sleep very little over the next two weeks. Luka was murdered on a Friday. His remains were discovered on a Sunday and identified on a Monday. A weekday funeral was out of the question because it would mean that many relatives and friends living abroad and in distant parts of the country would not be able to attend. The funeral committee chaired by Boro Tindi had initially considered holding the burial on the first Saturday after the murder. But that plan was dropped when it became clear that even five days was too short a period for many key people to be able to rearrange their schedules and attend the funeral. In the end, the committee settled on the following Saturday, two weeks after the murder.

Because of the nature of Luka's death, the press seemed always to be at hand, prying into why someone would want to kill him so gruesomely. But, honoring Rhoda's wishes, nobody in the family would discuss the matter.

Against the wishes of some people on the funeral committee, Rhoda was determined to let mourners view her husband's corpse if they so wished. But she did not think people would be able to stomach the full horror of what had happened to him. He had been severely beaten. Even reassembled, he looked hideous. A specialist mortician was flown in from Ghana to make the remains more presentable.

There was also initial disagreement within the committee over where to bury Luka. Rhoda, Soru, and Saks were for burial at Panderi Farm. But Panderi was not as straightforward a choice as they had hoped it would be. The farm lay outside the region of the country dominated by their tribe, the Luo. It therefore also fell out-side Uhanga, their ancestral home within Luoland. The Sollos were among several thousand families from across Kenya who, beginning in the late 1960s and early 1970s, had acquired farms in portions of the Rift Valley vacated by colonial settlers. But to some of their relatives, Panderi was not their home. Not their real home. That could only be within Luoland. How could a Luo of Sollo's stature be buried away from his ancestral home? What would people say? It was a thorny issue that had torn families apart, ruined lives, wasted hard-won wealth. In the end, the relatives in question dropped the matter, mainly because they lacked the support of Boro Tindi, the most influential male in the clan.

Across the country, friends and relatives had formed other funeral committees that were meeting regularly to raise funds to contribute toward funeral expenses and traveling costs. At Panderi, the Sollos readied themselves to host everyone for at least two nights – the night before the funeral, when the body would be brought in from Kisumu, and the night after the burial, when the family would need support as they came fully to terms with their loss. It was a huge undertaking. Thankfully, Rhoda and Boro agreed on almost everything. There was no war of attrition, no contest of wills, between widow and senior male in-law.

By the day of the funeral, they were all exhausted. When Madi died and similar preparations were being made for his funeral, Soru had said that it was just as well that she did not have time to think too much, for she would have been overcome with sorrow and longing for him. It was the same with her father's funeral. They barely had time to sit down, let alone reflect on the terrible fact that lay behind all the activity.

7

It was a colossal funeral. Luka Sollo had never been very popular among Luos. He had been seen by many as being too chummy, for too long, with a ruling establishment that was widely believed to have been responsible for the deaths of at least three prominent Luo leaders and banished others to the political wilderness for decades. It was said that while he acquired his enormous wealth in the Rift Valley, Luoland had remained impoverished, its huge potential – especially Lake Victoria – largely unexploited. Saks thought they should prepare mainly for relatives and close friends. But his uncle Boro insisted that they prepare for several thousand. He knew that, despite the mixed feelings about Luka, every Luo who could attend would do so.

Luka and Rhoda had put much thought into the location and layout of the Panderi homestead. The house sat about half a kilo-meter in from the Chemelil-Nandi Hills road, atop a hill that in less rugged terrain might have been considered a small mountain. The front of the house – where the large verandah, the living room, the dining room, the kitchen, and two bedrooms were located – faced eastward, to catch the morning light. The rear – where the smaller and more private verandah, two more bedrooms, and gym were placed – faced to the west, to collect the evening breeze that blew in across the Kano plains, having originated in Lake Victoria. The long driveway up the hill ended in a large pentangular lawn, bordered with the obligatory euphorbia hedge, and strategically sprinkled with carefully selected trees and shrubs. Sakawa's little two-room house stood near the gate, opposite the one that had been Madi's, which now served as an office for the farm manager.

Luka had a love affair with plant life. He always had a major gardening and landscaping project underway. No one fully under-stood that part of him. When pressed, Rhoda would put it down to his general optimism about the world – his way of leaving his mark on a place. Much as he would have been pleased to see the huge turnout for his funeral, he would have complained bitterly to see what the mourners did to his beloved plants, which were carelessly picked at, squashed, and trampled upon.

The graveyard lay in a lovely shaded spot to the south of the house. Rhoda took good care of it, always making sure that there were some flowers in bloom. Madi was buried to the left as one walked in. Luka's grave was dug in the center.

The grave diggers had begun their grim task the evening before the funeral. They were led by the old farmhand, Meja ("Major") Ben Omondi. Like many of his contemporaries, Omondi had been thrust into military service by the Colonial Government during the Second World War, in support of British campaigns in Egypt and Ceylon. He seemed to have learned just three English phrases from his army superiors: "Fackinell!" "Fayah! Fayah!" (Fucking hell!" "Fire! Fire!") and "Bladdy full, emi loh!" ("Bloody fool, aim low!"). And he used them as often as he could, especially when he had been drinking and wanted to remind everyone of the British Government's broken promises of support to African war veterans like him. He had gone to Saks the night before and asked for a little money to buy some of the local spirit, "So we can forget what we are doing, fackinell!" he had said in a comical mix of Dholuo and his special brand of English. Deep into the night, he could be heard exhorting his increasingly drunk team to push harder, "Dig, bladdy full! Emi loh! Fackinell!"

The committee had borrowed thousands of chairs and scores of tables and benches from nearby schools and churches. More than a dozen enormous tents had been rented; enough to cover almost the entire front lawn. On the day, it did not rain. It was sunny and hot. All the benches and seats were taken, every shaded spot claimed. Yet most of the mourners were still forced to stand in the sun, well back and outside the compound, following the proceedings through a public address system hired for the occasion.

The coffin was placed on a large table, a little to the left of the entrance to the house. The immediate family – Rhoda, Saks, his wife, Maaike, and their three children, Soru, her husband, Mark, and their two children, Jeremy and Catherine – sat at the front of the gathering, facing the coffin, their right sides to the congregation. Uncles, aunts, cousins, and several older relatives sat nearby, with their backs to the congregation, to the right or left, depending on whether they were related to Luka or to Rhoda.

There was much jockeying among relatives and friends to be included in the list of speakers. Funerals matter in Luoland – where the spiritual and material worlds flow in unison, cheek to cheek, conjoined at the heart. Where grief and grieving are inherently communal and loudly vocalized. Where everybody knows that the dead are living – forever watching you, forever watching over you. Where everybody knows that also everlasting in the collective imagination are the tone and content of the emotions expressed and messages conveyed as the dead are laid to rest. It is rare to see more satisfied looks on the faces of Luo men and women than during and after a skilled funeral address, nor more dissatisfied ones following a poor one.

The funeral event itself is a collective artistic production – a shared performance. The Master of Ceremonies is the Director. The closest and most senior relatives of the deceased are the Producers. The older the deceased, the more people he or she will have touched when alive, and thus the greater the number of potential performers. And even if a mourner does not make a formal tribute, there are opportunities to contribute to the drama from the sidelines, in unscheduled but tacitly encouraged interventions, either spoken or sung. The art lies not so much in what is said but how, and in what order.

High quality art is costly anywhere in the world. Luos pay dearly to produce and consume this form. Even the most impoverished family will spend its last penny to contribute to the collective artistic enterprise. If a funeral is to serve its purpose as a venue for an artistic performance, then the stage must be set, the audience large. And so Luo funerals are expensive. Luka's cost his family between six and seven hundred thousand shillings, and that was only a small fraction of all that was spent collectively by mourners in traveling expenses alone.

The day before the funeral, the Provincial Commissioner – the District Commissioner's boss – had paid the Sollos an unexpected visit at Panderi. It was unexpected because he had already dropped by to offer his personal condolences. His next scheduled visit to Panderi was not until the day of the funeral, which he would attend in his official capacity and deliver the Government's message of condolence. Rhoda, Boro and Mala, Soru, and Saks were in at the time. They all went out into the verandah to receive the important visitor. Once seated and drinking tea, the PC brought up the subject that was on his mind.

"Mama," he said to Rhoda. "The Government feels that you should not let the people see Mr. Sollo's body. It may cause unrest and lead to unnecessary violence at this sad time."

This statement was met with dead silence. Even Mala, who at first had been against a viewing, was appalled. This was the height of bad manners. Luka was not a Government employee. He had not been serving in any official capacity at the time of his death. Why did the Government feel it had any right to intervene in the family's preparations?

After a difficult silence, during which the PC looked very uncomfortable, Rhoda spoke.

"Was there something else you wanted to say to me, Mr. PC?"
Silence.

"In that case, let me just say that the Kenya Government has no right to dictate to me what to do with my husband's dead body. Instead, I believe it is the Government's responsibility to ensure – and my right to insist – that his funeral is peaceful and dignified. In fact, Mr. PC, I will hold you personally responsible for any violence or disruption of any kind that occurs on this compound tomorrow."

With that, she very politely bade the PC farewell and went back into the house, leaving the rest of the group to soothe his wounded pride. He had clearly not expected any resistance. But even he knew she was right. It had been an arrogant and insensitive request. It was indeed his responsibility to maintain the peace and not his place to interfere with private funeral arrangements at the eleventh-hour. He left sooner than was proper.

The PC need not have been concerned about inflaming the mourners during the funeral. On foot, by bicycle, in cars, they arrived already incensed. The official explanation for the murder – that the millionaire farmer and businessman had been killed by one man, an impoverished squatter with whom he had been engaged in a low-key dispute over a two-acre strip of land at the edge of his thousand-acre sugar estate – was roundly dismissed as absurd. The more stridently Government officials presented this version, the deeper became the conviction – not only for Luos but for all Kenyans – that the Government was hiding something.

There were unscheduled interventions aplenty that day. Some of them were downright reckless. But for the fact that it was a funeral, many an intervener would have been arrested on the spot by the large contingent of security personnel on hand. One fellow, Oluoch Rabuor, a Maseno High School contemporary of Luka's, was not on the original list of speakers until he pulled some strings with Boro, another Maseno Old Boy.

"Pigs! Goats!" Rabuor began. It was barely past noon, but he was clearly already drunk. "How many of our leaders are they going to kill?! Hyenas! We will kill them, too!"

At that, he was quickly pulled aside. But he was smiling hard. The crowd booed and heckled the Master of Ceremonies, Engineer Wanga Roche, the MP for Bondo and one of Luka's maternal cousins, when he tried to explain that such sentiments, while understandable, were not to be expressed that day.

Boro was the first scheduled speaker. He had been devastated by the murder, but he had worked harder than anyone to ensure that all went well. Earlier that day, he had looked so tired and worn-out that Soru and Saks had wondered out loud to each other if he would be up to making a speech. They need not have worried. As always, he was prepared. He wanted to pay proper tribute to his younger brother. Further, as MP for Kisumu East, any funeral in Luoland represented an opportunity to speak to his constituents wherever they might be, and sometimes even, as on this occasion, to the entire nation.

"Peace!" Boro began, in the usual greeting at funerals.

"Peace!" bellowed back the crowd, a little more loudly than Boro expected at that stage in the proceedings. The people were on edge. The day's events were already more than one hour behind the schedule in the printed programme.

"'I don't know if you knew this boy," Boro said, pointing to the coffin. "Did you know this boy?"

"Yes!" they thundered back.

"No, I don't think you knew this boy."

Smiles of anticipation all around. They could tell he was setting them up.

"Let me tell you who he was. This boy was Luka Sollo, son of Ang'awa, son of Osewe, son of Ogombe, son of another Ang'awa, son of Oyugi, son of Oweh, son of Silual and brother to the great Nwanji. Silual was the son of Kisanji, son of Boul, son of another

Silual, son of Manji, son of Ramogi Ojwang' – and you know Ramogi Ojwang', the one who brought our people to this land from the other side of the Great Lake."

The clapping lasted a long time. He knew how to move a crowd.

"Yes, I call him a boy because he was many years my junior. He even knew his exact birth date!"

Laughter all around.

"He also knew his place and position in the family. He respected his seniors; he gave me respect. Yes, I call him a boy, but he was bull of a boy! A bull of a man! Look at this farm. Look at this homestead. Look at this house. Only a bull of a man could do all this! He was my junior, but in many ways he was more of a man, much more of a man than I will ever be!"

Clapping again, nodding, smiles, shouts of agreement, the first sign of deep emotion from Rhoda since the day at the DO's office. She had loved that part of Luka – the confident machismo, the boundless energy.

"Luka Sollo died by the hands of other human beings. He did not die peacefully at home of old age like our father, Ang'awa, and our mothers, Anyango and Akoth. Or in a hospital of AIDS like our younger brother, Owiti. Or in a car accident like his first son, Madiany. No, Luka was killed. He was cut into little pieces like a sheep and then left for wild animals to eat."

Groans and shouts of anger.

"It is a painful thing, my brothers and sisters. What did Luka Sollo do to deserve that? I have seen many things in my life, but I never thought I would see anything like that."

He bowed his head.

Boro had spoken at two memorial services held for Luka, first in Nairobi, and later in Kisumu. He had been subdued and composed on both occasions. But he was shaking now, his tears falling freely. Luka's killers had taken not only his brother, but also his closest friend and confidante. The crowd, sensing the depth of his anguish, was visibly quaking. The PC was looking nervous. Both the DC and DO were sweating profusely. Boro stood there silently with his head bowed for many minutes. The sound of his irregular breathing could be heard through the loudspeakers. Everyone sensed his inner battle: the bereaved elder brother versus the politician. It was an important moment.

When Boro lifted his head, wiped away his tears with a handkerchief, and faced the crowd again, his mouth was set in a hard smile. Turning toward the PC and DC, he said, "The PC and DC are here. We thank them for coming to comfort us."

Hisses and angry shouts from the crowd. Boro raised his hand for quiet. The PC and DC were nodding hard.

"We ask them to assure us that those who did this to our brother will be found and punished. Mr. PC, will you do that for the people?"

The PC, still nodding – and seemingly oblivious to the fact that he was effectively contradicting the official version of the murder – stood up and said, "Yes, Mr. MP, I will do so."

The PC looked and sounded so terrified that someone toward the front of the crowd laughed out loud. Others joined and soon almost everyone was smiling, even Rhoda. The tension evaporated. The PC was embarrassed and deeply irritated. He could not leave, but nor could he bring himself to face the crowd. As he sat back down, he instructed his junior officer, the DC, to deliver the official message from the Government later in the programme.

The rest of Boro's speech was devoted to conveying condolences from his fellow politicians, and from a number of Luka's business associates who were unable to attend.

At Rhoda's request, the committee had agreed to a short list of scheduled speakers. After Boro, two other uncles and one aunt spoke. Then came the intervention by Oluoch Rabuor, Luka's ex-schoolmate. After that, only four more people spoke: the DC, Soru, Saks, and Rhoda, in that order.

The official message from the Government was short and as expected:

"Government wishes to convey its deepest condolences to the family of the late Mr. Luka Sollo upon his untimely and shocking death. Kenya has lost a respected and hard-working citizen. Kenya has lost a true patriot. Government assures Mrs. Sollo and the rest of the Sollo family that no stone will be left unturned in bringing Mr. Sollo's killer before the criminal justice system of this country."

Boos and hisses all around. "Sit down! Leave here!"

At any other funeral, the DC would have added some personal remarks. But sensing that anything he said would receive a hostile reception, he went no further and returned to his seat next to his still seething boss.

Soru and Luka had been good friends. With her large frame, smooth dark skin, wide smile, and calm yet intense demeanor, she resembled him both physically and emotionally. As a child she had been forced to grow accustomed to uncles and aunts on both sides of the family lamenting that had she been a boy, she would have achieved everything that he did. She certainly had his energy and, until her marriage, his deep self-belief. She spoke briefly that day. Briefly but very well.

"Peace."

"Peace!"

"I have to believe that if the people who took my father away from us had known what they would be doing to us, they would not have killed him. They could not have known. I just have to believe that. Otherwise, what kind of a world is this?"

Shaking heads all around.

"On my wedding day, my father called me his treasure. You are my treasure, he said. That was the best moment of my life. I loved him very much. I do not know what life will be like without him... He was almost like a brother to me... We understood each other... We disagreed just once as adults. I have come to learn that he was right, and I was wrong."

Soru was alluding to her very early marriage to Mark Awiti, a man she had loved, but whom Luka had immediately recognized as a weak man who would buckle at the first sign of hardship or pressure. Sure enough, Mark had made a costly mistake and lost his high-paying job as a Marketing Manager with Coca Cola. Rather than look for another position – which he would have found quite easily, since the mistake at Coca Cola had been an honest one – Mark had taken to self-pity and turned to drink. Luckily, they had invested well early in their marriage. Earnings from those investments, coupled with Soru's modest but steady income from her job with Capital Asset Holdings, meant that they lived a comfortable life. Comfortable but unhappy. Mark's self-image was so poor that he could not bear the thought of a joyful Soru. He was vicious to her and did all he could to demean and trivialize her dreams and achievements. It was sheer agony for her.

"He taught me that there are some mistakes that one must live with. I will bear my cross, just as he would have wanted me to do."

She looked and sounded so sad as she said these words that both Rhoda and Saks began to cry. Jeremy and Catherine wriggled off their seats and went to stand next to her. Mark looked on silently from behind dark sunglasses.

"I ask you to pray for his soul. I ask you to pray for all of us who loved him. We will miss him very much."

With that, she lifted both hands in a confident farewell salute – the one her father liked to give – and holding her children close, returned to her seat.

"Bull! Bull!" came the cries from the crowd. They, too, could see Luka in her. And despite herself, Soru smiled widely. Rhoda laughed out loud. It was not so much what Soru had said but how she had said it – with power, confidence, style, and real emotion – that had moved the people.

For several days leading up to the funeral, Saks had been trying to decide if he would speak in Dholuo and have a translator convert his words into English, like everyone expected him to do – like Soru and Boro had done – or if he would use English, which was by far his strongest language, and have the translation go in the opposite direction. Against his better judgment, he opted for the former. This partly explained the stilted, artless speech that he gave. It just fell flat. At one point, midway through it, he considered switching to English. But that would have lowered him even further in the people's eyes, especially given Soru's shining performance.

Saks spoke at some length of his admiration for his father, how much he had learned from him, how much he would miss his advice and guidance. The crowd clapped politely as he sat down. They could tell that he had said what was on his mind, not what was in his heart.

What was in Sakawa's heart was a deepening sense of missed opportunity. He had never been close to his father. Much as they both tried to fill the chasm between them, it never closed. The gap had been there for as long as Saks could remember. Whereas Luka's relationships with Madi and Soru had been light and easy, with Saks there had been a plodding heaviness marked by long periods of silence and averted looks. Neither questioned the other's love. But there was little affection between them. Their personalities clashed. They did not like one another too much.

"He is forever asking for advice, but when you start to give it to him, he stops listening," Luka would often complain to Rhoda.

"He always wants me to do what he wants. He doesn't have

opinions; he gives orders," a frustrated Saks would say to Maaike after each unpleasant encounter with his father.

In the back of his mind, Saks had always felt that he and his father had time; that they would work things out in the end. But now there was no more time. His father was gone. All the misunderstanding was totally irremediable. He was overcome with longing for another chance.

That was what was in his heart. Had he said it somehow, the crowd would have embraced him without diminishing him.

Rhoda's speech was so calm and measured that it surprised everyone.

"I knew Luka Sollo like the palm of my hand," she began. "I had touched every inch of his body. I had heard every tone of his voice. I knew and shared his greatest joys. I understood his fears and troubles. I will mourn this man until my dying day."

She had their attention. She continued with a moving narrative of their life together. Their days in Tororo, in Lusaka (where Madi and Sakawa were born), in Nairobi (where Soru was born), and there at the edge of the Rift Valley where they had built their fortune. Like many in their age-group, their marriage had been a good one, built on a shared view and understanding of the world and of their place in it. A strong partnership in a steady climb to wealth and influence. Everyone was moved, quite a few to tears.

But then she switched.

"You know how a child behaves when she is about to fall sick?"

Nods and murmurs of both understanding and curiosity. Where was she going with this?

"You ask her what is wrong, and she says, 'Nothing.' You touch her forehead and there is no fever. You check her stool, and it is normal. But you know that there is something wrong with her."

They knew.

"That is how it was with Sollo of late. Something was wrong, but he would not talk about it when I asked. Now I know that I should have pushed harder. But he is gone and all that is left for me to do is to celebrate and thank God for the life that He gave me with Luka."

Even as the mourners digested this bombshell, Rhoda switched again.

"Would everyone who was helped by Luka Sollo raise his hand."

There must have been a thousand hands in the air. Luka had been generous with both his money and his time.

"I want all of you to help me today. I want you to promise me that you will honor Sollo's memory. Mourn him with us, but please, please do not hurt each other or anyone else. It is too soon to jump to conclusions. There are things happening in this country that most of us do not understand. Sollo's death is one of these. I say this and I lived in the same house with him, shared his bed. But of this I am certain: Mr. Semoe Barsone did not kill Luka Sollo. We disagreed, yes, but as friends disagree. Why would Barsone kill the man who was educating three of his children? Does that make sense to you, my friends?

"No!" they thundered back.

But why was she making it sound like Luka Sollo was partly to blame for his own death?

At that point, Rhoda turned toward the Government representatives and said, "The people have agreed to mourn my husband peacefully. I would request that our Government show its own goodwill and from this day drop the story that Mr. Barsone killed my husband."

The still fuming PC did not respond. That decision was clearly not his to make.

Rhoda finished by thanking everyone who had helped with funeral arrangements, and promising that Luka's hard work would not be wasted. That she would always be there for those who had depended on him. That his home would remain strong.

Rhoda's speech was the highlight of the production. Most of the mourners did not stay for the actual burial but left immediately after she finished. This was just as well because even with the reduced numbers, the crush of people trying to get a final view of the body was so intense that a few people fainted before they reached the head of the multi-layered queue. The faintings not only added to the confusion, they also seemed to increase the determination and aggressiveness of those behind to see what could possibly have made someone faint. The viewing lasted for well over an hour.

There was space for only a few score people to join the family at the graveside for the final prayers. Each of those people was needed. The padre's choice for the final song took away whatever resistance Luka Sollo's family had left in them.

Night has come,
All lands have fallen silent.
The sky is dark,
The air is cool.

The cattle are penned,
The people have dined.
All are tired,
And readying to sleep.

Dear Lord, our Savior and Protector,
Come to the sickly this night,
Give them strength,
Give them courage.

And to those who will die,
Give peace and tranquility,
Even as they wrestle with their deaths,

Even as they wrestle with oblivion.

And when the eastern sun appears,
And the living emerge again,
Send them forth into the world,
To do your work in faith, dear God,
To do your work in faith.

2

CRAZY STORY

They met as graduate students at the University of California, Davis. She was one year into her studies in Anthropology. He had just begun his in Economics. She was born and raised in Fresno, California. He was born and raised in Uhanga Location, Bondo Division, Siaya District, Nyanza Province, Kenya. He had come to California four years before, in 1964, one of the third set of Kenyans in the student airlift program organized by Tom Mboya and funded by the Kennedy Foundation and several private American citizens with the aim of training Kenya's future civil servants and chief executives.

They saw each other for the first time at a National Farm Workers Association rally in Sacramento. His roommate at the time idolized Cesar Chavez, the NFWA leader, and pulled him along to the rally. She, too, revered Cesar Chavez, just as she did most of the world's then freedom fighters, including Kenya's Jomo Kenyatta. After the rally a large group of students went out for drinks. He found himself sitting next to her. They began to talk. She was very excited to learn he was from Kenya but alarmed to find that, at best, he was indifferent toward Kenyatta.

"Kenyatta is caught in the past. He only cares about Kikuyus."

"But he was jailed for Kenya, not for Kikuyus. He suffered for all of you. And look at him; he came out of jail with no bitterness toward white people."

"Yes, he certainly seems to defer to white people, despite everything they did to him. Meanwhile, he is not fulfilling our dreams of freedom and

self-reliance. He is selling us back to the British, and they are rewarding him with good publicity. He is busy grabbing land in Nairobi and the Rift Valley for himself and other Kikuyus, spending millions borrowed from the British. Why should I be happy about that? Why should my children one day have to repay money borrowed for that sort of thing?"

"He deserves the good publicity! He is a hero!"

"To you, maybe, and to Kikuyus. Not to me. Not to Luos. He is frustrating our leaders. I don't like that."

He was enjoying the banter and thus somewhat overstating his disapproval of Kenyatta. He understood the internal and external pressures the man was facing. But for him and many other Luos in the US at the time, condemnation and criticism of Kenyatta was a favorite pastime.

He had been unwillingly starved of non-commercial erotic physical contact with women ever since his arrival in the US. He did not know how to woo American women. So that evening he found himself eyeing her in the way he had come to eye most American women – interesting but totally beyond reach. She was well ahead of him. Not in his wildest dreams could he have imagined that later that evening he would be standing outside the football stadium kissing her lips and running his hands down her back and on to her buttocks, and then later still, cupping her cream-colored breasts in his hands as she moved above him, eyes closed, chin up, lips pursed in pleasure.

Four months and many more such encounters later, she was pregnant. They felt strongly enough about each other to be happy about it. Happy but scared. They were both students. He was black. She was white. Even in California, black-white marriages were rare. But they were determined to marry. Six weeks later they did, in her hometown Fresno, in front of her shell-shocked but intrigued family and childhood friends and a handful of California's complement of Luo Kenyans.

When the baby boy came home from the hospital to their one-bedroom apartment in the graduate student residence village, the proud father, embarrassed and apologetic, opened the old trunk he had brought with him from Kenya and took out a harp and bow. The new mother had never seen the thing before.

"What's that?" she asked.

"It is a harp. We call it orutu. It's played like a violin, but you hold it like this – low down by your ankles. You can play it on its own, but it sounds best as part of a three-piece band – a harp like this, a short narrow drum made from hard wood and leather, and another percussion instrument made from two pieces of metal. I want to play and sing for the baby... to welcome him home."

He started hesitantly but soon found a familiar furrow through which he moved confidently for almost an hour.

"You're so full of surprises," she said at the end, the baby asleep in her arms. "Nice surprises."

She liked the peaceful, deep-down happy look on his face as he played and sang.

"Maybe you should have studied music instead of economics," she said, laughing.

*   *   *

"Is that it?" his son had just asked.

How should he answer? Should he say, I have always loved music, it came easily to me. But it never seemed to fit easily with the rest of my life. At first, my father encouraged it, "Music is good," he would say. "It connects the mind and the heart. It unites you with the spirits." He wanted me to play the piano, the flute, and other such instruments. But I preferred the harp. Whenever I took it out to play, his face would change. He did not like it. I could not understand it. He liked harp music. In fact, he was my first teacher. But he did not like to hear me play it. He never stopped me, but he never encouraged me. I see now that I was always waiting for that acceptance from him. But he never gave it to me. I have been feeling bad about that of late. I don't know why it was so hard for him to do. Maybe *he was afraid I would follow a star he did not recognize? I don't know. I really wish he had accepted that part of me. It would have meant a lot to me. But maybe I should have followed my star anyway."*

Was that it?

Saks contracted gonorrhea within minutes of his arrival in California in 1982. Barely had he cleared immigration and customs at San Francisco airport than he was accosted by what he thought was a very attractive woman wearing a red mini skirt, a matching but almost see-through blouse, and no bra. Definitely no bra. He could not keep his eyes from settling on her clearly visible dark brown areola and nipples.

"Hi honey," she purred, moving in.

"Eh ... hallo," replied Saks, swallowing hard.

"Lemihepuwiyursookesweehar."

"Eh?"

"I said let-me-help-you-with-your-suit-cases-sweet-heart."

"Oh ... no ... no ... They are heavy."

"Oh no, no, they are heavy," she mimicked. "You talk cute. You look cute, baby."

"Eh... heh... heh..." laughed Saks nervously. He realized that he did not like her face. It was too hard-looking underneath the heavy makeup. He concentrated on her nipples. "Eh ... what is your name?" he asked them as the woman led him away from the crowd gathered around the baggage claim area.

"Call me CJ, honey, CJ Monroe ... as in Marilyn Monroe," she replied, laughing to herself.

"Thank you, CJ, but you need not carry my bags."

"It's OK, honey, I'm strong. Real strong. See," CJ turned and hiked up her skirt to reveal the remainder of her light brown thighs, along with one-third of her left buttock. "See, real strong ... and hot."

Saks was mesmerized. The Love Boat and Dallas had not prepared him for anything like this. He began to sweat.

"You got a ride, honey? Where you going?" CJ asked as she loaded his two suitcases on to a baggage cart.

"My cousin said he would come to get me. My plane arrived early. He will come soon. He may already be here, looking for me."

"Come over here and wait with me, honey. Keep me company." She took his hand and led him out of the main terminal and out to the parking lot, suddenly moving very quickly and purposefully, holding his hand with one of hers, and with the other either helping push the cart, caressing his buttocks, or rubbing his chest.

"Come over here and stand by my car," said CJ.

"Why don't we get in?"

"It's hot in there. I'm already warm enough. Aren't you? Look, it's such a pretty night." She turned and licked his earlobe and put her hand on his crotch, which had been out of control for many minutes. They did it standing, her legs wrapped around his hips. She robbed him at the very moment of entry, slipping her hand into the jacket pocket she had long since determined held the money. Six hundred dollars.

"Call me, honey. 415-555-1212. That's my number," said CJ as she disappeared across the parking lot, leaving Saks dazedly cleaning himself with the handkerchief his mother had given him to wipe his tears at the airport in Nairobi.

He worked his way back to the arrivals hall and found his cousin, Oremo, pacing back and forth in a near panic. It was not until much later that evening, as he was undressing himself in preparation to take a shower that he realized what had happened. He cried out so sharply that an alarmed Oremo came running and burst into the room.

"What's wrong?"

"I've been robbed!"

"Robbed? When? How?"

"By a woman... CJ Monroe .... a *malaya*... a prostitute... at the airport."

"No way! A *malaya*?! At the airport?! Did you ... you know ... have sex with her?"

Silence.

"*Aiya*! You've already screwed in America! It took me almost one year, man! I was dying! And you've done it already! But she stole your money? How? How much?"

The story poured out of Saks, whose sense of loss was only slightly dampened by his cousin's obvious admiration for his early foray into sex in the US. But any lingering doubts about his stupidity were dispelled when a week later he began to ooze a stinky, creamy substance.

Having been singed so early, Saks was celibate for the first two of his four years at UC Berkeley. He joined the rugby team and soon became one of the stars. Opportunities for sex came, but he let them pass by unexplored.

It was the length of Maaike that got to him. She was five feet ten inches tall, just two inches shorter than him. Within minutes of meeting her at an African Students Union gathering, he imagined kissing her lying down, stretched out, full length, both lips and toes touching. It proved to be an accurate image. But Maaike took a long time to do things. She was never late, but she reached each decision slowly. Deliberately. With finality. Eating. Dressing. Walking across campus. Kissing him, standing. Falling in love with him. Kissing him as he had imagined, lying down. Making love with him.

They both completed their Bachelors and Masters degrees in four years – both of his in economics, hers in chemistry and then statistics. They both applied to PhD programs and were accepted at different universities – he to continue with economics at the University of Minnesota, she with statistics at the University of Connecticut.

"Will you marry me?" he asked her the week before they graduated from Berkeley. They were at Hobbees in Palo Alto, their favorite restaurant. She was staring at the engagement ring at the bottom of her dessert dish. He had slipped it to the headwaiter, who was now beaming at them from across the room, giving Saks a thumbs-up sign.

"I love you Sakawa Sollo. You are my heart. I have been waiting for this day for a long time. Yes, I will marry you. Yes. But... only after we both finish our PhDs."

"But that'll be years!"

"We're only 22, Saks. There's no hurry."

"But you'll be at UConn and I'll be at Minnesota. Four years... at least."

"So? Are you willing to come to Storrs with me? Do you want me give up on UConn and come to St. Paul with you?"

Silence.

"Please put that ring on my finger, Saks. I said yes, remember! I'm going to be your wife! You're going to be my husband! I'm so happy!"

The four years apart were difficult, but they passed by more quickly than either of them could have imagined. Unknown to the other, each succumbed twice to loneliness and despair. He fell once to another stressed-out, similarly grateful, and surprisingly limber classmate in the weeks leading up to their qualifying exams, and then to the stunning leader of a Chicago-based Togolese dance troupe invited to perform at the University of Minnesota during Africa Week. She stumbled first with an irresistibly handsome Bolivian visiting mutual friends in Storrs, and then later with a jazz-loving Austrian diplomat during a summer internship in St. Louis. But even during these lapses of memory and resolve, neither lost sight of the vision of the other, and of the promise of their future life together.

That life began in earnest on Wednesday, September 26, 1990, when they left New York's John F. Kennedy airport on a plane bound for Paris, where they would board another one to Yaoundé, Cameroun. They had become Doctors of Philosophy on consecutive weeks in May, each one attending the other's graduation ceremony. Then they had spent the summer months working. Maaike had found them jobs in an ice cream storage and distribution plant in Willimantic, Connecticut, a short distance from the university. It was tortuous work in a huge, refrigerated acre-sized shed in which the average temperature was minus ten degrees Fahrenheit. But the work paid the then super-wage of fourteen dollars per hour. Working every overtime shift they could, they made twenty thousand dollars in three months.

Many of their fellow Kenyans and Africans living in the US northeast had secured similarly laborious but high-paying jobs that summer. Most were saving to buy cars and stereo systems to take back home after graduation. For Saks and Maaike, however, the money was for an overland trip around Africa.

It had been Saks's idea. "Let's use the money to see Africa... the whole continent!" he had declared during a weekend trip to see Maaike in Storrs. Coincidentally, their respective dissertation defense meetings had been scheduled on the same day the previous week. Both had passed well. They were celebrating. They had been thinking about next steps for some time, but other than the plan to go back to Kenya and get married, nothing more had been decided. "Let's see it all... North, south, east, west, central... Everywhere!"

Maaike agreed immediately. She loved the idea of traveling with Saks for a whole year.

"Maybe along the way we'll figure out what it means to be the 'Africans' the world has labeled us," she said with a laugh.

They failed on both fronts.

They had decided to begin the journey in Cameroun following an invitation to do so from a friend who lived in Yaoundé and had recently completed an around-Africa trip. From Cameroun they crossed into Nigeria, and then continued overland to Benin, Togo, Ghana, Cote d'Ivoire, Burkina Faso, Niger, back to Burkina Faso, and on to Mali, Senegal, and Gambia. They then hopped and skipped across North Africa to Egypt – Casablanca, Rabat, Algiers, Tunis, Tripoli, Alexandria, Cairo. Their plan had been to fly from Cairo to Cape Town, from where they would travel overland to Nairobi. But by then they were almost out of money, and both were suffering from recurrent bouts of malaria and dysentery. Lamenting the unavoidable end to their journey, they declared a partial victory and flew home to Nairobi.

They emerged from the trip exhausted but also exhilarated by all they had seen and heard. Yet at the same time they were even more puzzled by Africa and Africans than they had been at the outset. The continent was so huge, so diverse, so complex, so beautiful, so full of contradictions.

They saw great wealth and ease, mostly built up over decades of toil and discipline, but sometimes unexplainable in such terms. The livestock trader in Ouagadougou whose clients stretched over four countries and thousands of kilometers. The fruit trader in Dakar with a warehouse chock-full of apples, tangerines, and oranges sourced in the Mediterranean, and destined for tables across Senegal and Gambia. The cloth trader in Accra with row upon row of colorful bolts of fabrics, piled four-deep across her huge storeroom. Hoteliers in Rabat. Rubber plantation owners outside Kumasi. Famous painters, sculptors, and musicians in Oshogbo. Surgeons in Jos.

They saw great poverty and hardship, mostly due to accidents of place and time of birth, but at times linked to reckless hubris. They saw great effort, courage, and grace under that hardship. The young woman carrying an infant in downtown Yaoundé, walking up and down between rows of cars on a busy street, baring her chapati-flat breasts to motorists, hoping to elicit pity and donations, but laughing gleefully at Saks's embarrassed half-look. The one-armed shoe-shiner in Alexandria, whistling non-stop as he wriggled his body this way and that around dusty shoes and stinky socks. The disheveled child in Algiers slowly dragging his painfully deformed foot around as he walked, but quickly jumping up to run and join a game of soccer.

They heard hundreds of life histories, each one totally different from all the rest in its details, yet often so alike in theme and arc. They were harassed at border crossings. One time, they were mistaken for robbers and almost set upon by an angry mob. Another time, they were wrongly identified as wanted fugitives and almost gunned down at a police checkpoint. They were each courted by both men and women. Time and again they were rescued from disaster by stranger after stranger. Some, however, were not very kind and understanding about it. "*Nawao!* If you no get sense in Lagos, you no get sense anywhere!"

They grew to know one another.

It was the first time in their eight-year relationship that they had spent days, weeks, months on end together. They fought often, at first with a sense of disbelief at each other's cruelty in battle, and then with a deepening sense of each other's strengths, frailties, and insecurities. Seeing that their relationship could endure their disagreements, they grew happier and more content, each sure of the other's empathy and support.

They flew into Nairobi on Thursday, February 7, 1991. When they walked into the arrivals hall at Jomo Kenyatta International Airport, the looks on their parents' and siblings' faces confirmed what Saks and Maaike had already surmised for themselves. They both looked emaciated.

"You two look like AIDS cases, Saks." Not one to beat about the bush with her brother, Soru waited only until they were in the car and exiting the airport before asking the question that was on everyone's mind. "You don't have AIDS, do you?"

"No, Soru, we don't have AIDS!" replied Saks testily. "How would we have got that? We've been together for over four years!"

One of Soru 's married girlfriends had been sickly for some time. So had her husband. They had both just tested positive for HIV/AIDS. They both looked just like Saks and Maaike.

"Anyone can get it from anyone," Soru replied quietly, irritated but letting it go.

Saks and Maaike wanted to get married right away. The two families agreed. The wedding gown and tuxedo bought in New York the previous July and sent back to Nairobi with a friend were now at least two sizes too large for them. Hurried adjustments only made matters worse. Whenever Maaike lost weight, she did so first and foremost around the bust. For Saks, it was in his hips and shoulders. On the wedding day, she was unable to do full justice to her low-cut gown. He looked like a strawman in his tuxedo. But they were clearly so happy to be back in Kenya, and so thrilled to be getting married, that only the most mean-spirited of the three hundred invited guests noticed or cared.

*   *   *

Maaike's father, Benjamin Kosgey, had resisted the liaison for many years.

"There are so many Nandis in the US. Why must she choose a Luo?" he had protested to his wife, Maria, after she showed him the letter from Maaike bearing news of the engagement. Maaike had telephoned her mother three weeks before, on the day Saks proposed. Maria had been surprised. She had heard of the Sollos but did not know them personally, nor did she know anyone who knew the Sollos well. But she knew her husband well enough to advise Maaike not to inform him by telephone. She would keep the news to herself until the letter arrived.

"Why a Luo? Why? Why not a Luhya or Kikuyu? At least they are circumcised!" Maria also did not like the idea that Maaike had chosen to marry an uncircumcised Luo. She was circumcised herself and could not imagine sex with an uncircumcised man. She was told it was no different but found that hard to believe. Maybe it was because Maaike herself was not circumcised.

"Remember that Maaike is also not circumcised," she reminded her husband.

"She is a woman! It might be acceptable these days for women not to do it, but men must always be circumcised!"

"Yes, that's true. But we must not stand in Maaike's way. She is a grown woman and can make her own decisions."

"But what is this about marriage in four years? Why not do it immediately? What is wrong with these young people?"

"You have read the letter. She says that she still wants to do a PhD. They will not be in the same place."

He shook his head.

"If they have decided to marry, they should go ahead. Why tell us about something that is not going to happen for four years? If she wants to marry him, she should be with him."

"What do you mean, Ben? How is it wrong that Maaike has not given up her dream of a PhD? These days not all women are willing to do what people of our generation did. I think it is good that they have decided to delay the wedding. It shows that they are behaving responsibly."

"Enough," said Kosgey, getting up to leave. He did not like to speak with his wife when he did not know the direction in which the conversation was going. That night, they telephoned Maaike and gave her their blessings to proceed as she wished.

The families met formally for the first time two months after the engagement. Sakawa and Maaike were both back in Kenya for the summer break prior to returning to the US to commence their

PhD studies. The meeting took place at the Kosgey family homestead just outside Nandi Hills town, less than forty-five minutes from Panderi.

It was a bitterly cold July day. Dark, heavy clouds hung overhead, threatening rain that mercifully began to fall only as the Sollos drove off at the end of the gathering. The herd of semi zero-grazed Friesians normally roaming around the fenced paddocks that abutted on the driveway leading into the homestead were huddled together for warmth under tall acacias, whose leaves looked more gray than green in the gloomy light. The Sollos – Luka, Rhoda, Soru and Sakawa – were escorted by Luka's brother and sister-in-law, Boro and Leah Tindi, and by a close friend, Professor Mark Otieno of Kenyatta University, and his wife, Edith. Boro and Leah spoke on behalf of Luka and Rhoda. The Kosgeys – Ben, Maria, Maaike, her two brothers Ben Junior and Dickson, and her three sisters Cathleen, Anna, and Beatrice – asked Ben's cousin, Lieutenant-Colonel Matthew Bargetuny and his wife Susan to represent them. Also invited were three other couples, two from Ben's side of the family and one from Maria's.

"We agree to this... this arrangement. This marriage. Our daughter's dowry has yet to be paid, but to us she is now married. We have given her to you. We do not need to go to church for that. One year, two years, four years. It is the same to us. We have agreed. That is enough."

Lieutenant-Colonel Bargetuny was looking sternly at Honorable Boro Tindi as he said these words – words that everyone could tell did not capture his true feelings. To Bargetuny, the whole affair was highly improper, beginning with the Sollos being Luos. He had yet to meet a Luo he could trust. They were too carefree for his liking. In fact, he had yet to meet a trustworthy non-Nandi. And he saw all sorts in the army. All useless, utterly useless. And this business of having an engagement and dowry meeting for a wedding that would not take place for four years was absurd to him. To him, you either got married immediately upon announcing your intentions, or you waited and held this sort of meeting when the wedding was more than just an idea. He felt that his cousin was being stupid and violating Nandi custom. For Luos!

Bargetuny was driving a hard bargain on the dowry. Fifteen grade milk cattle, five of which were to be in-calf, bringing the actual total to twenty-five.

"You see those cattle outside?" he had said when he saw Boro visibly balk at the demand. "You see this farm? We have plenty of land. Plenty. We want to fill it up with cattle. We Nandi love cattle. We drink much milk."

The visible balk had been intentional. The terms were quite reasonable to Boro, especially since they had four years to deliver. But there was more at stake. Bargetuny's disrespectful tone was a signal that Kosgey – the man on whose behalf he was negotiating – was still not happy about the liaison. Boro sensed that tribal bigotry lay at the root of the problem. He was not keen to have Nandis as relatives, and nor were Luka and Rhoda. But they all knew Sakawa well enough to keep their feelings to themselves and support his choice. Any resistance would bring on a monumental and long-lasting sulk. They also saw that Maaike was a sensible woman who would be a good partner for their son. Boro suspected that Kosgey respected Bargetuny's opinion and would likely follow his lead. The Lieutenant-Colonel had to be won over early and totally. He knew where he had to take the discussions.

Up to that point, the exchanges had been in English. Now Boro switched to Kiswahili for effect. He also stood up.

"This son of ours is now twenty-two... no twenty-three years old," Boro began. "He is a clever boy. He has been clever from the day he was born. You know, he arrived early. He surprised us. His mother gave birth in the house. His father cut the umbilical cord himself. Himself. I say he is clever because as soon as he emerged, he turned his head and looked at his mother. He already understood the world! We named him after a woman, Sakawa, who was the daughter of man named Nwanji. We are told that Nwanji lived for only twenty-seven years. But by then, he had sired eight children from three wives. One of those women, Sakawa's mother, was known as Jebet."

It was Bargetuny's turn to look directly into his opponent's eyes in surprise. But in his case the surprised look was authentic. Jebet was a Nandi name. He nodded slowly and returned his gaze to a point just to the right of Boro's face.

"Nwanji," Boro continued, slowly, carefully. "Nwanji was a fierce warrior who loved cattle. He was a large man. A tall man. He loved milk and drank great quantities of it. You see, unlike some of us here today, milk did not trouble his stomach." Laughter. "Nwanji loved milk, and he knew how to identify a good milk cow. Now, some eighty to one hundred years before Nwanji was born, his great-great-great-grandfather – a man known as Silual because he was very light-skinned – settled in a place called Uhanga. The land around Uhanga was not good. The soil was thin and rocky. And there was little rain. But it was near the Lake. Fish were plenty. So Silual decided to become a fisherman. He made a good living from it. His descendants were strong and tall. But Nwanji hated fish and he did not care for fishing. He was a herder at heart. He wanted cattle, and milk."

Bargetuny nodded in understanding. That certainly made sense to him. He did not care for fish himself. Before then, he had been sitting up, leaning forward, knees apart, elbows on knees, fingertips forming a sharp pyramid under his jutted-out chin. Now he was sitting back, one leg crossed over the other, hands and elbows on the armrests of his chair. Listening. The story was getting through to him.

"Nwanji also wanted women. He began to yearn for women when he was still very young, maybe fifteen years of age or so – old enough to think that he knew what to do with a woman but still too young to compete with the older men in his clan for women in friendly villages nearby. He had to venture further away, into hostile areas. He knew he would have to steal women. He knew he would have to learn to fight. His father, who was also named Silual, was a peaceful and peace-loving man. But he saw that the only way to help his aggressive son achieve inner peace was to let him learn the ways of war. Silual did not know those ways. He could not teach Nwanji himself. He sent the boy to the home of his half-brother, Oremo Pala, a man who loved cattle and the violence needed to acquire and hold large herds. Pala was one of the best warriors in the clan.

"But even Pala moved too slowly for Nwanji. Soon, he was Nwanji's student in the art of waging battle. By the time Nwanji reached nineteen years of age, he already had two wives and over eighty head of cattle. Both of the women and most of the cattle had been won in battle. His chosen occupation was to acquire and trade cattle, and that meant going to war. It meant war and travel. He and the many men he led traveled widely, constantly, looking for allies, information, and victims. In time, he heard about a breed of cattle that was small in size but greedy and thirsty. That meant much milk. Nwanji wanted some bulls of this breed to introduce the characteristic for high milk output into his herd. The people who reared this breed of cattle lived in these hills where we are now sitting, eating, and drinking."

Bargetuny nodded his understanding. He was fully into Boro's narrative.

"These people were a fierce and proud people who knew how to deal with intruders. You can imagine the journey Nwanji had to make to reach these hills. As the bird flew, it was over one hundred kilometers between this place and Uhanga, Nwanji's homeland. But there were no aeroplanes those days." Laughter. "There were no roads. There were only trails. And those trails were few and unknown to him. He was gone for many months. He returned with Jebet and her sister, Jebkosgey, but with no bulls, and with only six of the thirty men who had traveled with him. They had met strong resistance to their progress starting from a place we now call Hollo but which used to be known as Pau Akuche. It is about twenty-five kilometers west of Kisumu, which, of course, did not exist at the time. The hardest part of the journey was in the area to the east of Kisumu, where bands of men based in the section of the Hills overlooking what we now call the Kano Plains attacked them repeatedly. They had hoped to find refuge with fellow Luos living in the Plains, but there was too much suspicion and competition. In the end, they raided a small homestead at the foot of the Hills, taking six bulls and the two sisters. They had to fight their way back. Three of the bulls were retaken. The other three succumbed to thirst and disease within a few days of entering the hot and dry zone west of Kisumu.

"Jebet was Sakawa's mother. While Sakawa married into another home, we have her mother's spirit in our hearts and in our minds. We are her sons and daughters. I am her child. This boy Sakawa is her child."

Boro sat down. He knew that his opponent was silently debating how to react to the story, trying to decide which part to carry forward. Boro hoped that Bargetuny would not ask about Jebkosgey, Jebet's sister, who, like the stolen bulls, had succumbed to an unfamiliar disease soon after arriving in her new home. Boro also hoped that Bargetuny would not make too much of Jebet's child being a girl and not a boy, which meant that Jebet's blood was not running through Sakawa Sollo's body, nor through that of anyone in his extended family.

"How did he die, this Nwanji... the husband of Jebet?" asked Bargetuny, still sitting back comfortably.

It was a brilliantly put question. Bargetuny already knew the answer. Nwanji would have died in battle. The details did not matter. That was an honorable death. A befitting death. By referring to such a man as "the husband of Jebet," Bargetuny was accepting Boro's implicit argument that the two families could relate at this deeper level and thereby move forward toward the eventual wedding with fewer reservations. By remaining comfortably reclined, Bargetuny was putting aside – for a moment at least – his aggressive stance and hostile tone. Those would soon return as the two men went back and forth on the size of the dowry. In the end they agreed on twelve cattle, four in calf.

Boro's story was told and retold in the years to come. It became the foundation of Sakawa's and Maaike's relationship in the eyes of the families, and sometimes even in their own minds. The story almost saved Luka Sollo's life. And it helped bring new hope to Nwanji's homeland.

With the funeral behind them, Rhoda Sollo was more open to discussing the circumstances surrounding her husband's murder. She remained adamant that the squatter, Semoe Barsone, was innocent. She wanted to visit him in jail to confirm this for herself. Perhaps to demonstrate how confident he was that the Government had an airtight case, the DC made all the necessary arrangements for a visit. But Rhoda could not yet leave the homestead. Friends and relatives who had missed the funeral were still streaming in to convey their condolences. She asked Soru and Sakawa to go and see Barsone on her behalf. It was the Tuesday after the funeral.

One of the reasons people believed that Barsone was being framed was that he was arrested within one hour of the time Luka's body was found. That was much too soon to be credible. Further suspicion was raised by Barsone's being remanded not in Kodiaga Prison in nearby Kisumu, as would have been normal, but rather in Nakuru Prison, a notorious place through which many a political dissident had passed. A place in which many a body and mind had been broken.

Nakuru Prison is located a few kilometers to the west of the town, up on one of the hills overlooking flamingo-dotted Lake Nakuru. But the magnificent view the prison commands belies the horrendous conditions inside, which, like those in all of Kenya's prisons, feature filthy, smelly, windowless, airless, dark, dank, overcrowded rooms teeming with all manner of contagious diseases.

Soru and Sakawa found Barsone showing the expected signs of physical abuse and mental distress. He had been badly beaten and seemed to be unable to fully use one side of his body. He could barely walk. Despite his long involvement with the family, neither Soru nor Sakawa had ever met him. But he seemed to know the two of them right away. As he was led into the grimy meeting room, he gave them a genuine but agonized lop-sided smile.

"Thank you for coming to see me," said Barsone in Kiswahili, as he settled gingerly onto the hard bench. "I did not kill your father."

"We know," said Soru.

"This is a bad place," continued Barsone. "Sometimes I can hardly breathe. Sleeping is almost impossible. There are people everywhere, touching, grabbing, licking, biting. Wanting to fuck you. It is too much. Please tell them to free me. I want to go back home. If I stay here, I will be killed by the guards. They beat me every day. I swear, they want to kill me."

Both Soru and Saks had developed claustrophobia after Madi's death and burial. Hers was more acute and unpredictable than was his. Barsone's words and the dark and clammy room suddenly became too much for her. She excused herself, saying that she would wait for Saks outside.

"Sorry, sorry," said Barsone as Soru walked out.

"We are the ones who are sorry," replied Saks in Kiswahili. "We do not know why they have chosen you. My mother has asked the PC to leave it, but he said you are the one. He said they have the... knowledge. The information."

"They have nothing, nothing at all. And they never will have anything."

"They say you said you would kill him."

"I threatened to kill Luka Sollo every week! It was part of my nature! Every squatter threatens to kill his landlord, but we never do it," he said, smiling his crooked smile again. "Yes, I said I would kill your father. But I was just talking-talking. Everyone knew that. They just want to be rid of me, to blame me."

"Who wants to blame you?" asked Saks.

Barsone was quiet for a while. Then he seemed to come to a decision.

"You must find out what became of the ring – you know, the ring," he said, drawing a circle on the dirty floor with the index finger of his still-functioning right hand. "If you can find out what happened to that ring, then you will know who killed your father. The answer is with the ring."

What he said made sense to Saks. Whoever had his father's ring – which, along with his hands, had not been found – had to know what had happened to him.

"We will try to find it," said Saks.

It occurred to Saks that Barsone would need a lawyer.

"We will also find a lawyer to help you."

"Thank you," replied Barsone. "But I think you are old enough to know that in this country, people like me do not need lawyers. We are always guilty. But I want you to tell your mother what I told you. She will understand. I am sure she knows, but tell her. And also please ask her to look after my family while I am in here. Even if I never see them again, if she is there, I know they will be fine."

Saks promised to convey the messages and hurried out. He, too, was beginning to feel sick.

He told you to find the ring?" asked Rhoda.

"Yes," replied Saks. "He said that if we found out what happened to it, then we would know what had become of Baba."

Saks and Soru were back at Panderi, sitting with their mother in the living room, recounting details of that morning's encounter with Barsone.

"Be very careful," said Rhoda, obviously troubled by the news. "Did he say, 'Find the ring' or 'Find out about the ring'?"

"You know what my Kiswahili is like, Mama," said Saks. Soru cackled. She was forever teasing him about how badly he sometimes found himself speaking the national language.

"I guess he wasn't sure he was getting through," Saks continued, studiously ignoring Soru. "He said it a few times in different ways. He said '*pete*' for finger ring, and '*mviringo*' and '*duara*' for circle. But I knew what he meant. He thinks we should find the person who has Baba's ring because that person must have been there at the time of the murder. Or, at the very least, such a person would know who did it."

"No, that is not what he meant," said Rhoda.

"Mama, I was there, I know what he meant," protested Saks.

"Yes, you were there, but that is not what he meant," she insisted.

"What did he mean, then, Mama?" asked Soru.

"It is a long and difficult story to tell," she answered. "But I have to tell you all the same."

Something in Rhoda's voice frightened her children. They wondered if this had something to do with the odd things she had said at the funeral.

"Did you notice that none of our immediate neighbors came to your father's funeral?" she asked.

It was true. Some neighbors had dropped by the house over the course of the two weeks leading up to the funeral, but none had come on the day itself. That was odd behavior, almost unheard of toward even the newest of neighbors, let alone long-term ones like the Sollos.

"What does that mean?" asked Soru.

"To be honest, I am not sure. I think they wanted to keep their distance. They must have been afraid to be seen here on that day. Do you remember that friend of your father's called Alfred Siromene, the one who used to come here every other week or so for drinks and roasted meat? He was building that huge house of his in Eldoret and used to spend almost every weekend there. Remember him?"

"Yes, I do," Soru said: "Weren't he and Baba quite close? We even called him Uncle Alfred."

"Yes, they were close, but mainly as business partners. We told you to call him 'Uncle' just to be polite."

"He's the President's doctor, right?" asked Saks.

"That's his official position," replied Rhoda. "He seems to spend most of his time as Executive Chairman of Mobi Holdings, which is a huge holding company with interests in most of the countries in this region. The President is supposedly the senior partner, but hidden. Anyway, he and your father had a disagreement a few years ago and grew apart. We might have stayed in touch with the family, but I never got along with Betty, Siromene's wife. Do you remember any of the others who used to visit when Siromene was here?"

"Yes, there was Uncle Tej, Uncle Dawa, Uncle Mwai, and Uncle Sadhru," recalled Saks. He was very good with names.

"There was one more: Malcolm Jura," continued Rhoda. "But he seldom came here to the house."

"What does this have to do with Baba's ring?" inquired Saks still puzzled, still a little irritated.

"Everything, Sakawa. They were the Ring, with a capital R," replied his mother. "The Investment Ring. You took Barsone too literally. What he meant was that if we find out what became of the Ring with a capital R, we will discover why your father was killed. I am surprised that Barsone knows about the Ring. He is not as innocent as I thought."

"What are you talking about, Mama?" asked Soru. Like Saks, she was confused by what their mother was saying. "Are you saying that this Investment Ring somehow had Baba killed?"

"No, I don't think so. But maybe some of them know something about it. Maybe Siromene does... I don't know."

She paused for a moment before continuing.

"We should have talked about this when your father was still alive."

She paused again and then asked, "Soru, do you remember that time you asked your father how we became rich? You were about twelve or thirteen. Do you remember?"

"Yes, I do. I was twelve, Saks was fourteen, Madi was sixteen. He said that you looked for good shortcuts and took them." Soru replied, smiling at the memory. Saks remembered it, too.

Their father was driving a brand new dark blue Mercedes – the first of many such cars the family would come to own. Their mother was in the front passenger seat; the three children were in the back. They really loved their parents at such times, especially their father. He seemed so in control of things. A look of pleasure appeared on Luka's face as he pondered his response to Soru's question. He liked that kind of question.

"There's only one way to make money in this world," Luka had begun. "You have to find good shortcuts. The shorter and cleaner the shortcut, the bigger the reward. Of course, some shortcuts are illegal, and the Government tries to block them. But most are legal and for a while they are there for the taking. And if you see one, you had better take it or someone else will take it instead. Or, worse, it might disappear before anyone has taken it. And that would be a waste. Your mother and I had acquired a few things

before we began to understand where the shortcuts were and how to take them. We had a few cars, a house or two. But we did not have anything this big. You do not get to be as big as we are by staying on the meandering path. You have to cut through the bush with a sharp axe. Shortcuts are the story of the world. Some people call it innovation. I call it shortcuts. Think of the sports that you play. The good players are the ones who see and take the best shortcuts. Remember Pele's goal in... was it the 1968 World Cup? The ball was booted in his general direction from well inside his own half. If it was a pass, it was a pretty adventurous one. But he made it look like an excellent one. He was fully airborne when he took the ball on his chest and barely back on the ground as he volleyed it into the goal. Two touches: chest-foot-goal. All of this was at full speed. See what I mean? Here's another example. When I was a student, this thing called multiple-choice did not exist. We didn't fill in boxes and bubbles. We wrote our answers to questions. I enjoyed those essay questions, but I remember that some of my classmates really struggled with them. They never understood that anything written for someone else to read must have at least two hooks: one to hang it on and another to deliver the coup de grace – the punch that ends it. I understood this very well. That was my shortcut. That was my path through the forest of essays. Whatever you are doing, you need to find a shortcut, otherwise you'll be forever ordinary. Of course, taking shortcuts is risky. You must do your groundwork first. Your mother and I did ours. We know the terrain and have found many shortcuts. That's how we have become rich!"

Saks had recently traveled to Brussels to attend a conference and while there had heard a cruder version of this theory. He was in a taxi on the way to the airport to catch the flight back home. Earlier that day, he had gone shopping and been flabbergasted by the astronomical prices for everything from food to clothing, to electronic equipment. He was complaining about this to the taxi driver and asked the man how he made ends meet from day to day as a taxi driver.

"I have to cheat, sir!" the taxi driver answered, laughing heartily.

"Oh, you mean you try to avoid paying taxes to the Government?" Saks prodded, expecting the usual complaints about that aspect of life in Europe.

"No, I mean everybody!" replied the driver, laughing even more loudly. "I have to cheat everybody!"

"That's right," said Rhoda. "Finding shortcuts was one of the main aims of the Ring. The seven of them had good contacts in many places, but especially in the Government. They knew the people to talk to and how to get things done. Most of the time, they tried to win Government procurement and distribution contracts. They were not always the lowest bidders, but they tried not to do anything illegal."

The looks on her children's faces betrayed their utter surprise to learn all of this about their parents. "Yes, children," Rhoda said, smiling. "That is the way of this world."

"How come we never knew?" asked Soru. "How come you never told us?"

"At first you were too young. Later, you were away in boarding school, or overseas in college. These days you are too busy with your own lives. Anyway, your father met Tej and Sadhru at Nyanza Club. They discovered that they had many common interests and plans. They also got along. Your father always got along with Asians. So they began to help each other. Each of them invited one more person and the group grew to six. Everything was fine until Siromene joined. Tej knew him and convinced the others that they would all benefit by adding him to the group. And to be honest, they did. Siromene was very, very well connected. But he was also very, very greedy. The deals he brought in were huge. The Ring members began to find themselves mixing with all kinds of odd characters. Your father, Jimmy Dawa, Patrick Mwai, and Sadhru grew concerned and asked Siromene to slow down. Siromene was very angry. He told them that they did not understand anything about making money. He said he did not need to be in the Ring to succeed and abandoned it.

"Siromene was very bitter over your father's role in the thing. He told your father that we should be careful since most of our assets were not in Luoland. He could arrange to have us kicked out of the Rift Valley. You know what your father was like; he told Siromene to go straight to hell!

"Anyway, Siromene left the Ring sometime in 1997. Before the elections. The Ring never recovered from the bad feelings Siromene brought in. It was disbanded last year. For us... for your father, business was still good overall, but it was slower and much smaller.

"The Ring lasted for sixteen years. I miss those days. I miss the get-togethers. I still visit Jane Mwai and Christine Dawa, but there are no more big get-togethers... with both men and women. The men always had such good stories to tell. Even Siromene. Those were very good years."

Rhoda stopped talking for several moments, her face turned toward the fireplace, where a large fire had been lit. Outside, a thunderstorm was forming. A cold draft blew into the room through the open sliding glass doors. Lightning flashed faintly, followed by a distant purr of thunder. The late afternoon light began to fade. The room grew dark. The storm would soon be upon them.

"Please close the doors and switch on the lights, Sakawa," said Rhoda, turning her sad gaze toward the sliding doors and the garden beyond. Sakawa jumped up, relieved that his mother was still in control of herself. For a moment, she had looked to be on the verge of tears.

"Oh, how I wish we had never met that man," continued Rhoda once Saks had returned to his seat.

"Who?" asked Saks, already knowing the answer.

"Siromene. He is such a vindictive man. After the Ring broke up, we heard from time to time that he was in the neighborhood, visiting his relatives and friends. But he never dropped in to say hello. Not even once. He was never a close friend, but we had done so many things together...

"The real trouble between us began during the ethnic clashes that began in 1996 and continued until after the 1997 elections. I am sure you remember that this farm was attacked more than once. The only reason we are still here is that we armed our staff and told them to shoot first and ask questions later. And they did. Many people died. We learned that Siromene was financing and arming vigilante groups based in the Hills. We passed on this information to the Central Intelligence Department, hoping that he would be stopped. But he was untouchable. That's why we were so surprised when his name was mentioned during the Commission of Inquiry into the clashes. But of course the Commissioners buried it immediately.

"Siromene threatened us again. He sent the PC to deliver the message. We should leave the Rift Valley. We did consider leaving. Remember? That was when we were talking about selling the farm. Remember?" Saks and Soru nodded. "But by then, the worst was over. The elections were over and the President and his people were still in control. Things calmed down. We decided to wait and see.

"We still have problems with those vigilante groups. While there is no more open violence or killing, those people still want this farm. They will never fully accept the idea that we Luos, and all the other so-called 'non-indigenous' people around here, own our land. The fact that we paid for the land and have title deeds to prove it does not seem to matter at all.

"But then last year we heard what we thought was just a nonsense rumor. According to this rumor, Siromene was one of the leaders – perhaps even the mastermind – of a plan to restart the tribal clashes on a massive scale in the Rift Valley. Your father asked Tej about it one day when they were playing golf in Kisumu. He knew that Tej had maintained contact with Siromene and was involved in some of

Siromene's projects. Tej's reaction was so extreme that it was clear that there had to be some truth in the rumor. Apparently, Tej could hardly wait to get off the course that day, and from then on he did everything he could to avoid your father.

"Your father thought this was very strange and tried to find out more about the plan. But he stopped talking about it after a while. I just assumed that everything had passed. But, looking back, I see that I was negligent. It could not have just ended like that. Like I said on Saturday at the funeral, I knew that something was worrying him. When I asked, he would say it was a troublesome business deal. But I sensed there was more. I should have pushed him for details."

The wind had gathered strength and was now ripping leaves off trees and sending them whirling into the verandah. The lightning was brighter and closer. The thunderclaps were sharper, following the lightning ever more closely. Large raindrops had begun to fall.

"Your father had some odd ways. When he wanted to tell me something difficult, he would grow silent for some days. Sometimes he would want me to prod the story out of him in pieces. Sometimes he would want to chew on it himself until he was ready to tell it in full. Looking back, I suppose I felt he was chewing on something that would come out in time. I was wrong.

"I think your father's death had something to do with this plan to restart the clashes. Remember the spear that was found with your father? The two people killed on this farm during the clashes had the same thing done to them – spears with little red flags on their ends driven through their chests and far, far into the ground. But just like for your father, there was no blood anywhere. It cannot be just a coincidence. Siromene or whoever... is still trying to intimidate Luos. But I am almost certain that there is more to this than just tribal animosity. Your father was too sensible a man to die for something like that. If that was all there was to it, we would all have been killed years ago."

"What does Uncle Boro say about this? Does he know?" asked Saks.

"We have talked. He knows as much as me. He cannot prove it, but he is convinced that Siromene was directly involved in your father's death. Apparently, people have come to mean nothing to the man. Money is everything."

The storm was immediately overhead. Blinding lightning flashes and deafening thunderclaps were arriving almost simultaneously. The wind-swept rain was turning the windows into shimmering translucent sheets through which Luka's beloved trees and shrubs – fighting to stay upright under the bombardment from above – appeared as swaying dark-green silhouettes against a hazy light-grey background.

4

Raju Ahluwalia, the Sollos' long-time lawyer and friend, was a pioneer in many dimensions. He was the first in a family of Kisumu-based Asian traders and merchants to enter the professions – in his case, law. The first to leave the country to study abroad – in his case Aberdeen, Scotland. Soon after his return to Kenya in 1959, he made his name as the first lawyer of Asian descent to be employed in the Solicitor-General's Office in the Colonial Government, and in 1960, as the first lawyer of any race to resign in protest over that Government's prejudicial and opportunistic interpretation of the law he so cherished. Thereafter, he built a successful private practice in Nairobi, specializing in commercial law. And then, in 1973, he became the first big-name lawyer to establish a permanent practice outside the capital. He chose Kisumu largely because he had been born there in 1929 when his immigrant parents were small-scale merchants in Kamito, a tiny trading post in Kisumu's hinterland. His parents had lived their final years in Kisumu and were buried there.

Many of Ahluwalia's relatives still lived in Kisumu. The older ones were unwilling to leave the town. Like his parents, most of these older relatives had moved to Kisumu in the 1950s and 1960s following years of small-scale trade in remote rural centers scattered around the Lake Victoria Basin – Holo, Akala, Ndori, Kamito, Kendu. For many years, fearing that Asians would out-compete European-owned businesses, only in such places had the Colonial Government allowed most Asian traders to operate. The political opening-up that began in the early 1950s meant new economic opportunities for Asians in major towns. Some Asian families moved from their rural bases to Kisumu. And then following Independence in 1963, and soon thereafter the passing of the Trade Licensing Act that decreed that small-scale rural trade was to be the preserve of

Africans, all Asian traders were ordered to move to large towns. Kisumu became home for many. Most never left.

For Ahluwalia's younger relatives, Kisumu was the only home they had ever known. To them, the town's easy pace and good weather were difficult to top or replicate elsewhere. The understanding and goodwill from the local populace cultivated by the older generation during years of toil in remote outposts were still strong. Relations with Kisumu Luos were relatively tension-free. And most important of all, with their trading skills brought to Kenya from India, with their privileged positions relative to Africans in colonial Kenya, with their forced but path-breaking relocations to Kisumu, and with their abilities to adjust quickly to new surroundings, Ahluwalia's older relatives and their contemporaries had bequeathed to future generations of Asians total domination of economic life in Kisumu. In how many other places would the typical young Asian with no post-secondary school education be able to say that? Theirs was a closely-knit community, determined to maintain a long-cultivated way of life.

As a practicing lawyer in Kisumu, Ahluwalia was the first professional of any kind to set up an office outside the town center. He selected an old colonial-era house overlooking Lake Victoria in Milimani, which by the late 1980s had become the most rapidly expanding middle-class residential area in the town. He was the first lawyer in East Africa to open a branch in a neighboring country, in his case Uganda. And even in Uganda, he chose to locate his office not in the capital, Kampala, but in Jinja.

"You just watch," he would tell his skeptical Nairobi-born, US-educated children when they questioned the wisdom of foregoing booming Kampala in favor of sleepy Jinja. "Places like Kisumu, Jinja, and Mwanza are going to be goldmines in another ten or fifteen years. First, they will be rewarded by their proximity to the Lake and its water, since, more than anything else, access to water is very soon going to define economic and social welfare in this region. Second, all those people you see working in Nairobi, Kampala, and Dar es Salaam today are soon going to be looking for places to retire in comfort. The big cities will be too expensive for them. Many of them will continue the practice of returning to their rural villages to retire. But for a good number, those rural villages will be too remote and full of hardship. Such people will choose places like Kisumu, Jinja, and Mwanza to spend their retirement years and retirement incomes. And then anybody who owns land in these places will be very happy. You don't believe me now, but you just wait and see. You will thank me for it one day."

On the Thursday after the funeral, Ahluwalia telephoned Rhoda and requested that she pay him a visit in his Kisumu office to discuss what he described as, "Various details about Luka's estate." To Rhoda, this was a very odd request. She and Luka had a joint will in which all assets reverted to the survivor. There should not have been anything to discuss. Troubled, she decided to go the very next day. Soru and Saks were still on compassionate leave from their jobs and able to accompany her.

Ahluwalia greeted them warmly, his diminutive body almost disappearing into Rhoda's large frame as they hugged.

"Your daughter is just as beautiful as you, Rhoda," said Ahluwalia, standing back a little to take in both women.

"Oh stop it, Raju!" said Rhoda. Ahluwalia never failed to compliment her. It was always in good taste, but it always embarrassed her.

"Oh no!" protested Soru. "Please go on, Mr. Ahluwalia! Nobody has said anything like that about me for ages!"

After a surprisingly easy conversation about the funeral, Ahluwalia turned to Soru and Saks and in his high-pitched voice, which his advanced age and abstemious lifestyle were rendering increasingly hoarse, said, "I want you to know that I thought very highly of your father. One could count on him."

"He thought very highly of you, too, Mr. Ahluwalia," replied Saks and Soru at the same time.

"Thank you for that. Thank you very much." Ahluwalia seemed to want to say more.

"I don't know if you are aware that for the last year or so your father and I were spending a lot of time together – not as lawyer and client but as friends and colleagues. We had helped found the Lake Victoria Action Group. Our aim in the group was to make the case to the Government that it should take more seriously its responsibility of managing the Lake and its resources. I love this lake. One of my first memories is of traveling with my father and brother by tugboat from Kisumu to Jinja, where we boarded a train on the old Busoga line north to Namassagali on the shores of Lake Kyoga. What a wonderful trip! But my goodness, that was a long time ago! In those days, the Lake was just there. So big. So full of life. So full of resources. Dangerous, yes, but devoid of problems. Not anymore. These days, the Lake is the resource centerpiece of major agricultural and industrial activity in eastern Africa. That means there are several competing interests. Artisanal fishermen and their cooperative societies, large-scale illegal trawlers, irritable islanders out there in the middle of the lake, small-scale fish and cargo loaders and unloaders, small-scale fish assemblers and dressers, large-scale processors, small transporters, large transporters, conservationists, administrators and tax collectors, and many more. Conflicts among them are growing sharper and more complicated. There is more and more pollution. Whether planned or not, a new development path is inevitable. Your father and I believed in planning.

"The difficulty is that while the Lake is a source of sustenance and livelihood for all of these local interests, it is not a local re-source, not even a national one. It is an international one. Only the national Governments in this region have the authority and power to force the competing interests to work toward more sustainable use of the Lake. But they must do that together. Each Government must be proactive. Unfortunately, over the years ours has not shown any interest at all in doing so. This region and the Lake have never been a priority. But your father was a persuasive man. He somehow managed to convince the Nyanza Provincial Commissioner and the Permanent Secretary in the Ministry of Environment and Natural Resources to jointly fund and convene a Conference on the State of the Lake Economy and Ecosystem aimed at getting each interest group to air its grievances or dreams and thereby build mutual understanding, if you know what I mean. We had begun to make progress. A few politicians from the region – including your uncle Mr. Tindi – had opened informal talks with key people in State House to gauge the likely reaction to the Conference. They knew that it that would most probably be interpreted in strict geopolitical terms. Through a tribal lens."

"Exactly!" said Saka, excitedly. "I have been trying to find a way to introduce material on the impacts of tribalism into my course on Kenya's economic development. Tribalism is so clearly a major driver of uneven progress across the country. But not one textbook deals with it directly."

"Yes," agreed Ahluwalia. "Sad, but true. You may have to write that textbook, Saks. No matter how good an idea, it must further the Government's tribe-based interest in a region. It was the same with the previous regime. OK, OK, we do not expect them to work against themselves. But we must find a way to help the President and his people see that they gain politically by investing in this area. And that the whole country gains, not just Luos. It will be hard work. We will miss your father's advice, his ideas, and most of all, his energy."

Ahluwalia seemed to grow embarrassed and turned to Rhoda and said, "Forgive me, Rhoda, I had not intended to go into all that.

But seeing you and the youngsters has resurrected lots of different emotions about my old friend."

"That's alright, Raju, I just thank you for being such a good friend to Luka."

Ahluwalia nodded slowly, then stood up and walked to a safe at the rear of his office. He opened it and took out a small envelope and hand-held tape recorder. Rhoda, Saks, and Soru recognized the tape recorder as Luka's. He would carry it around with him to catch, he said, half-thoughts before they flew away forever – half-thoughts on which he claimed many rewarding business ventures had been built.

Very gently, Ahluwalia handed the envelope and tape recorder to Rhoda and said, "Rhoda, Luka brought these to me a few days before he was killed. His instructions were that they be passed on to you in the event of his death or disappearance. He also instructed me to not allow the contents of the envelope to leave this office. Please take your time. I will be in the next room if you need me for anything."

Rhoda began to open the sealed envelope as Ahluwalia left the room. Her hands trembled a little. Inside the envelope she found a small cassette tape with her name on it, written in Luka's tiny hand-writing. She took out the cassette and inserted it into the player. She pressed play.

"Hello, Rhoda," said Luka, clearing his throat a bit. "If you are listening to this, I am probably no longer alive. Please forgive me for putting you and the family through everything you must be going through. But there could be no other way. I am being forced to take some terrible risks. I want to explain it to you. I have asked Raju to destroy this tape once you have listened to it. Please make sure that he does that."

Luka cleared his throat again. They heard him shuffle some papers.

"Do you remember that rumor we heard about a plot to restart the clashes in the Rift Valley? Alfred Siromene and some others were mentioned. I have discovered that there definitely is a plan to cause trouble in the Rift Valley. But the plan is not to restart the clashes. It is for a secession! Yes, the Rift Valley's so-called indigenous peoples are planning to secede from Kenya during the President's next term. Yes, the President is hoping to manipulate Parliament into changing the Constitution so that he can run again. He may not be able to twist things so that he himself gets another term. That would be difficult. But the Opposition is split. Anybody the President chooses to be his successor will win. The plan will remain the same.

"Everything begins with the cattle wars going on in the north Rift Valley. Apparently, the wars are being staged by Siromene, but with the President's full blessing. The idea is to get large numbers of military personnel stationed in the Rift Valley well ahead of the secession. These troops will then enforce the split following a mock *coup d'etat*. They believe that this is the only way to ensure that the President and his people will be safe forever. Safe from what, you ask. I have no idea. But that is the plan. These are some callous people, my dear. This explains the international airport and munitions factory in Eldoret. It explains those superb but barely used roads running north-south within the Rift Valley but next to nothing running east-west across it. And it explains why they insisted on building the new dam in the Rift Valley and not here along the edge of the Lake Basin where it would have made much more sense for the country. Siromene was so impatient with the Investment Ring because he really was in a hurry. You can just imagine what kind of capital these people feel they need to have to run the wars they are running and finance the country they want to create. There is only so much they can steal. They will have to earn some of it. I think I finally understand the man.

"So do I," thought Rhoda.

"This Alfred is bloody impossible!" That was three years before. Luka had just returned from a Ring meeting in Kericho. Rhoda knew something rotten must have happened because Luka seldom lost his cool or cursed like that. "He has bought off people at Customs Mombasa to delay the release of the shipment of tractor tires Patrick found for us. He wants a bigger share. Why? Because, for the first time, we went through his bankers for the guarantee. The first bloody time! Everyone has done it. Sammy, Patrick, Tej, Malcolm, me... Everyone! The shares are always equal, no matter what. But now Alfred wants 30 percent and the rest of us are to split the remaining 70 percent between us. Can you imagine?! I tell you, Rhoda, this fellow is going to destroy the Ring."

"I found out about all of this purely by chance, from Barsone, that squatter we have been feuding with for a while. You know him better than I do. The other week I caught him taking his landlord's name in vain (chuckle). I was buying petrol at Chemelil. He was walking by, apparently on his way home. He was very drunk and looked like he would not arrive safely. I offered him a lift, just for a laugh. I was not disappointed. Even after he was in the car and we were well on our way, it took him many minutes to realize that I was the donkey to whom he was referring! And when he did realize it, he became so disoriented that he started rambling on about all kinds of things – whatever came to his mind. I did not pay too much attention until he said something about being paid to steal cattle from Turkana communities in the far north of the country, drive them west across the border into Karamoja in Uganda, a good distance southward, and then back into Kenya, where they'd be abandoned in Pokot grazing areas. The Turkana would then attack the supposed Pokot cattle thieves, who would themselves be on the warpath over the apparent intrusion into their grazing lands. He said that he hated to do it. It was causing death and suffering among previously peaceful peoples. But he needed money. He knew of at least twenty other men who were being paid to do the same thing.

"By the way, are you paying school fees for Barsone's children? He thanked me for that as he got out of the car. That is good. He needs help. He has a good heart."

A pang of envy and self-pity cut into Soru's heart. If she did anything like that, Mark would be very angry with her... even though she was bringing in all the money. It was all so horrible. She did not understand him anymore. When she tried to talk to him, he would shout at her. "You think you are what? Eh? Just because your father is rich, you think you can talk-talk stupid things! You bugger off!" Mark's voice was always hard these days. Everything about him was hard. He spent hours on end in the gym. His body was like a rock. Yet being in excellent physical condition did not seem to give him any pleasure. He was scary. Thank God he wasn't the hitting type. One blow from him these days would probably kill her! But where were they going? How could they go on like this?

"Anyway, it was a crazy story, but it did explain those puzzling cattle wars. When I asked him who was paying him to do all this, he didn't want to say at first. But when I reminded him of his...um... his squatter-hood (chuckle) he revealed that it was Alfred Siromene and a few others just as close to the President. I asked him why they would want to do something like that. He said it was because these people want war. He said it just like that, "These people want war." He was not too coherent after that, but before I dropped him off, he said enough for me to be able to piece things together in the following days.

"It's a clever plan, but very callous. Siromene and company were too clearly implicated during the tribal clashes at the Coast and in the Rift Valley to go down that route again. Remember that their names came up during the inquiry. Their aim is a purge of us so-called foreigners from the Rift Valley. They will have some so-called indigenous Rift Valley people fight a bit. Then they will call in their future army, supposedly to help cool things down. In actuality, the army will be moved in so that it can practice its secession maneuvers for a few years. And all this will be on the unified Kenya's budget. It is clever but sinister and brutal."

The tape ran on for a while. Only the soft sound of Luka's slow breathing was audible. Rhoda, Saks, and Soru could picture the stern look on his face as he gathered the words he wanted to say next.

"You know, I've thought again about Tej's reaction when I asked him about the rumor about a new round of tribal clashes being planned for the Rift Valley. In retrospect, I see that he wasn't being cagey. He was scared. He was totally, totally terrified. I don't blame him. I was also scared when I found out about it. What does one do with this kind of knowledge? I could not go to the press. Too many journalists are either in the pockets of Siromene and his cronies or working for dishonest editors. Most of all, I could not tell you, or Boro, or anyone else close to me. I knew this thing would endanger lives.

"My solution is not a comfortable one. It has been on my mind for many weeks. On my own – and it must be on my own – I cannot stop them. But I think I can tie their hands for a few years. But to do that I must reveal that I know what they are planning. That is the dangerous part and the reason why you are listening to this."

Another long pause.

"You know me, Rhoda. I have never been one to take myself too seriously, especially when it comes to politics. For me – for our family – politics has always been something to get into to help relatives and friends with their election campaigns and whatnot. And it has always helped us to know a few senior officials when we are competing for Government contracts. But this story – this plan of Siromene's – has done something to me that I cannot explain. For the first time in my life, I am prepared to give my life for something other than you and the children. And what is that thing? It is this nation. This country they want to destroy. This country they want to split apart. This Valley they want to claim for themselves. I know you're surprised. To be honest, so am I. But this country has given us so much. Our family came to the Rift Valley many, many years ago. My grandfather lived most of his life here. He died here. He is buried here. My father was born here. We have as much of a right to live and work here as anyone. My father chose to build his life and family in Uchanga... in Luoland... because he saw big possibilities there. But he was still young when he made that choice. His vision of big possibilities in Luoland could only have come from here. His commitment to educating Uhanga's children came from what he saw education meant for Kenya, and he could only have seen that here. He changed thousands of lives with that vision. What these people are trying to do would have made him very angry. Just think about it. One day we are one nation, the next we are cut into pieces – families are split, businesses are ruined, people like us are driven from our homes. No way. It is within my power to help prevent it. I must try. I may lose my life, but I must try. I must honor the spirits of Osewe and Ang'awa. Heh heh, imagine Luka Sollo saying that!"

Saks was forever having to put up with innuendo and insinuation from his university colleagues about his father – the farm, the businesses, the behind-the-scenes influence, the immense wealth. He knew they just wanted to draw him out. They wanted to know what he thought about his father. He had learned to hold his tongue. "Why don't you just ignore them?" Maaike had asked a few weeks before when he had returned home in a rage. The Department Chairman had rejected his request to be put forward for a promotion to Senior Lecturer. "You don't need the money anyway, do you? Your father has plenty." It made him mad. But it cut in another direction, too. His father did have plenty of money. Was that all that counted? Was that all that life was about? Was that all that his father was about? Saks had begun to think that perhaps it was. Yet here was his father talking about honor, principles, and ideals. What should he make of it?

"What do I think I can do about it? I don't know if you remember a job we did in ninety-three and ninety-four for that Swiss telecommunications company, AMCOT Incorporated. We supplied them with the materials they needed to build those small sheds for what they said were three thousand digital-signal boosters along the length of the Valley. This was another one of those north-south investments. I remember at the time thinking that it was an odd project. But to be honest, I did not wonder for too long. The money we were earning was too good. Then the other week, what I had been too lazy to see back then came to me. The sheds were not for boosters at all! They could not have been! One large booster receiving satellite-transmitted signals would have been sufficient to serve an area ten times larger than the zone covered by those three thousand small ones, and at much lower cost. They could only have been building a land-based surveillance system. I have been digging further. I now know that those sheds contain highly sensitive audio monitors to track movements in key spots in the Valley. They are to be used to monitor troop movements. I know this because last year I saw a model of something very similar when we visited the City of Science in Paris. You went to another part of the museum, but I think I described the model to you when we got back to the hotel. Remember?"

Rhoda nodded, her thoughts flashing back to that vacation. Three weeks. They had flown first class from Nairobi to Cairo via Khartoum.

Five days of sightseeing in Egypt. A luxurious boat trip from Alexandria to Marseille. A train ride up to Paris. Two weeks in that wonderful city. And then back home by plane. She had loved it. She had never imagined it would be their last vacation together.

"Anyway, bit by bit, more of my memory began to return. I remembered a conversation I once had with AMCOT's Chief Engineer on the Project. His name was Heinz, or Henning, or something like that. A nice fellow. I think you may have met him, too. He had pushed for us to get the job mainly because we had visited his hometown, Lausanne, and had eaten lunch at his favorite restaurant. During that conversation, this fellow had revealed that the contract had been improperly awarded to AMCOT. It was the same old story. They had over-bid in the knowledge that they would win. The amount over and above their real bid would go to Siromene and thus also to the President. AMCOT was more than happy to do this because they were having trouble finding takers for their technology. They were very confident in the technical sophistication of their product, especially its ability to simultaneously receive and distinguish among very low-frequency signals over a wide area. I know, I know, I wasn't listening! But their system had a major flaw. Its hardware and software were exclusive to each other. Permanent damage to even one of the components of either would destroy the entire system. Few governments wanted a telecommunications booster system so vulnerable to damage and sabotage, let alone a land-based surveillance system. Worse still, the French firm subcontracted to build the hardware had withdrawn from the partnership because the number of orders for the system was too low. But then few countries are being run by the likes of our Alfred Siromene. AMCOT was on the verge of collapse. Like us, they were going to close their eyes, do the job, take the money, and run.

"That's the background, Rhoda."

Luka paused again, seemingly to catch his breath and clear his mind.

"This is what I have done. Since we built the so-called booster network, I know it inside out. But all I needed was a few of the boosters, as far apart from each other as possible. I have destroyed each one's relay switch. That alone should be the end of the system. I remember that the Chief Engineer mentioned that those switches were going to be the first casualties of the withdrawal of the French sub-contractor. There is a good chance that Siromene and company will have ordered extra. I will need to disable the software as well.

"Again, I think I can use something the Engineer told me. He described how the so-called boosters would eventually be adjustable remotely using a unique set of digital codes. But these codes would each have to be entered into a number pad on the relevant booster. The initial coding sequence for the three thousand boosters was going to be very simple, beginning with 3-0-0-0-1 and ending in 3-3-0-0-0. To activate the system for the first time, this simple initial coding sequence had to be in place. It would be customized once the system was up and running. What I plan to do is to change the coding on a few of the boosters. The only way they will be able to run the initial setup routine will be if I give them my new codes. I won't. So they will have to rely on pure chance or scrap the entire system and start afresh. That will set them back at least three years, maybe more."

Rhoda often found herself marveling at how some of the little things in one's life – the things one learned as seemingly trivial asides while living one's real life – how those things could suddenly and irreversibly move to center stage. Luka had embraced computers like an excited child. He could see that they helped the businesses. But for him it was more than that. He liked to play with them. He became an expert, fully steeped in the jargon, nobody's fool. Rhoda knew that there was no way that system would ever work properly once Luka Sollo was done with it!

The tape ran on silently for a long time. More than five minutes. At one point, they heard footsteps. And then they heard a door being locked.

"Where were you, Luka?" whispered Rhoda out loud, capturing her children's thoughts as well. As if responding to her, Luka continued with his devastating monologue.

"By the way, I am at our house in Nakuru. I drove here this morning from Panderi. I am starting from here. But for this to work, they need to know what I have done. Otherwise, they will continue with their plans as if nothing is wrong. In a few years we will have a poorly coordinated secession, but a secession all the same. So once I have changed the codes, I will have to go to Siromene and company – perhaps with the destroyed switches in hand – and tell them of the damage I have done to their system. If they do not kill me, then I still do not know Siromene.

"That is what is going to happen... that is what has happened. I am not afraid. I know I should be, but I am not. Perhaps the fear will come soon. It is an odd feeling to know that you are probably the only person able to do something that will almost certainly change the course of events in your country. It is a strange feeling, but it is sitting well in my mind.

"I am most probably dead now, but you are still alive. And the only reason you are still alive is that you must be behaving as confused by my death as everyone else. Things must continue to look that way. Do not be fooled. You are being watched very closely by the likes of the DO, DC, and PC. As you know, all of them are on Siromene's payroll. If they get even a little suspicious, you, too, will die, and so will the children. I do not want that to happen. The time to speak out will come.

"I must stop now, my dear. Please talk to Boro for me. He must be careful. They are watching all Luo politicians very closely. Tell the children that I prize and cherish them. I am very proud of them. I know I speak for you when I say that Sakawa needs to settle down. Life is short. He does not have as much time as he seems to think he does. Please assure him that we want him to be happy, but he must make up his mind about his life and commit himself to something.

"Soru feels that I want her to stay with Mark. To be honest, for a long time I did. But, Rhoda, she is no longer the daughter we raised. That man is destroying her spirit. Please tell her that I have changed my mind. She must not waste her life. It will be hard for her to begin again, but her children will thank her for it one day.

"Tell them both to be careful, but also to seize any opportunity to get engaged politically. They know my mantra. We do not have much time on this earth as adults so we must spend that time doing important things. I now see that a sure sign that something is important is if it is politically charged. But please tell them that as they get involved, they must not do so in isolation, like their father has done at sixty years of age (chuckle). And they should remember what their grandfather Ang'awa used to say. "To climb your ladder you must first plant it on flat ground." His point was they there is no naturally flat ground. You must create that for yourself through hard work and sacrifice.

"And you, my dear..."

A long pause, the first trace of uncertainty in his voice. It seemed like the tape was stopped and restarted. His voice was deeper. His words came out shakily... haltingly.

"You, my dear – you, I thank for... for every minute of our life together. Thank you for everything. Everything. Thank you for your love and care for me. Thank you. I hope... I hope you always felt mine for you. I hope you always felt safe... and protected. You will be in my heart to the end."

The tape ran on silently for a few more minutes. No one made a move to stop it. Each of them felt battered, but none of them felt bad. They were not that surprised by it all. It was just like Luka Sollo to take things into his own hands like that. It brought tears to their eyes. But it warmed their hearts as well. And when they looked at one another, they were all half-smiling. Nobody said anything.

After a while, Rhoda got up and asked Ahluwalia to come back in. He did not ask about the contents of the tape but instead reminded them of his agreement with his client. Rhoda handed him the tape and asked him if he would kindly destroy it in their presence. Ahluwalia seemed relieved and did so immediately, using a hammer that, to their surprise and amusement, he pulled out of his shiny leather briefcase.

"Muggers, you know," Ahluwalia said, smiling self-consciously.

He threw the shattered plastic and mangled tape into his large fireplace and put a match to them.

5

"Eat, fool! This is your last meal. Your last supper! Ha!" snarled Spike. He was on edge. He could never understand why Geoffrey lingered like this before a job. Why not just get it over with?

Luka had not eaten for a long time. Not since lunchtime the previous day – right before he had gone to State House and confronted Siromene. The man had been infuriated.

"So help me God, you will pay for this with your life!"

"So help you God?" It was so absurd that Luka had laughed out loud. "Alfred, do you really believe that God is on your side? You are already causing death and destruction. You are planning for more. And you believe that God is on your side? You are truly sick."

Luka had not seen Siromene in person for almost three years. He had to admit that the fellow looked well. He was clearly working out. When Siromene joined the Ring, they had bonded quite quickly due to their mutual devotion to weight-training. Like him, Siromene had a full gym in his house. They had often worked out together. But that felt like a long time ago. The last time they saw each other had been at Gilani's Supermarket in Nakuru where they were both buying meat. Luka had been on his way west to Panderi. Siromene was going the other way to Nairobi. They had greeted each other warmly enough but nothing more. The break in the friendship was complete.

So here they were. Perhaps it was always going to come to this?

"What I believe is between me and my God.," hissed Siromene. "And I am telling you now... You primitive Luo... I am telling you that, *so-help-me-God*, you will die for what you have done!"

"Me primitive? You, Alfred Siromene, are calling me, Luka Sollo, primitive? You? You thug... you brute... you are calling me primitive? What a joke!"

"You are laughing at me? I will tell them to kill you slowly. You will beg for your life."

Two State House security officers had marched Luka to a rear exit and pushed him into a waiting police van. He was handcuffed and pushed down on to the van's cold floor. The van set off. It was an old vehicle, so it moved slowly, laboring through the gears. Luka could not tell where he was being taken. There were no windows in the van. After some hours he asked to be allowed to relieve himself. The van slowed and turned on to a very bumpy road. After a few minutes, the van stopped and he was let out into a small thicket. As he urinated, he recognized the surrounding landscape. They were near Rongai, about forty kilometers northwest of Nakuru. He breathed in the cool air and thought of his grandfather, John Mark Osewe, who was buried in nearby Njoro. He had visited the grave two weeks before, on his way to destroy one of the signal boosters outside Elburgon. As he was led back to the van, the memory of the visit gave him comfort. "I honor you, *Kwaru*. I honor your life. I honor your spirit. I honor your sacrifice."

They did not stop again until they arrived at the DO's office in Londiani. He had driven past the building many times before on his way to Panderi but never entered. Given the dirt and grime on its outer walls, the office was surprisingly clean and tidy inside. "Admirable," thought Luka as he was led in. "This fellow must be good at his job."

He had not eaten for a long time, but he was not hungry. He was thirsty.

"Water. I need water. Please."

DO Kimani handed him a cup of something hot. Tea. Very sweet. Very strong. Too strong.

"Please, just water."

"No. You drink that tea. All of it." They wanted him to stay alert.

Luka drank it with difficulty. He lips were badly cracked, his tongue and throat swollen, his wrists still handcuffed in front of him.

At Geoffrey's signal, the other five stood up and walked out of the room, leaving Luka alone with their leader. It was also part of the routine. Geoffrey always spent some time alone with the prisoner, right before the exercise commenced.

"Sollo. What kind of a name is that?"

"Eh? I mean, pardon me?"

"Your name. What sort of a name is it?"

"I do not understand you. I think you know that I am Luo. It is a Luo name."

"Where did it come from?"

Luka looked up over the cup at Geoffrey, who was leaning against the wall, watching him. It was a strange question. The man was strange. What did he want to know? On a hunch, Luka said in Dholuo, "Why do you want to know?"

"I just want to know," replied Geoffrey quietly, also in Dholuo. "Where did it come from?"

Luka set the cup down on the table and very slowly and carefully told Boro's milk-cow expedition story, replacing "Nwanji" with "Sollo."

"Good story. Very good story," said Geoffrey, continuing in Dholuo. "Almost good enough for a reprieve. Almost. They want you to disappear. There are many ways to disappear. Look at me." He walked across the room and stood in front of Luka. He held up his hands and flipped them back and forth in front of Luka's face. Light side. Dark side. Light side. Dark side. Luka saw that they were the hands of a much older man. Much older than the face, which was also being presented for close examination. Facelift.

"Why are you telling me this? Who are you?" asked Luka.

"I am a killer, my friend. I kill people who annoy governments. I kill people like you. I used to kill people who annoyed Botha's

Government in South Africa. I worked for Amin. I worked for Obote. I worked for Mobutu. Now I work here... at home."

"Why are you telling me this?"

"I sometimes let people go and help them to disappear... I have done it many times... if I like their stories. But your story was not quite good enough. Don't say I didn't give you a chance." He walked out.

"You are disgusting!" Luka called out after Geoffrey, shaking his head and trying to regain his concentration. The woman in book about life as a prisoner in the Soviet Gulags had said, "I became stone." He had been concentrating on that for the last several hours – becoming stone. He knew he was going to die, he remained oddly afraid of that. The journey to his death was what frightened him. "Stone, stone, stone..." he silently repeated to himself in Dholuo. "*Kidi, kidi, kidi...*"

They waited until it was completely dark and then led him outside, still handcuffed, but now from behind. They put a black hood over his head and tied it just tightly enough around his neck to slightly restrict his breathing. They marched him out in front of the Range Rover, kicking him back to his feet whenever he stumbled and fell on his face, which was every few steps. They laughed.

It took him three hours to get to the shed. Once inside, they stripped him naked, tearing off the shirt with "LS" embroidered on each cuff. They used the *sjambok* for the first time. Still hooded and handcuffed, the lash took him totally by surprise and he fell to the floor screaming. They laughed and whipped him many more times, stopping only when his screams had become whimpers. They removed the handcuffs and hood. They shone a powerful flashlight directly into his eyes, scorching his retinas and partially blinding him. They forced him on to the table, face up. They donned heavy latex gloves. Fifty punches to the stomach, fifty blows to the head. They demanded the codes. They saw him shake his pulpy head.

"*Kidi.*"

They opened the trunk that had been in the back of the Range Rover. They took out the battery, the cords, the pliers. They zapped his soft spots: earlobes, lips, nipples, foreskin, testes, in between his toes. They demanded the codes.

"No! *Kidi!*"

They removed each of his toenails with the pliers.

"No!! Please, please!! *Kidi!!*"

They took out the small drill and bored into his incisors. They saw that he had fainted. They revived him with five cc of adrenaline injected directly into his jugular. They circumcised him. The codes!

Head shake... "No... *kidi...*" now just a whisper.

They turned him over, pulled his arms wide apart, his legs, too. They sodomized him with a massive dildo. They saw him faint again, shitting blood."

They knew he was almost dead. They gave him another adrenaline shot, this time ten cc directly into the heart. They saw his eyes fly open.

"Rhoda... "

They took out the ice chest and removed the flask. They took out the electric saw.

3

THE END OF THE WORLD

The man was angry at the boy – his six-year-old son. It was his daughter's birthday party. She was turning four. The party was at their house, outside in the garden. The man disliked children's parties. The many shrieking children annoyed him, as did their parents who would hover around, watching, not saying much beyond hello, I'm so and so's father or mother, and then expecting him to keep the conversation going. He always just wished they would leave.

His wife was clearly enjoying herself. She was in her element. He envied the ease with which she was moving between groups of children playing the games she had planned for them. Smiling brightly at parents and inviting them to join in or help themselves to the tea, coffee, and scones she had prepared and laid out on a linen-covered table in a shaded corner of the garden. He had yet to learn how to play his role during these events. It was his house, and it was his daughter's birthday. But he felt out of place – like a stranger.

And then there was his lingering frustration at having allowed his nemesis at work, Jake Bosnich, get the better of him at the previous week's planning meeting. He had been arguing for a quick decision on his proposal that Shasta County create an open space district with a range of outdoor recreational activities. The aim was to lure in campers, hikers, and bikers by-passing Redding en route to more northerly sites in California and Oregon. There was potential for Redding to capture some of that business. He had sounded out their boss, Gerry Carr, on the proposal and been assured of support. But at the meeting, Carr had heeded Bosnich's inevitable call for a delay to allow for further consultations with Redding's business community. He knew that Jake had personal relationships with Redding's business leaders. He knew that Jake's primary objective always was to ensure that the companies led by these individuals captured large shares of any new commercial opportunity in the city. With these forces at play, it would now be many months before a decision could be reached. And the eventual plan would be nothing like the original proposal. He was still irritated at himself for not being prepared, and for not finding the words to resist Jake's skilled assault.

He was on edge.

So when the man saw his son bounce a toy dinosaur off the head of another child, and when he heard that child let out a distressed yelp, the man was suddenly infuriated. In no time he was across the garden. And suddenly his son was at his feet, looking up at him with eyes wide open, screaming in pain and fury, clutching the spot at the top of his head where the man's open palm had landed, stiff and hard.

The party was ruined. His daughter began to cry, as did his wife. As usual, the boy had stopped crying almost immediately. Everyone left within ten minutes. For some days after that, the man waited in apprehension for a visit from the Redding police. He was sure that one of the parents would report his cruelty. The police never came. But his punishment did. And it was worse than any fine or jail sentence. His daughter forgave him for ruining her special day, but frequently and opportunistically reminded him why four was her least liked number. From his wife he lost a bit more of the soft feeling on which their marriage had been founded. And he lost his son altogether, for many years.

And so how should he answer this question from his son?

*   *   *

"Is that it?"

Should he say, "It's like this. Remember that time at your sister's birthday party when I hit you and knocked you over? Well, that was a mistake. I made a mistake. I should not have done that. I did it to protect myself. You were six. I was thirty-seven. You did nothing wrong. What does it mean? It means I am sorry for that."

But he knew that would not help. The boy had seen right away how wrong it had been. He had never again called the man "Daddy." From then on, it was, "Dad," or "Father." Hard and flat, like a hand slapping a head.

Was that it?

Oweh began to whistle loudly as he approached the upper entrance to his homestead – the entrance in between the huts of his fourth and sixth sons. He preferred this one to the main entrance, which stood directly in front of his own hut, across the width of the circular homestead of sixteen huts – his, one each for his seven wives and their unmarried daughters and young children, and one each for his eight post-adolescent sons. But Oweh always approached noisily, aiming to avoid finding any of the young men in compromising situations. He knew they were up to young men's games, which he encouraged. Their serious years would come. But he did not want to know any details.

The tune Oweh whistled was a lively one, but it did not jump to his tongue and spring from his lips as would normally have been the case. There was a heaviness in his chest, a tightness in his throat. Jebet was ill. Oweh could see that she did not have much time left. Her once plump and supple body was gaunt and wrinkled. She had lost almost all her teeth, and with them had gone her beautiful smile. Oweh saw all this and wept inside. Jebet, his third wife, inherited from his brother Nwanji, who was killed in battle. Jebet, the only woman he knew who would serve herself more food than she did him and other men. Jebet, who refused to cook fish for him. "That is not food," she would declare. Jebet, the mother of just one child – a daughter, Sakawa, who had not married well and was now so busy toiling in her fields and caring for her children that she seldom came home to see her mother. Jebet, an aging woman without sons and thus a woman increasingly reliant on charity and good will from others – from the husband she shared with six others; from her co-wives who cared for her but still felt compelled to compete with her; from her stepsons and stepdaughters who loved her but loved their mothers more. Jebet was dying.

Oweh went straight to her hut, which stood to the left of his, with one hut in between.

"Jebet?" Oweh called out at the entrance. No answer. He called out her name again, a little louder. Still no answer. But he noticed that the removable door made from newly cut branches sewn together with strips of bark stood closed from the inside. Closed from the inside?! It was already mid-morning. Oweh felt a rush of concern. He crouched down and pushed at the door. It fell inward loudly. He thought he heard a moan. The five hens and eight chicks that spent nights in the hut scrambled out and into the light, clucking angrily at having been left indoors for so long.

"Jebet?" Oweh called out as he stepped into the hut, closing his eyes briefly to quicken their adjustment to the darkness. But he knew the layout of the room and went directly to her. "Jebet?"

"Friend," she croaked back.

"How have you awoken?"

"I have awoken. I am thirsty."

Still only half-seeing, still crouching but ignoring the pain in his creaking knees, Oweh moved quickly across the small room to the covered clay pot of drinking water. He half-filled the drinking calabash and brought it to her. She gulped at it. When had she last drunk any water, he wondered, suddenly livid at Achieng, his youngest wife whose responsibility it was to tend to the ailing Jebet. Achieng would see!

"Slowly, slowly," Oweh cautioned her, holding back the calabash.

"I am thirsty!" snarled Jebet, grabbing at his hand and directing the gourd back to her mouth. Oweh smiled to himself. There was no pleasing Jebet. He remembered the day he first saw her – the day Nwanji returned from the disastrous milk-cow expedition. Nwanji's homestead had stood about twenty long throws away from his, in the direction of the evening sun. Nwanji's expeditions always took him in the opposite direction – toward the rising sun. On his return, Nwanji would pass through Oweh's homestead on the way back to his own homestead. And before that, he would have passed through their father's homestead. So that day, as always, it was their five mothers Oweh heard first.

Oweh was sitting outside his hut repairing a fish trap when he heard the first yelp. Then came two more, less surprised it seemed than the first, and then a rhythmic high-pitched chant, growing louder by the moment. The return of an expedition brought both excitement and trepidation. What had been won? How many cattle? How many women? What had been lost? How many men?

Nwanji's weary party of men, women, and livestock entered his younger brother's homestead through the main entrance. It turned left and wound its way twice around the large field at the center of the compound and then departed, taking with it Oweh's two wives, already chanting and ululating along with the other women.

"I see you," Oweh had called out to his elder brother each time Nwanji passed in front of him.

"There!" Nwanji had responded, spear in hand, back as straight as a mature papyrus shoot, body even leaner, darker, and harder than it had been the many moons before when he and his party had passed through the home in the same way, but moving in the opposite direction, to mark the start of the expedition.

Oweh did not see his brother again for many days. In addition to taking time to visit and pray beside the graves of relatives who had passed away in his absence, Nwanji had to visit the homes of men lost during the expedition. It was a delicate matter. Widows, parents, children, relatives, friends wanted details of the men's last days. News of their final wishes. Words of comfort and understanding. Shares of spoils. Nwanji took this responsibility seriously, always taking with him two items of value – one living, one dead. Maybe a he-goat and a throwing spear. Or a guinea fowl and a stool. Or a calf and a wooden drinking cup. And with each item he brought a story about the fallen man. Everyone knew he made up the stories, but that did not matter. The stranger the story, the better – better for keeping the departed man's spirit alive.

After the three remaining stolen bulls died, Nwanji had traded his prized hunting spear – a spear so well-balanced that it sat almost weightlessly in the palm – for four goats and ten chickens. He knew he would need them for the stories.

"When Olloh fell, he threw his spear toward a bush with his last action. Like this. This he-goat here – yes this very one – this he-goat appeared from behind that bush as if it had been watching him. It followed us all the way here. You know, this animal has never made a sound – not until I brought it here to this home. Now listen to it! It will not stop talking. Just like Olloh!"

"Where we went, there were no guinea fowl. But there were great trees with dark, hard wood. Okeyoh made this stool from such wood. He hungered for the sweet meat of guinea fowl and talked often about how he would come and gather his children around him as he sat on this stool and told them war stories."

"The day before he died, Omoreh told me of a dream in which a calf was flying above his head trying to piss on him. The piss was raining down like huge beads, but slowly-slowly. He knew that if the droplets touched him, he would die. He knew that if the droplets touched the soil, the crops would die. He ran to his hut and found a drinking cup and caught each drop of piss. The calf was pleased and came to live in his home and promised to bear him many fat offspring in the years to come."

Nwanji spent a full day at the home each of the six fallen adventurers. Drinking. Eating. Talking. Singing. Playing his harp. Dancing. Consoling. Telling story after story, in one way and then another, and another. To men, to women, to children. Individually. In groups. He did it with great care and skill. To them, he was the man they had lost – their memories of the man. By the time Nwanji and his escorts arrived at each home, their hosts would have heard of the expedition's return, and of the absence of their loved one. Nwanji and his escorts would be met at each homestead with wailing and chest-beating from dust-covered, shaven-headed widows, wild-eyed and terrified at the uncertainty wrought by the death of a husband. Who would inherit them? Would they be better or worse than their fallen husbands? Would they be richer? Poorer? Kinder? Crueler? Better lovers? They felt all this, and wailed it, as they raced round and round their homesteads, temporarily maddened by the upheavals in their lives.

Only after Nwanji had fulfilled these duties did he feel free to visit the homes of his father, Silual, and brothers, Oweh, Madiany, and Miganga. There would be small gifts and mementos for them, too. A new stool. An unusual rock. A new medicinal herb. Some new seeds. And when the expedition had been especially rewarding, some livestock. The milk-cow expedition had not yielded any exotic livestock, but it did bear two women – the sisters who called themselves Jebet and Jebkosgey. So Nwanji took the two women with him on his round of visits to family homesteads.

Right away, Oweh saw that Jebet was the stronger of the two.

"This one has a strong spirit," he observed. "She will produce strong children."

"Maybe," said Nwanji, smiling at his brother. "But first I need to find a way through. She is still fighting. The other one has been no problem, but she is not well. She has been vomiting. And she is also... damaged... down there. Everything has been scraped away. You touch it and it is as if she feels nothing. But her breasts are very sensitive."

Nwanji got through to Jebet only after her sister passed away following two moons of almost non-stop vomiting. Nwanji was a keen observer of moods. He sensed Jebet's vulnerability. The night following Jebkosgey's burial, Nwanji let himself into the hut he had built for Jebet. She did not resist. But his pleasure was diminished by the discovery that she, too, showed little responsiveness to his skilled touching below the waist. She, too, was damaged. Unlike with Jebkosgey, focusing on Jebet's breasts did not appear to arouse her. But when it was over, she would not let go of him. She wrapped her arms and legs around him and held on as if terrified. She held on to him until morning came. That was how it would be between them. In time, their lovemaking was less about the brief intercourse than it was about the lengthy holding, which soon he also came to need from her.

Jebet conceived four times in three years, but gave birth only once, the fourth time, to Sakawa. Nwanji was away on an expedition when the baby came.

"You see, she is now ready to become one of us," whispered one of Jebet's co-wives to the other as they watched the new mother smile at her new baby, following a long and hard delivery during which she had ripped badly. "*Aiee*, now there will be no stopping her. We are in trouble! Wait until Nwanji returns and sees what she has produced for him!"

But it was not to be. Nwanji never returned.

*   *   *

Jebet had not liked the stories brought back to her about Nwanji. The storyteller, Ogutu Kochido, had been lazy, careless, and unimaginative.

"What do you mean Nwanji dreamt he was a fish?!" Jebet had spat out, staring angrily at the black mudfish flip-flapping lazily at the bottom of the half-filled water pot. "He would never have had such a dream! Never! His dreams were always of war, cattle, and women. Not flat ugly fish! He hated fish!"

Jebet had dropped the pot in disgust, turned away and bolted for her hut. But for Oweh's quick reflexes and sure hands, the pot would have fallen to the ground and broken. And that would have been scandalous. Rejecting a gift was unheard of, let alone damaging it in the process.

"Don't worry," Oweh consoled the angry Ogutu. "She is a foreigner."

"Yes, but she has been here for almost five years! She should know our ways by now."

"Yes, yes. She should. But Nwanji was away too much. He did not take the time to teach her. She needs a husband who will take the time to teach her our ways. Who will inherit her?"

"The elders are saying it should be you, Oweh. You are Nwanji's immediate follower, and he loved you very much."

"Me?"

"Yes, that is what they are saying. You are a stable man."

Oweh was not being fully open with Ogutu. Nwanji's death had shaken the entire clan. A promising leader had been lost. Still only midway through his first maturity, Nwanji already owned over eighty head of cattle and had taken three wives. Jebet was his third. Oweh knew that he would be expected to inherit one of them. It could only be Jebet. Whenever Nwanji went on expedition, he would ask Oweh to look after his homestead. Oweh therefore knew each of Nwanji's wives well. Jebet was the youngest, but he knew her the best. She had picked up Dholuo quickly from her co-wives and other women in the clan. But she wanted to understand what men meant when they spoke. With Nwanji's frequent absences, she came to rely on Oweh for that instruction. Taking care to meet with her only during the day and only in plain view of his own two wives, Oweh spoke often with Jebet. Her intensity meshed easily with his calmness and generosity. In time, she stopped referring to him formally as brother-in-law. "I will call you friend," she had said. "You are Nwanji's friend and my friend." It could only be Jebet.

"But why are you leaving when Jebet is so heavy?" Oweh had asked Nwanji on hearing of the planned journey.

"I must go now," Nwanji had replied. "I was here when she lost the other three. I had a dream two nights ago. In the dream, I was away from home when this child was born. The child lived. I called her Sakawa. My brother, this child must live. I must go."

Oweh knew how much Nwanji hungered for a child with Jebet. She was his favorite. Everyone could see. A decision to leave when she was so heavy must have been very difficult.

"Please look after her," said Nwanji, resting his hand on his brother's shoulder. "Her tongue is sharp, but her spirit is tender. Her home in the Hills and the three lost ones are always on her mind. I know you understand her wounds. You are a friend to her."

Oweh nodded. "I will take care of her."

"When the child is born, speak for me and name her Sakawa."

"I will."

"And if I do not return, take Jebet into your home and care for her as I would."

"You will return, my brother."

"Look after her."

It could only be Jebet.

"Yes, it should be you, Oweh," repeated Ogutu. "But will she cook your fish?! Ha ha!"

Jebet heard the men's laughter from inside her hut. The sound of it enraged her. Who did they think they were?! Why had Oweh caught the pot? She had wanted it to break. Oweh was her friend, but he was too kind and polite. And who did that fool, Ogutu, think he was, bringing her a stinky mudfish and water pot from Nwanji? A fish? From Nwanji?! What a lazy, disrespectful, foolish man! His pot should have fallen and broken!

Nwanji had taken Ogutu into his expedition party only after weeks of unrelenting cajoling from the man's uncles and elder brothers who were concerned that he was maturing too slowly.

"Only you can form him into something that might become a man," they had flattered him.

Nwanji had not been keen. Expeditions were serious affairs for serious men, not learning trips for aimless ones. Eventually, he had capitulated under the flattery and taken Ogutu into the group. He had begun to regret it almost immediately. The man did not have a single drop of adventurous blood running through his veins. No warrior spirit. No predatory instincts whatsoever. Afraid of battle and death. No real hunger for the sweetness of livestock and women won by force. No music in his heart. No singing voice. Nothing to contribute to the many songs composed by Nwanji and the other warrior-harpists and warrior-drummers Nwanji always included in his expedition parties. So Ogutu's usual job on expeditions was to prepare campsites, cook, and clean. He never went into battle. And thus it came to be that he alone returned from the doomed expedition.

Ogutu had few stories for his fallen colleagues' families. He had not actually seen any of them fall, so he had few facts to work with. Moreover, he had a poor imagination. And most of all, he had no real love for Nwanji or any of the other men in the party.

The brutal end of the expedition came after they had been traveling for almost four full moons, as always heading in the direction of the rising sun, toward the unknown. Their advance men had been skillful negotiators. They met little resistance along the way. Nwanji had no wish to confront the fierce hill people from whom he had won Jebet ten rains before, so he led his group of thirty-seven heavily armed men on a path parallel to the hills but well inside the flat plains inhabited by Luo communities – some friendly, some not.

The long rains came while they were in the plains. With the

rains came flooding. Torrents of muddy water rushed down from the hills, submerging plants, drowning animals, and forcing the party to cling precariously to trees and sturdy shrubs for days. They emerged from the muddy plain sodden, hungry, thirsty, and fewer by two men who had been bitten by venomous snakes competing in the dark for perching spots.

Long marches without food and heavily laden with weapons were part of regular training drills for Nwanji's expeditions. The men were accustomed to the extra weight they were carrying, and also to the severe food deprivation they had endured while fighting with the mud. It was the thirst that did them in. They had been surrounded by water for days but unable to drink any of it. Bloated bodies of animals floating by told them as much. Their hands and feet swelled both from internal dehydration and lengthy immersion in water. Their tongues filled their mouths. Their eyes grew sandy and bloodshot, their vision blurry.

The attack was sudden and ferocious. Two men – Ogutu Kochido, the sole survivor, and Owino Kajulu, another man deemed by Nwanji to be too timid a fighter to be given any combat duties – had been sent to look for drinking water while the others took stock and discussed the way forward. Nwanji had chosen what he felt was an ideal site for a temporary camp. It sat midway up a small hillock and had an uninterrupted view of a shallow valley through which he was sure a spring with clear potable water ran, emptying eventually into the larger river that traversed the plain and broke its banks every long rainy season.

Had he been less tired, less thirsty, more clear-headed and alert, Nwanji would have sent two more men further up the hill to make sure that others with more permanent occupancy aims had not already acted on a similar favorable assessment of the site. He would have noticed that the shrubs and bushes around them were too well-browsed to be the work of only wild animals, the grassy patches grazed a little too low. He would have recognized that there were domesticated livestock nearby, and thus also human settlements. He might have saved more of his men. He might have saved himself.

From well-hidden spots further up the hill, their attackers had been watching the group for some time, as it trudged its way out of the mud. They saw everything. They could tell who was in command. So when they attacked, silently, in three groups of twenty men each, one coming in from directly above, one from the left, one from the right, they slew Nwanji first, literally chopping him to pieces with their bitterly sharp axes and machetes.

Nwanji heard the shrill war-cry and knew right away that an attack was underway. He had heard it before – during the doomed milk-cow expedition when his party had been assailed repeatedly as they made off with the stolen cattle and kidnapped women, Jebet and Jebkosgey.

Jebet.

Right before the deluge, Nwanji and Ondiek Pith had been composing a love song. The song had been at an early stage. The tune had stabilized, but the words had yet to settle.

I am calling you, come
Come quickly to me
The river is swelling
I will hold your hand as we cross

We are crossing together
Together we will cross

Bring your baskets
There is grain to carry
Bring your gourds
There is milk to drink

We are crossing together
Together we will cross

I have left my spear
There will be no battle
Here is my hand
Hold it to your breast

We are crossing together
Together we will cross

It had been raw and incomplete, but everyone in the group had liked it immediately. An initial drumbeat had been added as Nwanji and Pith continued to work on the words.

Pith's inspiration had been the new bride he had taken a few months before the start of the expedition. For Nwanji, it had been Jebet.

Jebet.

It had been Jebet for a long time. Her grasp of Dholuo was almost complete. But when listening to him sing, she wore the expression of sharp concentration that had been constantly on her face during her early days in his home as she learned the language. More than anything else about Jebet, Nwanji loved that searching look on her face, and the way her eyes would light up with pleasure whenever she grasped the message he was sending her. On such days, he knew she would be waiting for him in the evening. He would go, even if another wife was expecting him.

The bond between them was almost sacred.

"You are a kidnapper who sings love songs to his prisoner," she would whisper as he moved inside her. "You want to comfort me. I want to satisfy you."

As he fell, Nwanji's final thought was of pregnant Jebet's searching look.

Those in Nwanji's party who could, ran downhill but were quickly overhauled and killed in stride, their shouts of fear and agony drowned out by hoots and whoops from the attackers.

Nwanji had underestimated Owino and Ogutu, the two men he had sent off in search of clean water.

Owino was a braver man than Nwanji had assumed. When he saw a terrified Ojal Kotieno sprinting downhill, obviously running for his life, Owino had turned uphill, toward the danger. He was the only one to inflict a casualty on the attackers. He saw Ojal's three pursuers a few seconds before they saw him – enough time to launch his spear toward them, felling one but turning the other two on him. He crouched down, ready to defend himself, but was slain immediately.

Ogutu was a more cunning man than Nwanji had imagined – a better battle tactician. He, too, spotted fleeing comrades and knew immediately that the party had been ambushed. He guessed correctly that the attack could only have come from above. He also correctly imagined the claw-like maneuver to block off a lateral escape and leave only a downhill outlet. So he sprinted hard down the hill, away from danger, about thirty paces, turned to his right and raced twice that distance straight across the face of the hillock, and then turned right again, uphill, into the clearing at the top that was sprinkled with huts but which at that point contained only women, children, and old people – all the younger men having gone down for the kill. Within moments, Ogutu was through the clearing and into the thickets on the other side, well before the startled cries from the women and elders, and even longer before word of his escape reached the ambushers. He ran all day until the sun set, toward the sunset, toward home, stopping only once for water. The next day, he ran again, toward the setting sun again. Only on the third day, only when he was sure that he was safe from the rear, only then did Ogutu settle into the quick walk that led him home.

2

Never again did Ogutu Kochido leave Uhanga. His children, grand-children, and many generations of great grandchildren were raised on terrifying stories of the perils of travel into distant, foreign lands; of the possibility of total loss; of the virtues of limited ambition. It was not until 1983 – almost two hundred years after Ogutu's death – that any of his descendants left Uhanga to make a life elsewhere in Kenya. Fifty years too late. Only extraordinary luck or immense effort would prevent his descendants from being anything but followers in a rapidly changing world.

Oweh, son of Silual, brother of Nwanji, inheritor of Jebet, was not a well-traveled man. He had few good stories that extended beyond the time and space covered by half a day's walk in any direc-tion. Oweh's stories of adventure and daring were stories of solitary challenges overcome on the lake – stories that were difficult to share with those who spent most of their time on dry land in the company of others. Oweh's descendants might have suffered the same fate as Ogutu's had he not accepted the responsibility of inheriting Jebet following Nwanji's death in battle. By doing so, Oweh inherited for his family Nwanji's stories of adventure, cunning, and negotiation in distant, hostile lands. Jebet had loved those stories and committed them to memory almost as soon as they left Nwanji's lips. She had also loved to retell the stories. And she loved to sing Nwanji's songs. Through her, Oweh's descendants grew up with Nwanji's stories and songs throbbing and beating in their minds and hearts.

Oweh's lineage also inherited Jebet's infrequent but intense sullen periods that everyone came to understand were brought on by hunger and longing for a distant home. Emerging from Jebet's dark days was gruff disaffection and impatience with the way things were in Uhanga. "There are people who do not see the world the same way as you," she would say in irritation. "There are many, many other people in this world."

The full impacts of these intangible inheritances were not felt for more than one hundred years. It took that long for their basic messages to be winnowed out. By then, Oweh, Jebet, and all their age mates had long since succumbed to the march of Time. By then, many stories with previously unfathomable roots and tips had taken hold of the lives of their descendants. By then, Uhanga's destiny was increasingly driven by rules and imperatives with distant origins and unfamiliar patterns and rhythms.

*   *   *

The year was 1904. Both rains had failed in 1903. Without the long rains, the sorghum and millet crops had died without yielding a harvest. Without the short rains, the forage that sustained the livestock had withered and died, and so had many of the animals. Without enough sorghum and millet, milk and butterfat, the people also began to waste away. Forced to share shrinking watering holes with cattle and wild animals, the people began to develop explosive intestinal ailments that dehydrated and weakened them further, and then began to kill them.

The first human casualty came midway through the long dry spell that would normally have been interrupted by the short rains. She was the one-year-old first child of Atieno Diang'a and her husband Osewe Rodi, the son of Ogombe, son, of Ang'awa, son of Oyugi, son of Oweh, son of Silual and brother to Nwanji. Many more children died before the long rains came. But none of their fathers had inherited the stories and images that loomed large in Osewe Rodi's active mind – stories and images that defined his reaction to the loss of his daughter.

We came here the setting sun behind us. Our history lies with the setting sun. We must respect that history. But our destiny points toward the rising sun.

There is a land where the rain never stops falling from the sky, where the grass is forever green, and where the cows are always fat and full of milk. But those cows are always hungry and thirsty; there is not enough land. So the people are thin, mean, and fierce.

Never give up on an idea – not until you have pressed it dry of all its juice; not until you have sucked out its very marrow; not until it has become an ordinary thought.

Never be afraid to set out in a new direction. Never be afraid to walk away from your mistakes. Never be afraid to run away from bad luck.

There are many, many other people in this world. Most of them do not see the world in the same way that we do.

The end of the world is marked by a huge black hole – a hole so deep and wide you cannot see its bottom or its edges to the left or the right or in front. You know it when you see it. With the black hole before you, you discover who you really are. But you must travel many moons to reach it. Many, many moons.

Osewe's first memories were of riddles, proverbs, and stories told by his grandfather, Ang'awa, and his grandmothers, Adhiambo, Kisumo, and Adero. The riddles, proverbs, and stories were told to the Ang'awa homestead's young children who each evening would gather in the elders' huts for this purpose. The stories came after the riddles and proverbs and were intended to calm the mind in readiness for sleep – after the effort needed to solve the mind-bending riddles:

I am a jaw without teeth, but I can eat a stick as big and thick as a leg. What am I?

I am water on a long journey, sunshine after the rain. Who am I?

At one end of your tongue I am sweet, at the other end I am bitter. What am I?

If you let me escape from you before my time has come, you will never catch me again. What am I?

And to dig out the meaning in complex proverbs:

Smoke bothers not only bees but honey gatherers, too.

Slowly, slowly, bit by bit, porridge is poured into the gourd.

A lazy man grows hungry and then sees ghosts and evil spirits all around him.

Ignore the old man's directions and walk all day in the hot sun, hungry and thirsty.

The sequence of riddles-then-proverbs-then-stories would work with the other children, who would doze off one by one during the riddles and proverbs, needing to be carried off by their mothers, who always seemed to appear at the very moments their children's eyelids began to droop. But for Osewe, the riddles and proverbs had the opposite effect. They sharpened his imagination in readiness for the stories, which for him were always the highlights.

One day as he walked through the bushland, a hunter named Atho Randa came upon a massive goat that was talking to itself in our language from a lipless mouth. It was a terrifying sight. Atho Randa was sure it was an evil spirit. Not wanting to confront such a thing, he turned to run away.

"Stop! Do not run. Do not be afraid," the goat called out to him. "Help me. I need some water to drink."

Atho Randa's mind told him to run, but he felt his heart being pulled by something in the goat's voice – something that reminded him of a safe and warm place; somewhere in between the memory of his mother's embrace and his father's approval. Atho Randa turned and walked back toward the talking goat.

He was carrying a water gourd on a leather cord hung from his shoulder. He unslung the gourd and held it out to the goat.

"I have no hands," said the goat. "Please come and pour the water into my mouth."

Atho Randa moved closer to the goat. Soon he was standing right next to the creature. The goat opened its terrible mouth and Atha Randa poured in the water. The goat drank and drank. Atho Randa grew less afraid. Soon the water was finished.

"Thank you, Atho Randa, son of Opok Ochieng," said the goat quietly. "You are a kind man."

"How do you know my name?" asked Atho Randa, once again growing afraid. "How do you know my home?"

"Do you not see?" replied the goat. "There is only one man who would have done what you just did, and that man is Atho Randa, son of Opok Ochieng. It has been known since time began that you would meet me here today to face your fears and overcome them with kindness and empathy.

It has been known. Go now and live in that way – confronting your fears and showing kindness."

Atho Randa returned to his home. He never again saw the talking goat. He grew to become the most fearless and successful hunter of his time. But when he died, it was the loss of his kindness that the people mourned the most.

So, children, never be afraid of the unknown; it is there that your future lies.

Years later, Osewe would come to realize that the memories from those evening gatherings were the only ones he had of his grandfather, Ang'awa. The evening riddle-posings, proverb-framings, and story-tellings were the only times he could recall having heard his grandfather speak. The old man died well before Osewe reached his first maturity at fifteen years of age. The age at which Osewe's six lower front teeth were pried out one by one as his initiation into adulthood. The age at which Osewe's father, Ogombe, through one of his uncles, Ouma, invited Osewe to begin to attend the monthly gatherings of men at which family and clan affairs were discussed. It was at such gatherings that adolescent men learned how to think and speak like men. But by then, most of the talking was done by one of Osewe's granduncles, Andiego Koluoch – a man with a small voice, limited diction, poor grammar, and scanty imagination. Andiego's tenure as chief spokesman for the clan yielded a cohort of men with similarly hampered powers of communication.

Osewe's command of Dholuo therefore astounded everyone. Nobody could understand how it could be that a product of Andiego's term would say, "I am delighted" rather than, "I am happy," or, "That is exceptional" rather than, "That is very good," or "That is a splendid point," instead of, "That makes sense." Osewe spoke deep Dholuo, like an old storyteller. He had internalized not only the contents of his grandfather's stories, but also the old man's extensive diction and polished speech patterns.

And so Osewe won Atieno's heart through her ears – with his words. It helped that he was tall, handsome, and a good wrestler. But the way he expressed himself was the key to her affection.

"Your proportions fall well within my limits."

When Osewe's cousin, Matar, walked up to Atieno and her sister, Abugo, uttered these words to Atieno, and then revealed that the words had been sent by the wrestler they had just watched throw Olloh the Snake, Atieno managed at first to keep from laughing. But then when she looked over at Osewe and saw him beaming at her, she let go, trying to think of a befitting message to send back. She, too, was good with words.

"His girth is surely catching, but first looks can be deceiving. A closer viewing would be most welcome, even if brief."

"But why only a brief look? Why sip slowly on a small gourd when you could swig at will on a large one? Come over here and listen to the story of the rest of your life."

Atieno went.

She found that up close, Osewe was indeed more physically impressive than from across the wrestling enclosure – his shoulders broader, thighs thicker. His smile and laugh came easily and genuinely. His look was relaxed and unguarded. "He seemed unafraid of the world," Atieno would say many times to her children in the years to come. On his side, Osewe was very taken by Atieno's striking upper body and shapely calves. He also liked her smooth complexion, calm playfulness, and seeming immediate comfort in his presence. While Matar kept Abugo entertained, Osewe and Atieno mischievously tested each other's command of riddles, proverbs, and stories. They lost track of time. At dusk, for the first time ever, Atieno's heart failed to feel the familiar pull of her father's home. It was a delicious recognition. She knew then that Osewe was the one to whom she would give herself. "Why wait?" she thought to herself. She sent word home with a delighted Abugo that she had found her husband.

Atieno's parents would have preferred to be more directly involved in her choice of a family into which to marry, but they were thankful that she had not been grabbed against her will and eventually forced into a union, as was sometimes the case. The two families knew and respected one another. The dowry discussions that took place soon after Atieno had begun to cohabit with Osewe were conducted without acrimony or bitterness.

It seemed to be a blessed union. They quickly settled into the typical life of a newlywed couple. Opening new cropland. Acquiring livestock. Visiting relatives and friends. Bringing baby Awino into the world. But then came the drought, and the heavy blow of Awino's death from dehydration brought on by endless diarrhea. Yet even then, the commonly held view was that while the loss of Awino was devastating, there was little cause for major alarm. Osewe and Atieno were young. Other children would soon come. Osewe's words the night after they buried the scrawny remains of Awino in the little clearing behind their hut therefore took Atieno totally by surprise. But she was too exhausted and heart-broken to protest.

"Our child is resting now. Her spirit has flown up to join the ancestors in the stars. There is now too much pain here. Let us leave this place to seek our destiny. That destiny lies toward the rising sun."

The next morning, Osewe repeated his vision of their future. Still traumatized by the image of dry soil being thrown on top of the leaves covering baby Awino's lifeless body in her tiny grave, but more alert than the night before, Atieno was shocked by his words. She had never imagined such a thing and told him so. She did not want to go. Where would they go? What would they do there? What would *she* do there? What did women do where they were going?

But Osewe sounded so sure of himself that she feared he would go anyway and leave her behind. She did not want to lose the promise of their life together. For three days she tried without success to get him to change his mind. In the end, uneasily, yet also trusting her own judgment about Osewe's commitment to their marriage and love for her, she agreed. She also agreed not to speak to anyone about their decision until Osewe had informed his father, Ogombe.

They did not plan to leave right away. Food was still scarce. Like everyone else in Uhanga, they were weak and sickly. There was also great tension in Uhanga as more people were dying, both children and adults. Mercifully, the long rains arrived on time and were plentiful. The next harvest was good. Health and calm returned to Uhanga. Osewe and Atieno regained their strength. They prepared themselves to leave.

One morning, after supervising two of his nephews as they milked his cows, Osewe gathered up his courage, stepped out of his hut, and walked slowly across the homestead toward his father's hut. He found the old man sitting outside, cleaning his teeth with a twig from a medicinal shrub.

"Where are you going?!" asked the shocked Ogombe, spitting out a mouthful of pulpy saliva. Ogombe could not believe what Osewe had just told him. He did not want to believe it. Osewe had been so easy to raise, so easy to teach, that Ogombe had come to rely on him even more than he did on his older sons. "Where are you going?! Do you not see that I need you here?"

"I am not sure where my journey will end, but I know the direction I want to take," replied Osewe, unable to look into his father's eyes. He did not want to take in the sight of the old man's breaking heart. The sound of it was already almost too much for him to bear.

Ogombe was silent for a long time. Osewe remained seated at his father's feet, unable to move, unable to speak, hoping that the old man still had some words to give him.

"Go, my son," said Ogombe in the end. "You are a man. You have made your decision. You did not come for my permission. You go with my blessing. We will miss you here. Look after your wife and give her many children. I will look after your cattle."

Ogombe rose slowly and held out his hand to help Osewe stand up. Ogombe hugged his son for the first time in many years, holding him tightly, patting the back of his head.

"I will come back, father," said Osewe tearfully when his father finally ended the hug.

Ogombe half-shook, half-nodded his head in response.

"You go well, my son," said Ogombe with finality. "I will look after your cattle." He turned and stepped into his hut.

The partings from the rest of the family were more outwardly emotional yet less difficult for Osewe. His brothers and sisters were stunned and saddened but supportive. His mother, Agono, wailed uncontrollably, refusing to be consoled. It was the same with Atieno's mother, Achola, when Osewe and Atieno stopped briefly at Atieno's pre-marriage home in nearby Kapiyo. Atieno's father, Odhiambo Oliech, was largely unmoved. His daughter had ceased to be his responsibility the moment she chose to leave his homestead.

By the end of that day, Osewe and Atieno had traveled farther in the direction of the rising sun than either of them had ever been before.

3

The year was 1904. The month was April. The date was April 1. April
Fool's Day – a Friday. Reverend Justin Harrison was having a bad
day. Another one. He had been suffering from an upset stomach
for two days. He was feeling dehydrated from diarrhea, which had
turned his anus red-raw. Not for the first time since his posting to
the British East African Protectorate, he was questioning his faith.
He needed a sign of some sort. A sign of His presence and power.

"Certainly not here," he muttered to himself, glancing around
distastefully at his seven Indian travelling companions – six porters
and a guide. Heathens. Terrified of their own shadows. Totally
worthless. Not one of them knew the area at all.

"West of Port Florence." That was what Harrison had been told
in answer to his question about where he was supposed to set up the
new Church of Scotland mission post in the Protectorate. Sitting
across the shiny oak desk in the vestry of Knox Kirk, Edinburgh,
watching Archdeacon Alwyn McLeod mouth the words without
missing a beat, any trepidation Harrison might have allowed himself to feel fell away.

"West of Port Florence," the senior clergyman had confirmed.
"That's where we want you to go. The Church of Scotland is now
almost fully recovered from the Disputes of 1843. We are reunit-
ing quickly, and Presbyterianism is taking hold across the country.
Soon the Church of Scotland will be the largest Protestant church
in the country. The battle at home has been won. That is clear for
everyone to see. We are ready now to take our message to the rest
of the world. And that is why you, Reverend Harrison, and all the
other young men about to venture into lands where heathens and
heathenism dominate – that is why you are so important. That is
why we want you to go to British East Africa."

"Thank you, Archdeacon McLeod," said Reverend Harrison. "I am ready to serve the Lord in that way."

"Very good," said the Archdeacon. "Very good indeed. Some history for you. I'm sure you know it, but here goes anyway. European missionaries began settling in that area in the 1840s, under the protection of the Sultan of Zanzibar. The Imperial British East Africa Company began its operations in 1888, also by permission of the Sultan. But from the very beginning the Company had deep problems. It never turned a profit. Eight years ago, in 1895, the British Government declared a Protectorate. A British Protectorate must be buttressed by Christian principles. That is where you come in, Reverend. Your job for the next several years will be to build Christianity in the region west of Port Florence, which, since completion of the railway two years ago, is now part of the modern world."

Before setting sail for Mombasa on December 15, 1903, a typically cold winter's day, Reverend Harrison made one last trip to Iona Abbey on Iona Island, the birthplace of Christianity in Scotland. After praying in the chapel, he took a walk on the beach. A bitter wind cut straight through his greatcoat. But the cold made little impression on his body, so preoccupied was his mind with his impending departure.

He would miss Scotland, of that he was sure. But he also saw that leaving would not be as difficult as it would have been a few years before. With his mother's death in May 1902, his father's death two months later, and his brother's emigration to America in January 1903, he was alone in the country. He was almost happy to be leaving, keenly looking forward to the challenges that lay ahead.

But nothing could have prepared him for this.

"West of Port Florence!" Harrison shouted out in frustration, startling the ever-silent porters. "Where?! Where?!" he continued, waving his arms about. His men looked on silently, no longer surprised. This was not the first time the white man had behaved in this way. He seemed always to be shouting, if not at them, then at his many books, or his mule, or his many suitcases. Back home in Krishna District, Andhra Pradesh State, they had been told of a new town, Port Florence, which lay at the end of the railway their fellow Indians had helped build in British East Africa. A new town meant new opportunities. Any such opportunities in Machilipatnam, the nearest town to their village, had long since been snatched up by men with better grasps of the English, French, and Dutch spoken by the European traders who had been operating in that port city since the seventeenth century. Any new opportunity – even in faraway Africa – was better than nothing. So they had left home, all nine men in the Jyothi family, first on foot to Machilipatnam, then on a dhow down the Bay of Bengal, around the southern tip of India, and across the Indian Ocean to Mombasa.

Mombasa had been fascinating but dominated by local Arabs and railway Indians who had stayed on. There were still one or two opportunities for newcomers, so they had decided that two of them, Rajesh and Srinu, would remain in Mombasa. The others – Sujata, Bharati, Aruna, Chandra, Prasad, Sai, and Rama – would continue by train into the interior, hoping to set up a trading business at Port Florence.

They arrived at Port Florence parched and almost starved from the twoweek journey across the plains past Voi, up to cool and swampy Nairobi, down into the Rift Valley, up out again, and then slowly down to Lake Victoria. Within days of their arrival, they saw that their plan would have to change. Port Florence was a town only in name. Barely eighteen months since its creation, the place comprised nothing more than the railway station, a few sheds and houses for British administrators, and a few plain-looking hotels and restaurants that served those same administrators. Nothing else. However, the Jyothis knew enough about the British and the construction and commerce they brought with them to see that the picture would be very different within a few years. Soon there would be movements and collections of people who would demand goods. The Jyothis' long train journey from Mombasa convinced them that most of those goods would need to be produced nearby. They saw that to be able to take advantage of the opportunity when it came, they would have to venture out into the surrounding countryside and develop the supply-side of the market they knew would soon appear. But how?

The Jyothi brothers came to understand that Christian missionaries were being sent to the Protectorate in large numbers, first to pave the way for British authority and later to affirm that authority. They heard that the young, single-minded men sent out as missionaries needed guides and porters. So they took to waiting at the train stations for the arrival of travelers. The train came only once a month, so their chances of finding work were limited. When they spotted Reverend Harrison step out of the First Class carriage with a bewildered look on his face, they descended on him like fruit flies on a ripe mango.

"Help you, sir?" said Sujata in his limited and heavily accented English while his brothers stood off to the side, ready to move into action at his signal.

"My luggage," replied Harrison, relieved to find someone with whom he could communicate. "I need my luggage."

"No problem, sir. I get it for you, sir. Come with me, sir," said Sujata waving in his brothers.

Within a few hours, Sujata had convinced the Reverend that he and his six brothers were just the people he needed to help him identify a site for his mission, map the surrounding area, and serve as interpreters with the local populace.

Almost immediately after their departure from Port Florence into the surrounding bushland, Harrison began to have reservations. Sujata, the supposed guide, had been charting a zig-zagging path that seemed at first to be wisely exploratory but which by the fifth day was clearly confused.

"Sujata," barked the Reverend at the end of the sixth day, during which he was sure they had gone in two complete circles. "Which direction is north?"

"Sir?"

"North. Point it out to me. Where is north?

"Of course, sir. That way north, sir," said Sujata, pointing southwest, according to the Reverend's compass.

"I see," said the Reverend, suddenly aware of his predicament but still too appalled to be angry. That would come later. "Dear God," he called out. "I am lost. I cannot see the way forward. Please help me see it. Please help me find it..."

4

Legend had it that the end of the world was marked by a huge black hole – a hole so deep and wide you could not see its bottom or its edges to the left or the right or in front. You knew it when you saw it. Then you discovered what kind of a person you were. But you had to travel many moons to reach it. Many, many moons. What, then, was this massive black thing hurtling toward them, as tall as the sky, wider than their eyes could behold?

*   *   *

Osewe and Atieno were seventeen days into their journey. They had been moving slowly, stopping often at homes to talk, eat, drink, ask for directions, learn. They took care to arrive at each home well before dark – well before the night sentries were at their posts, on edge, spoiling to hurl their battle spears at anything that moved. They were usually met with surprise and suspicion. But by and by, as their peaceful intentions became clear, suspicion would be replaced by genuine curiosity and generous hospitality.

Their most fruitful and enjoyable encounters with strangers occurred at points where major footpaths crossed – Kambajo, Maranda, Nyamira, Bondo, Ndori, Ajigo. They would stop at these crosspaths and wait for someone to appear – a herdsman and his livestock; a woman on her way to collect water; a young man out gathering firewood for his mother. They quickly learned how to position themselves at the crosspaths in unthreatening ways (seated side by side, apparently in easy conversation), how to hold their faces when the person saw them (smiling, but not too eagerly), how to rise and approach (slowly, hands upheld, palms showing), what to say in opening ("We greet you, dear brother/sister. We are travelers from Uhanga, Yimbo on our way to the new world. We come in peace and friendship, in a spirit of discovery. Do you have time to talk?). Again, they took care to stage such encounters only in the bright light of day, ending even the most enlightening conversation well before dusk to ensure daytime approaches to homesteads of prospective overnight hosts.

Several crosspath meetings led to invitations for overnight accommodation. But they always declined such offers, sensing that the magic of the chance encounter would not be sustained. They also knew that the highly refined and courteous interactions associated with being invited guests in homesteads would not accommodate their need for flexibility and informality, and, more practically, their desire to make early starts each day.

So they would bid their informants farewell and continue on their way until the time came to enter a homestead.

"We greet you, dear brother..."

They heard news of the strange group of eight on the fourteenth day of their journey. Three days before they saw the end of the world. Ten days before, still traumatized by the events of the seventeenth day, they met face to face with the group itself. The news of the group came to them at the Ajigo crosspath, from a livestock trader traveling in the opposite direction, back home to Bondo. The story was that the tall one – the angry one with white hands and a red face under a big hat – carried something that made a loud sound and could kill a wild pig from several times the distance any man could throw a spear. Osewe's heart leapt in excitement at the thought of such a thing.

The seventeenth day would have begun as any other – early and without formality – except that Atieno's menses had set in and she had begun to feel some slight discomfort in her feet and lower back. She would have preferred not to move that day, but she knew that Osewe was in a hurry to see the strange group. So she boiled some painkilling herbs, drank the broth, placed some fluidabsorbing leaves in her vagina, and they set off, bidding a quick but sincere and thanks-filled farewell to their still sleepy hosts.

By mid-morning, Atieno was in severe pain, feeling bloated, and struggling under the quick pace being set by the eager Osewe. Her inner thighs were sticky with coagulated blood. The absorbent leaves were effective only when a woman was seated or moving about slowly.

"I cannot continue today, my friend," she said at last, stopping to sit on a flattened rock at the top of the hillock that the livestock trader at the Ajigo crosspath had told them offered an unmatched view of the terrain to be traversed over the next few days. She expected a sharp rebuke from Osewe but was prepared to stand her ground. It felt so good to sit and take some weight off her feet and back.

"Dear departed ancestors help us! Our time to die has come!" Osewe fell to his knees beside her, grabbed her hand, and began to pray.

"Please, Osewe, please. Just let me rest here. I cannot go on," Atieno pleaded, relieved that he was not upset but seemed instead to be making a silly joke of it.

"Oh my wife," said Osewe, gripping her wrist even more tightly and pointing out in front of him with his other hand, "Don't you see. It is the end of the world. It is the black hole."

Atieno looked up for the first time since reaching the hilltop. She had been too exhausted to do anything but close her eyes. She saw that Osewe was right. They had reached the end of the world. But the hole was not in the ground as she had imagined it would be. It covered the entire horizon and went straight up into the sky.

"It is a black wall!" she cried. "It is going to crush us!"

The black wall was rushing toward them at an alarming speed. There was no escape. They were going to be swallowed.

Holding on to Atieno's hand, Osewe threw himself on the

ground. He buried his face in a tuft of grass, stretching his arms out in front of him. Atieno did the same, shouting, like him, at the top of her voice, too afraid to look.

Soon they felt the thing descend upon them. First, a fierce wind, strong enough to pick them up and threw them a short distance down the hill. And then water, a torrent of it, creating copious streams that snaked around their still prone bodies, filing their nostrils, mouths, and ears with copious amounts of the deep red soil Osewe had been admiring the previous afternoon and morning. And then suddenly it was over. The hole – the wall – had passed.

"Atieno!" Osewe cried out, blinking open his mud-caked eyelids and looking to his left and right for Atieno, she was nowhere to be seen. The wind had ripped her hand from his. "Atieno!"

"I am here!" Atieno called out from directly behind him. Much lighter in weight than Osewe, she had been flung further down the hill. "Are we dead? Did it swallow us?"

"No," replied Osewe, spitting out a mouthful of reddened saliva, "We are not dead. Look."

He was pointing behind her. The black wall had passed over them and was continuing its destructive path. From behind it, they could now see that it was massive storm cloud that stretched wider and taller than their eyes could yet behold. But as the wall proceeded into the distance, they began to be able to make out its edges and find mental measures for it. Millet field upon millet field, thought Atieno. Herd upon herd of cattle, thought Osewe.

Repeatedly giving thanks to departed ancestors for sparing them from death and injury, they watched the wall move on over the bushy landscape until it had shrunk to barely the size of a palm. And then they turned around to take in the view that had been excitedly described to them in great detail by the eloquent livestock trader.

"Until you reach that hilltop, you will have no thought that such a view could exist. The first thing you will notice is the bay. It fills the scene. The local people call it Asembo. Like the rest of the lake, it has its moods, depending on the speed and direction it wants to send the wind. When it is angry at the land and land-dwellers, it will stir up a fierce gale that will suck in every drop of rain in the sky and thrust it all down in fury. At such times, Asembo will be like a jealous wife seeking revenge on her husband for taking a mistress or an unwelcome new wife. No mercy. All hatred. Waves as tall as you lashing the beach, splitting boats into small pieces. But just as with the right look, or word, or touch from her husband, a wild-eyed and spitting wife returns to her former self, so, too, will Asembo – once it has emptied itself of its frustrated desires and irritations. And then it will be all grace – gentle waves stroking the shoreline, tickling the toes of the reed stalks, which will be slowly straightening their backs after the beating from the wind and rain. A light breeze will be putting just enough of a ripple on the deeper water to blur the reflected image of islands in the distance. Fishermen will be busy preparing their boats for the evening's pursuits. I hope you see Asembo on such a day. You will remember that view forever."

With the black wall now a small spot on the horizon behind them, it was indeed such a day for Osewe and Atieno.

"The area in between the bay and the hill where you will be standing will at first look like nothing but empty bush. But of course it will not be empty. There will be all kinds of wild animals in there – just like anywhere in this land of ours. If you look closely, you will see a few very tall trees scattered here and there. Those trees mark spots where families have established homesteads. You will see a huge, heavily leafed tree at the water's edge. That one is home to a pair of fish eagles that the locals revere and protect.

"For travelers like you who are not in a hurry, a few days spent in Asembo would be worth your while. There is a good livestock market every three days. Traders like me bring news from across the land. And every day, the fishermen and lake traders bring news from the islands and from the other side of the lake. You will find that the people are accustomed to welcoming outsiders."

They spent the night on the hilltop, curled around each other on the light but firmly woven reed mat that was their bed, next to a small fire that served to keep away wild animals.

"There are so many ancestors, Atieno," said Osewe, looking up at the stars. "Look at all of them winking at us. There are so many of them. But maybe there are more people living in the world today than there are ancestors in the sky. Could that be, Atieno?"

Atieno did not respond. She had fallen asleep. Osewe gently stroked her back. Instinctively, she moved in closer. He turned back to the stars and, as he had done at the end of the each day of their trip, he offered up a silent prayer of thanksgiving that he and Atieno were still alive. And then, as he had done the last few nights, he fell asleep to the image of the man with a stick that could fell a wild pig from several times the distance of a spear throw.

The next morning Atieno felt better but not well enough to move. She continued to bleed heavily. Her menses had resumed two moons previously, when hunger and thirst had caused her breast milk to dry up and she had been forced to stop breastfeeding baby Awino. Nothing Atieno did would make the milk return. Reluctantly and fearfully, she had begun to feed the baby porridge made from finely ground millet. Awino had developed diarrhea almost immediately. Within no time, she was gone.

Atieno had been told that the pregnancy would change the nature of her menses, so when her first one after giving birth had been almost painless, she wondered if that would be the case from then on. But the familiar pain and discomfort had returned with this second one. She was bleeding heavily and in almost constant pain. Osewe made a short excursion down the hill in the direction of the bay. He returned carrying wild berries and medicinal herbs and telling a story about how he had been rushed by a boar and felled it with a hard punch to the forehead. Atieno knew that the story was made up, but she still allowed it to lift her spirits.

The next day, the bleeding stopped, but Atieno's energy level remained low, her spirit deflated. So it was not until the next day – three days after the black wall passed over them – that they began their descent toward Asembo. Their unthreatening routines at crosspaths and homesteads allowed quick progress to the water's edge where they rested for three days at the homestead of a fisherman, feasting on fish, millet, and stories of Asembo and its people.

"This lake – we call him Lolwe – this lake has no mercy on fools. If you do not respect him, he will throw you up into the air and swallow you like a seed. And he has no ending down underneath. He goes on forever, especially out there in the middle, where the waves are as tall as three huts standing one on top of the other. I once tied a big, big rock to a long, long rope made from many, many reeds tied together. I wanted to find his depth. But my rope was too short. And through the rope I could feel the rock being thrown about like a feather down there. Lolwe is not to be played with."

"There is a beautiful breed of cattle over there on that island. It has huge horns, big udders, big buttocks, and, best of all, black-edged eyes that look straight at you from in front, not jutting out from the side like most of our breeds. It has a gentle nature. But it does not live for long if taken from that island. The people of the island say that the breed is only for them. They have bewitched it to die quickly when it leaves the island."

"You see that man over there? His name is Owuor Podho. He is the greatest wrestler this area has ever seen. But look at him. He is tiny. Yet he cannot be thrown, not even by men twice his size and weight. The bigger his opponent, the quicker Owuor finishes him. It's like magic. They say his wife gives him strong magic – strong medicine before every fight. Who knows? He is very, very tough. That huge man there is called Odhiambo Malit. He drinks milk like it is water. And his stomach does not bother him at all. So look at the size of him! He can pick up two full-grown sheep at the same time, one under each arm. He is also a good wrestler, but he refuses to fight Owuor."

"Come, let me take you to greet my first wife. She is not well. She began to go blind with white-eye about ten long rains ago. And then her mind began to go bad. At first, it was a little funny. She would tell visitors that a snake had spat into her eyes and blinded her. But then it grew more serious. She began to wander off. First, it was for short periods, and then for days. Once she was lost in the bush and was badly gored by a wild pig. She almost died. But she was strong. Anyway, please come in and greet her... come... no, do not worry... she will not respond... she does not talk anymore. She just writhes and thrashes around on the floor like that. She is in pain, but I do not know where on her body is giving her pain. She has become so small. It is hard to believe. She was a fine woman once. Very, very fine. You can greet her. I think she knows we are here."

"You are traveling at a fortunate time. There is peace among the Jokamireji, Jokamito, Jokandenga, and Jokakuodi clans. Two rains ago, you would not have been able to move through here as quickly. The hunger was beginning. People were fighting and killing each other. The fighting was over the usual two things – grazing land for cattle, and women. Fighting over women I can understand, but cattle! Why?! Look at the lake. There is enough meat in that water to feed many, many more clans than these four. Why bother with ugly, foolish creatures that fall sick and die when you need them the most? But where is the common sense? There is so little of it remaining in the world these days."

"Now, these eight strangers. What does one do with them? The people around Pau Akuche have been watching them for many days. When the one with the big hat killed the wild pig with that loud stick, the chance to drive them away was lost. Now everyone is afraid. How do you approach such a man? How do you reason with him? What if he points that stick at you?"

By the time Osewe and Atieno left Asembo, Atieno was back to full strength. The women of Asembo had embraced her generously. They could not believe that she would leave her house and home like she did. But they also saw the firm determination and self-belief in the way Osewe spoke and carried himself. None of them would have left his side either. Yet still they wondered what she would do by his side without land to be tilled and cattle to be milked. She did not know and could not tell them. But she had made her choice four rains before, under a tree next to the enclosure where Osewe threw Olloh the Snake. Her heart was troubled, but it still told her that her original choice had been a good one.

They made quick progress toward Pau Akuche. By nightfall they were almost there. Rather than approach a homestead after dark, they slept out in the open, once again beside a small fire, under a low thorny tree unlikely to be home to snakes.

They awoke at dawn, hungry, thirsty, but excited. Their overnight resting place stood atop a rise overlooking a landscape considerably less lush and less thickly bushed than the area surrounding Asembo. The soil was thin and sandy, much like theirs back in Uhanga. Large boulders worn smooth by centuries of exposure to wind and rain lay scattered around in all directions, like oily eruptions on an adolescent's face. It was not an appealing scene. Now they understood why they had been told that the force of Pau Akuche's appeal did not draw from its physical beauty. That force apparently sprung from its position and value in regional livestock trading routes. For a decisive period right after the onset of the long rains – following the hot dry spell that set in after the short rains – Pau Akuche's normally undesirable tough, knobby, but exceptionally water-responsive grasses were the only ones available to herders and traders driving hungry cattle between grazing areas. During periods of inter-clan peace, those grazing areas spanned a region that extended two to three moons of non-stop movement in all directions. But for a while each year, only Pau Akuche had grass aplenty.

Pau Akuche's men had long since incorporated this seasonal opportunity into their activities. At first, they had merely altered their own grazing practices to ensure availability of fresh grass to incoming herds, in return for stud services from the choice bulls in those herds. In time, the men had entered the livestock trade themselves. Through their control of grazing land during a key period each year, they had gained greater than proportionate strength in the trade. Pau Akuche was thriving.

Even under the best of circumstances, Reverend Justin Harrison would have been too early into his assignment to have gained more than a cursory comprehension of such aspects of the underlying tempo of his surroundings. As it was, he was struggling to keep from abandoning the mission altogether. With little new information to work with, his understanding of the area around him and his group differed very little from one day to the next. His attempts to bring more direction to their movements were frustrated by bunches of men watching silently and unseen from the thickets. Whenever the group's aimless path took it near a homestead, the huddled men would rustle the bushes violently. The porters and guide, fearful of the wild animals they heard each night, would veer away, taking the irritated and shouting Harrison with them.

That day, his frustration was extreme. He had awoken to find his suitcases invaded by red ants. As he furiously beat them away, many had leapt on him. Some had found their way into his underwear. Even now, many hours later, he could still feel the burning and itching from the stings, his penis and testes swollen and blistering.

"Dear God, give me a sign of your presence and mercy! Give me a sign!" shouted the Reverend, grabbing his rifle from the half-trotting gun-carrier beside him, unlocking it, and shooting a frustrated blast of thunder into the sky above. "Please dear God, give me a sign!"

*   *   *

The old fish eagle and his mate had been eyeing the strange formation for several days, puzzled by the stop-start nature of its progress. Neither of them liked that kind of patternless movement. Even from the great height at which the birds preferred to hold themselves, they could tell that the formation also had a strange color to it. The more recognizable movements of the more familiarly colored groups were oddly truncated and menacing. The old bird had lived through many days and seasons. He had seen everything there was to see, eaten everything there was for him to eat. He and his mate had no enemies or competitors other than younger birds of their own kind, none of whom could match them yet. The bird-eaters down below left them alone because, he knew, their diets had too much in common.

He was alone this time, having left his mate tending the two new eggs in their nest in the thick tree by the water's edge. He decided there was nothing to be learned from the odd goings-on down below. So he swept into a slow, wide turn back toward his mate whom he knew would be wondering what had become of him. The turning arc he chose would cut his elevation by onethird. One final look would do no harm, he thought to himself.

The grey bullet ripped into the center of the old bird's white chest and out the middle of his black-brown back, taking all his breath and most of his life with it. His wings went limp and disobeyed his conscious command to return them to the great width his long and careful life had allowed them to attain – the width his still functioning brain knew was needed to retain height and complete the turn.

*　　*　　*

Acting purely on impulse, Osewe had suggested to Atieno that they wait a while before commencing that day's movements. He had a feeling that patience and stealth would bring rewards. They found some berries growing nearby. They ate those, briefly taking the edge off their hunger and thirst. And then they sat down under a tree and waited for something to happen.

They heard Harrison and saw one of the groups of hiding men at almost the same moment. Like Osewe, the men wore beaded leather headbands and thick iron anklets and bracelets. There were five of them. They were about twenty paces away, moving quickly from right to left from Osewe and Atieno's vantage point, their attention fixed ahead.

"We see you," Osewe called out to them in a sharp whisper. The men whirled around in unison, crouching down even lower, clearly readying to defend themselves. One of them, slightly older and more heavily set than the others, whispered to the others and approached quickly, a smile on his face.

"Are you the travelers from Uhanga?" he asked in a whisper, extending his hand in greeting. "Are you the ones who were in Asembo?"

"Yes, we are the ones," replied Osewe, also whispering. "I am Osewe Kogombe from Uhanga, and this is my wife Atieno Diang'a."

"Welcome. Welcome. I am Atho Kolloh, this is Otieno Karaudo, Migiko Kowino, Odhiambo Karemo, and Oruko Kokoth. You slept outside?" Osewe and Atieno nodded. "You should not have done that. We were expecting you. This is a time of peace, but it is not a time to sleep outside. The men with the loud stick are still here. We are trying to scare them away, but they are taking a long time to leave."

"Where are they now?" asked Osewe.

"They are behind those rocks over there," replied Atho, pointing in the direction he and the others had been going. "You stay with us until evening. Then you can come with us to our settlement."

Osewe and Atieno joined the group. As agreed with nine other such groups, this one had been moving toward its assigned spot in the wide circle intended to surround the group of eight intruders, who were already on the move.

From their hiding place, Atho Kolloh's group could see and hear everything clearly – the frustration on the face and in the voice of the man with the loud stick; the odd mix of fear and patience in those of his companions. As on the previous two days, the hiding men's strategy was to leave an opening in their large circle toward which the intruders would be guided, bit by bit. The plan was working well. Throughout the day, the intruders were herded in a direction that in three more days would take them out of Pau Akuche forever.

Nobody expected the stick to shout this time when the man pointed it to the sky. He had made it shout twice before, but only when pointing it at a wild pig. So when it let out its terrifying crack, all eyes in the vicinity except four were transfixed on the now terrifying Harrison – all except Harrison's and Osewe's, which were turned upward, locked on the rapidly falling bird.

Instinctively, Osewe knew that what he did those next few moments would define the path of his life thereafter. He grabbed Atieno's arm and set off in the direction of the fallen bird.

"Bring me that bird!" Harrison yelled at his group. Nobody moved. There was no way any of them was going anywhere without him and his gun. "I want that bird! It is the message... the sign from the Almighty God! Go and get that bird, you ... you stinky, foolish cretins! I want that bird!"

The many eyes behind the bushes began to retreat. It would soon be dark. Nobody wanted to be near the red-faced, wild-eyed man at night.

Osewe found the bird quickly. It had landed head-first, but now it lay on its side, its neck twisted backward so that its sharp, curved beak pointed back toward its wrinkled heels. To Atieno's horror, Osewe bent down, picked up the terrifying object, and set off immediately in the direction of the bird's killer.

"Why?" pleaded Atieno. "Please, let us go back to the other men. It is almost night. They said they would give us a place to rest."

"We will go back," Osewe lied, speeding up to quicken her breathing and silence her voice. "We will go back... someday..." he muttered under his breath. "Someday we will go back."

5

It took uncommon self-control for Reverend Harrison not to gun down the naked savage who hurtled into the midst of his party from behind a clump of bushes, holding aloft the massive bird. And then came the naked woman, clearly terrified, breathing hard, eyes wide open.

"Shoot them, Revrin! They want to kill us!"

Harrison's thinking was clear but conflicted. These were the first natives he had seen since leaving Port Florence. He was curious to learn about them. But their appearance bearing the bird meant they had been watching his band. So he was fearful and suspicious of them. And there was their nudity. Neither one had anything on, other than the man's headband and amulets and the woman's beaded necklace and bracelet. He had never seen anything like it. He was both revolted and deeply aroused by them. But most of all, he was grateful to them. Through them, God had answered his prayers.

"Please, Revrin! Shoot them!"

"Shut up!" snapped Harrison, laying down his gun and slowly approaching the naked man holding the dead bird.

6

"If a *kaffir* could be great man, then this man, John Mark Osewe, would have been such a person. I knew him for forty years. That is a long time. Forty years. I think that's long enough to be able to say you knew a man... even a *kaffir*.

"He was introduced to me by a Scottish priest... What was that fellow's name? Dammit! I don't remember... Anyway, this priest was on his way back to Scotland. He couldn't stand Africa. Couldn't take it. Went to America in the end. Bloody hell, what was his name? Anyway, on the way here from Kavirondo he had baptized John Mark and his wife and wanted to make sure they continued to receive Christian guidance. Sheila, my wife at the time, was also Scottish. She promised to provide it... the guidance... that's how they came here to Njoro... to Waterbuck.

"*Ach* man, I knew right away that he would be a useful *kaffir*. You can tell right away with *kaffirs*, you know. Some want to leave, some don't. Some are curious about the world, some aren't. John Mark was a quick learner, and he always wanted to know more. He started out as a game tracker on my hunting trips to Mt. Kenya. The Aberdares. Tanganyika. He did that well. But then he annoyed me, so I moved him into the fields. I put him in charge of the oxen and plough. He did that well, too. Then he moved to the stables as an ordinary stableman, and then as the foreman. All of this he did well. That would have been 1920 or so. After that, he became a sort of handyman around here. He could fix anything... a broken fence, a leaking pipe, a faulty hammer mill, bicycles, even cars. He had a good eye, and good hands – very good hands. Good with words, too. Picked up English in no time at all.

"I had to whip him only a few times. Just a few. I remember each time... four times... always for pretending he did not understand something when it was obvious that he did – someone like him... he understood everything. How could he not have known that I wanted that rhino's head and tail? He just left them there on the animal. So, of course, bloody Carrington's men took them, and I had to behave like it was just fine with me that Carrington kept them, even though I'd shot the rhino myself... a hard shot, too. He just left them there! The head and the tail, for fuck's sake! They would have looked splendid on the wall in the study – next to the leopard. The stupid *kaffir*! So I whipped him when we got back here to Waterbuck. I should have done it right there, but fucking Carrington would have blubbed about it. That's why I moved him to the fields.

"And there was the time on his first day as a field hand when he brought in sacks of maize of different weights – eighty pounds, one-hundred-and-twenty, one-hundred-and-five, one-hundred-and-eleven, and so on. Who would have bought those, for God's sake? I had to whip him for that.

"I also whipped him when he fed the horses too much oatmeal and gave them the runs for two days. And then again when he came back from leave one week late. Some story about too many graves to visit and pray beside. I'd given him two whole weeks! That should have been more than enough time for all the praying he needed to do.

"He is gone now. Too bad... too bad... But he lived a good life here on Waterbuck. Whenever he was ill, he was treated with modern medicine. His wife over there gave birth many times here, and each of my wives was always there to help with the births. His wife wanted a plot to grow vegetables. That was fine as long as he did his work properly. He never went back to his home in Kavirondo after that first trip, even when he had the opportunity. I think he came to think of Waterbuck as home.

"I do not believe in God anymore. But I know that John Mark was a Christian to the end. It was an odd kind of Christianity, though. All those amulets, the praying by gravesides and so on. Always singing those strange songs. I never understood it.

"This morning, my wife, Jocelyn – she's my third wife – Jocelyn asked me what would be the one thing about John Mark that stood out for me. I have been thinking about that. He was just a *kaffir*, so the standard is different. But I think it was his ability to adjust without being diminished. He was always growing. Imagine where he came from. Imagine what this farm looked like forty years ago when Reverend Harrington – yes, that was his name – when Harrington dropped him off here. There was just the one house – the main house for my family – a shed for the horses, and five or six huts for the laborers. *Ach* man, life was bloody tough back then, but it was also simple. If you didn't fall sick or get injured... if you worked hard... if the weather was good... It was that way until the first war. That changed everything. After that, there were many more settlers, many more new ideas coming in, many more changes. Lasting change always comes in packages. And people must shift in many ways at the same time. Well, we certainly had to, here at Waterbuck. By God, I've seen all kinds of changes in this country. And I've seen all kinds of reactions – from indifference, to delight, to sorrow, to suicide. But I tell you... it's 1943 now, right? Well, I tell you, when I look back over all those years and all the people who came through here and all the people I met, only from John Mark did I see both total engagement with change and absolute equanimity under it all. There must have been lots of inner turmoil. There must have been. But it never showed. He would just listen, nod a few times, and get on with it, humming to himself. Always humming to himself. You take that sort of thing for granted – that ability to adjust and seize a moment. You come to expect it, even demand it. But it couldn't have been easy.

"I should know. I am a Boer. And being a Boer means knowing what it's like to feel no security over life or property. It means knowing what life on a frontier is like. You go and ask the de Klerks in Kitale or the van den Brinks in Eldoret. They'll tell you. Well, back home the Afrikaner National Party is in power now. We're all going back. Then those Brits and *kaffirs* will see what it's like to eat their own shit. My children – my step-children – Vincent and Victoria might come with me. Vincent is about to be released from the army. Why he agreed to join the British army is beyond me. But his letters say he's sick of them and wants a change. I hope I can convince him to come home with me to South Africa. Victoria and her husband, Jason, are having Maasai problems out in Laikipia. Fucking Maasai. They agree to move to reserves and then change their minds. Want to come back to our ranches, now that we've done all the hard work and made them look like places where human beings live. We knew how to handle the *kaffirs* here in Njoro, boy. But these Brits are too soft. What right does a *kaffir* have to anything? Eh? What right?

"I have said enough. Like I told my wife this morning, John Mark wasn't a bad *kaffir*. Not really. Not really. May he rest in peace."

7

It is not easy to follow White Boss when he speaks in English. This other language he began to whisper to himself after the third madam died is impossible to catch. Even those of us who can read and write do not understand it. They say it is the language of whites from a place called South Africa. Only those terrible whites from Kitale can speak it. I wish White Boss would finish and leave us to bury Osewe in our own way. But he always comes to our funerals and talks and talks even though nobody listens to him anymore.

My friend Osewe is dead. Sometimes I wonder how he lived for as long as he did. From the day the first white man left us here, White Boss was terrible to us. He was that way with all the staff, and even with the three madams. The difference with Osewe was that he survived it all, year after year, even when White Boss seemed to be trying to kill him with that long whip. What a proud man he was! So, so proud. So rigid, even when the world curled up its hard fists and beat them into him. He never bent. He was strong-strong!

The other men in the first white man's group – the seven brown ones with shiny black hair – they did not want to come this way. In the beginning, they would not move away from him. They ran behind him when all the people came out from behind the bushes and crowded around. They kept shouting at the white man, but he was not listening to them. He was interested only in that bird. He and Osewe began to make signs at each other. It always makes me laugh when I remember that. But on that day, all I could feel was fear. Soon Osewe understood that the white man wanted a place to rest, water to wash, and a place to skin the bird. I was very happy when Osewe decided to lead the group to Asembo. I loved Asembo. I wish we had stayed there. The people of Pau Akuche were very happy to see us leave. They did not like the white and brown men.

The brown men stayed behind in Asembo when we left. They

were good men. One of them saw the way the white man was looking at me and gave me one of his dresses to cover myself. Another one did the same for Osewe. After some days in Asembo they were no longer afraid. The people of Asembo were very kind. The brown men wanted to go out in the boats with the fishermen and traders. I have always wondered what happened to them.

We left Asembo with the white man after he had made the dead bird stand up again. I remember being very afraid of the way it stared straight ahead from empty eyeholes. It looked so angry. Osewe carried the one bag the white man decided to take back with him. He left the rest with the brown men. They were very happy. The white man carried his gun and a small bag. I carried the stiff bird. At first, it terrified me – the way those empty eyeholes looked at me. I was also afraid the bird's mate would come looking for it and attack me. But nothing happened.

We walked for many days. I was always tired and hungry. But the white man was in a hurry and always seemed to be in a bad mood. But then one day we stopped by a small river. He poured water all over our bodies and touched our foreheads with a soft black box he kept in the small bag. Only after many months did we understand that the box was a Bible and that he had baptized us and given us new names – John Mark and Priscilla. After he did that, he was happier. It was as if he had made peace with himself. But still he was in a hurry. Osewe told me his name many times but I never learned it properly. It was something like Harrisee.

We came to a place with other white and brown people, and also some people like us. Later, we came to understand that this was Port Florence – the place we knew as Kisumo. We stayed there for many days, waiting for something. The white man ate and slept in a white house with other white people. He took the bag and stiff bird with him. Osewe and I ate and slept with the people who cooked and cleaned for the white people in the white house. Some of them spoke Dholuo. They were very friendly to us. They asked us many questions.

"Where are you from? How did you meet the white man? What does he want from you? Where is he taking you?"

Some of the questions we could answer, some we could not. We also asked them questions. We wanted to know about Port Florence. They said it was changing. They did not know much. We saw people carrying dried fish. They asked us what we had to exchange with them, but we had nothing. One day we walked to the lakeside. One of the men pointed to the center of the lake and said that sometimes boats came that way from Asembo. I was excited. I did not like our situation. I wanted to go back to Asembo. I would tell Osewe. But he would not listen to me. "We are going with the white man," he would say. He would say it in a way that meant I should not say anything more. I did not like that. I would tell him so, but he would be silent.

After some days, the white man sent someone to get us. We followed him to a noisy place with many people moving here and there. He wanted us to enter a room where other women and men like us were already sitting. It was very hot in the room. I fell asleep leaning against Osewe's back. I can still remember how straight his back felt. It was always like that. Straight. Even at the end. I awoke sweating and confused. The room was even hotter than before. The door had been closed. Through the small windows I could see trees moving past the room.

"Why are the trees moving!" I shouted out to Osewe. I was very afraid.

Osewe said, "No, it is this thing we are in that is moving!" His voice was shaking. He was trying to help me calm down, but I could tell that he was also afraid.

"What is going to happen to us?"

"I don't know. But do not worry."

I did not feel comforted. The room shook this was and that way. The trees outside passed by faster. There was a sharp clapping sound coming from below, faster and faster. Soon, everyone in the room had vomited – on the floor, against the wall, out of the small windows.

We stopped many times, but the door to our room did not open. The smell of vomit was terrible. I still remember it to this day. I needed to urinate and could barely hold it in. But somehow I did. Finally, at a stop that was longer than the others, the door opened. It was dark outside. It was also very cold. I had never felt so cold. A white man in red and black clothes shouted something. When nobody moved, he grabbed the leg of the nearest person and pulled him out, shouting again. The rest of us jumped down painfully. Our legs and backs were stiff from too much sitting.

"Look," said Osewe as he helped me out of the room. He was pointing in the direction we had been moving, "There are many more rooms like ours. We are all joined together... like a snake." Later we came to understand that we had been on a train. We used to laugh about it with Osewe and the children.

A man who was the same color as us but spoke a different language washed the room. He looked tired. But he was kind. He gave us water and showed us where to relieve ourselves. I pissed for so long that the woman who was squatting next to me finished before me, and she was shitting!

The white man in red and black returned and pushed some of us. He wanted us to climb back into the room. He was shouting all the time. I was very hungry and tired. But there was no food. I felt like crying, but I knew it would upset Osewe. We climbed back into the room. It was cleaner but still it smelled bad. I closed my eyes and tried to think of something else. But all I could see was little Awino. It might have made me sad, but her face was happy. I fell into a deep sleep. Again, I awoke confused. The snake had stopped again. It was morning. Bright sunlight was shining through the small windows. The door was opened and again the white man dressed in red and black was there. He shouted and waved his arms at us to get out of the room. We found our white man waiting for us. He smiled when he saw us and called us to him with his hand. I did not like the look in his eyes as we came near. The dress was filthy with vomit and dirt, but I put it on. We followed him. He climbed on to the back of an animal we later learned was a horse. We had never seen one before. It was so large! Its neck, face, and legs were so long! Our white man waved his hand that we should follow him. We walked behind him for a long time. The white man had tied the two bags to the horse. Osewe carried the stiff bird. We were very tired and very hungry.

When we arrived here at Waterbuck, the first madam greeted the white man. She was wearing a bright green dress. She smiled at the white man and embraced him. She looked at us from time to time while talking to the white man. Then she pointed to the huts. We still live in the same one we took that day.

The white man waited three days for White Boss to return and then he left. He shook Osewe's hand. He touched my shoulder. I did not like that.

One day the first madam jumped into the well. She was wearing the bright green dress. White Boss had killed her spirit. She could not have any children. But when even the second madam also could not have children, everyone saw that the problem was with White Boss. One day, when White Boss was away on a hunting trip, the second madam left and never returned.

That time between the second and third madams was terrible. The whippings. Nobody escaped, not even the pregnant women. Osewe and I talked about leaving. But where would we have gone? We were not ready to go back to Uhanga. Osewe was not ready. And we heard stories of even worse white people. What if we found work with a worse White Boss? We stayed.

We went home to Uhanga only once. It was very painful. Fifteen or sixteen years had passed since we left. So many people had died. We had to pay our respects. As soon as we stepped into the old homestead, we were pulled to one grave after another. Both of our fathers, both of our mothers, some of our brothers and sisters, many cousins, uncles, and aunts. All of them had died. That visit almost broke Osewe. Everyone begged us not to leave again. They could not understand what was so good here that we could not come back home. I could not say it, but the answer was that Osewe loved the work. For him, everything was still an adventure of some sort – like a long trip. I could never have said so to him, but the problem was that he never had any idea about the reward that would be ours at the end. Even when White Boss whipped him, Osewe would not admit that he might be wrong. Look at all the new things we have learned here, he would say. I could never have said so to him, but what good thing was there to learn from being whipped in front of your children? What good thing could have come from the children seeing their mother slapped by the madam just because a teacup was chipped?

But time is a strange thing. It pushed on without mercy, but it allowed us to change and bend our lives. So even when we seemed always to be blowing like butterflies in the nasty wind that blew out from White Boss, we always found some beats and shapes of our own. We chose to stay here. We could have left. But we stayed. It was our life. It was our choice to spend it here. Nobody forced us. We grew our crops. We kept our chickens. The children ate well. We were happy to be together here.

It was the third madam who helped us the most. She was a widow. She came with two children – a boy and a girl. Even though her hands liked to slap, her heart was good. Osewe used to say that White Boss still talked to her, long after she died. When she began to school her two children, she included all the children on

the farm. Oh, what a joy it was when Ang'awa wrote his name –
Mathew Ang'awa Osewe. And then he taught us how to write ours –
Priscilla Atieno Diang'a Osewe and John Mark Osewe Rodi. Osewe
been so proud that he did not even question why the boy was using
"Osewe" as one of his names, instead of his own Luo name, Ang'awa.
Later, we came to learn that this was how white people named their
children.

Yes, that third madam's heart was good, even though she was not
a Christian and did not attend church. She had seen that Ang'awa
was quick. He told us he was even quicker than her two children.
She sent him to a school in Nakuru. And then she sent him to a
teacher's college. Our son became a teacher! I was so proud. Osewe
was also proud. But the boy disappointed him deeply.

When Ang'awa first started to talk about settling in Uhanga, we
took it as a joke. But soon we saw that he was very serious. We could
not understand it. Why would he want to build his life in Uhanga
when everybody knew that the future lay in places like Nakuru,
Nairobi, and Mombasa? But what a strong-willed boy! As soon as he
had finished at the college, he went straight to Uhanga. He opened
a school. He married. He had children. He settled. Osewe forgave
him for that, but he could never forgive him for convincing his two
brothers, Otiende and Mala, to join him in Uhanga. Osewe and
Ang'awa never spoke again.

So in the end the two of us were left here alone, just as it
had been in the beginning. Ang'awa wrote to me every month. As
each letter was being read to me I would find myself hoping that
he would ask me to greet his father. But he never did. They did
not understand each other. It was as if their faces were turned in
different directions.

White Boss has finished. Good. Good. Look at you. Bend over
slowly, reach down for some soil to grab, throw out your hand,

stand and watch as the soil falls down on to the box. Limp away. Good. Look at you. Leave us alone. Now we can begin to sing.

Ang'awa is here. He looks well. He is almost fat! They all look well – Ang'awa, Otiende, and Mala. I sent word that their father was ailing. I wish they could have come in time to see him before he died. Especially Ang'awa. But at least he is here. He came with both his wives, each with her eldest son. Otiende and Mala are also here with their women and eldest sons. All of them except Ang'awa have visited us here before. Both of Ang'awa's wives came last year. Mathlida came again this year by herself. I did not say anything then, but I think she could sense that he was not well. She wanted to see him again. She only met him two times, but she loved him deeply. She told me that when she spoke to him, she understood Ang'awa much better. She was right. They were different but also the same. They both approached life like an adventure. Like mine, her tears are still falling. But I am very happy to have all of them here at the same time like this.

Osewe, my friend, I think we did well. We shared many memories in our adventure. You never wanted to think about Awino, so you always said that our first memory together was the view of Asembo after the black wall passed over us. From then until now we were together making our story. We were happy to be together. But, my friend, I know you. I know that even the sight of all your children and grandchildren healthy and prospering would not have been enough for you. Where – you would have asked – where was their ambition? Where was their sense of adventure?

8

He missed the views the most. The main view – the one from the living room and verandah, which he had seen just once when he was an eight-year-old, during a mathematics tutoring session with Mrs. Terreblanche, ten-year-old Vincent Terreblanche, and eight-year-old Victoria Terreblanche – the main view was the best one. This view faced north from the top of the small rise, leaving the verandah shaded throughout the day. The verandah wrapped around the house on both sides, so that Terreblanche could sit in his rocking chair and watch the sun rise and set each day.

To the left, the north-facing view took in Waterbuck's wheat and barley fields. To the right lay the sectioned-off paddocks for the Guernsey cattle and Merino sheep. Beyond, stretching to the horizon, were the McFarland and Armitage farms. To the east was the Njoro Country Club's golf course, and to the west was the rest of Waterbuck – still unopened forest. To the south, behind the homestead, down the rise, and across a narrow valley, was Lord Egerton's estate, also mostly unopened.

He remembered that main view... and the cold juice and biscuits Mrs. Terreblanche had given him that day. He had gulped down the juice painfully. But he had been too nervous to eat. Mrs. Terreblanche had let him take the biscuits back with him to the servant quarters. It must have been awkward for her, too. She never again invited him to the tutoring sessions, which he knew went on week after week. Baba and Mama were upset with him. But how could he explain? How could he have understood that she felt she had gone too far with her kindness to a worker's child by inviting him into her house and treating like a white child. That understanding came to him much later. But not to Baba. Baba never understood. A few weeks after he came home with the biscuits, it became clear that he would not be invited back again. Baba whipped him.

The servant quarters. These were located to the south of the main house, a short walk down the rise, just out of view for someone looking· out the kitchen window.

Servants.

Baba, did you think of yourself as a servant? What about Mama? Was she a servant, too? It is 1943. You came here in 1904. Is that what you did for forty years? Is that why you left Uhanga? Where was my ambition, you were always asking? Where was yours?!

He wished Terreblanche would stop talking. What made the man think they would want him there to begin with? And then why speak in Afrikaans when it was obvious nobody could understand? The man was still such a brute.

He used to whip Baba and Mama. And then Baba and Mama would not want to look directly at anyone for many days. Baba's back had marks on it.

To think that Mama actually thought he had named the boy Luka Sollo after that beast. Never! Luka – not Lucas – was from the Book of Luke, which was the mother's favorite gospel. Sollo was for Ojok Sollo, uncle to Nwanji, cousin of Oweh from whom they all descended. How could Mama even imagine he would do such a thing? What did this Lucas Terreblanche man ever do for him?

Mrs. Terreblanche, maybe. He should have come to her funeral. She was kind. For her, he might. But Lucas Terreblanche. Never. Never.

They had never really argued ... he and Baba. They just never agreed. At first, he assumed it was because he went away to school in Nakuru. He knew the way he spoke had changed, because the way he thought had changed. But Baba's bad reaction to the news that he would be going to start a school in Uhanga had reminded him of a much earlier parting of ways. It had happened in 1922 when he was about nine years old – at least five years before he left for Nakuru. The family's one and only visit to Uhanga was almost over. He had not seen his parents for many days. On the family's unannounced arrival in his grandfather's homestead, they had all been swept up into one fervent embrace after another. He and his brothers had ended up in the homestead of Joseph Oremo, one of his uncles. While his parents fulfilled their many social obligations, he and his brothers played with their many cousins and drank in unconditional outpourings of love from aunts, uncles, grandaunts, and granduncles. He had never felt so warmly loved and accepted. The days flew by.

"Come," his father said one day, finding him tending sheep and goats with two cousins, throwing pebbles at a tree in a contest of strength and accuracy. "We are leaving today."

He had never seen his father looking so tense. Red eyes. Shaking hands. Lips cut thin and tight. Voice hard.

"No, Baba!" he had shouted out in disbelief. "I don't want to leave! Please, Baba!"

"We are leaving today. Now! Come here!"

His first instinct was to run, but he had never seen his father so upset and irritated. So he let go of his handful of pebbles and trotted over to his father, who took hold of his hand and marched him roughly to where his mother and younger brothers were already waiting.

"Why must you leave now?" Uncle Joseph Oremo had asked, smiling. "Why not stay for a few more days. We have hardly spoken to you."

"We are already late," Baba had snapped back, not returning the smile.

He had begun to cry. He did not like the way his father was behaving. His mother and younger brothers were also crying. The look on his father's face did not change – not until they were on their way, at which point his father's usual calm and pleasant demeanor returned, as if by magic. His father began to hum and sing again. They all joined in. But he never viewed Baba in the same way again.

Not until many years had passed without a return to Uhanga did he understand the biggest difference between him and Baba. He yearned for the place and how it made him feel, but Baba had no love for Uhanga's routines, rules, and tones. Those were firmly in the past. Those were old things that belonged to history and played no role in shaping the future. But for him, they were everything. The root of life. The heart.

"Baba wanted to know why you have taken a second wife." The previous year, his brother, Otiende, had gone to Njoro to visit their parents and returned with this question.

He had been furious. What was it to the old man, anyway? It was a very normal thing. He had reached his second maturity. His first son from his first wife was almost twelve years old. In his father's continued absence, he was being asked to take on more responsibility in the clan. As headmaster of Uhanga Primary and Secondary Schools for almost fifteen years, he was well respected. The time had come for him to take his life to the next level. He wanted to position himself as the clan's spokesman and leader. He wanted to be selected as the new Chief by the Colonial authorities. He did not like the idea of being the one to enforce the hated poll and hut taxes, or the one to compel free labor for road building and other Colonial Government projects. But he would do it very happily if named Chief. In addition to these political ambitions, it was obvious to everyone, including his first wife, that it was time to bring another woman into the homestead. His first wife did not want to add to her four children. And her body no longer brought out the best in his. It was clear that he should take another wife. But taking care not to drag his brother into the long-running disagreement with their father, he had forced himself to laugh and reply, "Brother, you know that we Luos have our ways."

He looked over at his second wife, Magdalena Akoth, and felt a warm glow inside. She looked fresh and tender. The baby boy, her first born, Samson Okello, was asleep in her arms, his soft hair just visible underneath a bright orange blanket. His first wife, Mathlida Anyango, had been knocked down by the news of her father-in-law's passing. She still looked stunned. Her first born, Boro Tindi, was by her side. As always, the boy was watching his every move. A good boy. Sensible. Good with words. A good singing voice... like his grandfather. Like his grandfather. His grandfather.

He raised his eyes to look around at the homestead. He could see his father's hand everywhere. No holes in the fences. No rotting posts. No peeling paint. No overflowing latrines. Nothing carelessly done. Nothing out of place. Everywhere he looked, he saw the meticulous hand, the painstaking touch, the unwavering pride.

"Oh Baba! Baba! Baba! Baba... "

9

Two days. We have been tracking this rhino for two days. It is not interested in us. It is just wandering freely, eating its food and drinking its water. I think it can hear us and smell us from very far away. We never surprise it. We must be silent and keep following until we get close enough for Terreblanche and Carrington to shoot it. They are very hungry for that. I cannot understand it.

It is now four years. I miss father. I think of him most days. I think of how I disappointed him. He needed me so much. What would he say if he knew what I have done for four years? What would he think if I told him that I have been chasing wild animals for Terreblanche? Where are your crops, he would ask? Where are your animals? What would I say? Would he understand if I said that life is measured differently here? Would he agree that what a man does can be different from what he owns? Only if the man is building himself, he would say. Are you building yourself, Osewe son of Ogombe?

I miss you, father. I miss hunting with you and Oremo and the other men. I miss the way you sharpened your spear and knife on the smooth rock next to your stool. I miss the sound of your voice as you greeted us and told us what you wanted from us during the hunt. I miss the sound of the dogs barking ahead of us, chasing the deer and wild pigs. I miss the jubilant shouts when we hit and killed one. I miss the careful slaughtering. I miss the division of the meat, and how serious and precise you were about it. To each his proper share, you would say. The hind legs, innards, and spine to the one who dropped the prey. The forelegs, chest, ribcage, and head to the others. I miss the proud and tender look on mother's face as you handed her your share of the kill. I miss the smell of roasting meat. I miss the stories as we feasted on it.

That was hunting. There was purpose to it. The company of men. The love of women. The meat to feast on.

I will never understand this hunting of Terreblanche and Carrington.

Why chase an old rhino like this? What for? Why kill something that has no interest in you. Why kill something you will never eat. It was the same with the leopard. We followed it for three days. Terreblanche killed it. He told me to skin it without removing the head. He killed it, yes, but he was afraid of it. I could see. He thought I would not be able to do it. It was easy. A leopard is not big. I did it quickly. But the meat smells bad. Bitter. It made me want to vomit. We left it there for the hyenas. Terreblanche was so proud of himself. But what for? What had he done to be proud of? When we returned to Waterbuck, he told me to help me place the hide on his head and shoulders and then he called Madam from the house to see. He looked like a demon with two heads. She was smiling as she came out but screamed when she saw him and ran back into the house. He laughed. That was the first Madam. It was the next day that she jumped into the well. I went down there and brought her out. She was cold and swollen. I will never forget it.

I must find a way to change. This meaningless hunting is not why I broke my father's heart. I must find a way to build myself.

Last night I heard Terreblanche tell Carrington that he wants to shoot the rhino for its head and tail. He is good with the gun. I am sure he will be the one to shoot it. Carrington is very thin and weak. The big gun is too heavy for him. There is no way he will be able to control it.

When Terreblanche shoots this one, I will tell Carrington's men to take the head and tail.

4

TERRIBLE SMILE

The boy had left the harp behind! The man grabbed it from the kitchen table, jumped into the car, and sped off after them. He found them already at the airport, standing in line at the United Airlines check-in counter. Only the girl returned his smile. But like his, hers was forced. The boy would not look at him. Their mother's glare asked, "What do you want now?"

"This is his," he answered out loud, holding up the harp and handing it to the boy.

"I don't want it," mumbled the boy, still not looking at him. "I don't like to play it."

"That is not true. You love to play it."

"Stop pestering him about that harp." This from the mother. "When was the last time you played it yourself? Leave him alone."

"Here," said the girl, winking conspiratorially at her father. "I'll take it."

"No!" snapped the boy, jumping forward and grabbing the instrument from his father. "It's mine! He gave you the drums!"

"Okay, okay," said the girl. "You said you didn't want it." She chuckled and winked again at her father. He winked back gratefully.

"Please play it sometimes," the man pleaded with his son. "You are talented. But you must play regularly to reach your full potential."

The boy did not answer, but his father noticed that the way he was holding his shoulders was less closed.

The boy had left the harp behind on purpose, hoping his father would see it and come after them. They both loved the harp. For a long time, it had been the only thing they could share without animosity and irritation. But then his father had stopped playing. So even that was lost. It had been around the time his mother began to commute from Redding to Davis each week, trying to finish the PhD studies she had abandoned during her pregnancy with him. Six long years. She did it. But then she and his father stopped talking to each other. No more music for him. No more words for his mother. It hurt.

"I love your father very, very much. But we've been growing apart for years. This is just part of a bigger problem."

That was how his mother had described it to him. He could not bring himself to ask his father. Now they were leaving his father behind. It hurt.

The line was moving slowly. The man wondered if he should stay or leave. It was awkward. He should leave.

"Bye, bye again. Have a good flight. Please ring when you arrive."
He left.

*   *   *

"I have been offered a job at Georgetown." She had been very excited. He could tell. But she would not let it all show. They had been speaking so little those days. "I am leaving... I mean... I am going to accept it. I think the children should come with me. The schools in the Washington DC area are better... Maybe you could find something there ...?"

"No," he had cut in sharply. "I cannot leave Redding now. Everything is just beginning to come together."

Ever since they moved to Redding from Davis in 1973, right after he finished his PhD, they had been plowing every extra cent they earned into real estate, speculating on Redding's one day becoming an attractive and affordable destination for retiring baby-boomers. THeir gamble had begun to pay off. Property values in Redding were rising rapidly, as wave after wave of retirees from California's big cities sold their houses to the next generation of middle-class homeowners and moved north. If everything went according to plan and expectation, they would be very rich within ten years. Maybe even millionaires. But he had to be there to make it all happen.

So he had to stay, and the family had to be split.

*   *   *

Is that it?

Should he say, "I should have come with you to Washington. I did not know it at the time, but I was depressed and confused. It was that trip to Kenya in 1980 that did it. So many irritating questions and demands. 'When are you coming home?' 'When are you going to marry a real woman? We want a Luo! That white woman is not enough.' 'You must teach your children Dholuo or they will be lost. Don't you want them to be Luos?' It was all too much for me. It took me a long time to make peace with myself. I am sorry for hurting you."

Was that it?

"I've been asked to be the new Organizing Secretary of PNN " said Saks to Maaike. The children were asleep. Saks and Maaike were sitting in the living room. It was a Sunday evening. Maaike was tired. The maid had fallen sick and been allowed to stay in her room all day. Saks had been away in Nakuru since Saturday morning. He had returned just before dinner. The children had monopolized him after dinner. This was the first chance to talk about his trip.

"Sorry?" asked Maaike, slightly disoriented. "I'm so tired. I think I dozed off. What did you say?"

"I said I've been asked to be the Organizing Secretary of PNN."

"Oh... How do you feel about it? Are you going to accept?"

"Actually, I already did. I felt I had to give them an answer right away."

"Why? Surely they could have waited a day! And if not, you could at least have phoned me."

"I didn't know where to find you."

"That's rubbish, Saks! I've been here all weekend!" She was wide awake now. Very upset. "This will affect me, too."

"I know, I know. I'm sorry. But listen, I..."

"No, wait, Saks. I'm still upset." Maaike stood up, went upstairs to their bedroom and lay down on the bed. She hated this trait in Saks. He was too impulsive. He never thought things through fully before committing himself, and his family, to costly or risky ventures. Eight years into her career, Maaike was well on the path to becoming a senior manager at Central Pharmaceuticals and Chemicals. Eight years into his, Saks had changed jobs three times and did not seem to be interested in stopping. Maaike traced his restlessness to their trip around west and north Africa. She had emerged from the journey ready to settle down. He seemed to have picked up an impatience with sameness – a desire to be constantly on the move.

They had nothing to show for their years of work – only two old cars, one of which was forever breaking down. No house of their own. No serious investments. Hardly any savings. It frustrated her. This business with PNN was his latest fixation.

The Party for a New Nation was Kenya's newest political party. It had been formed by friends and colleagues of one Brother Josef Bonde – a Franciscan monk who had been murdered just outside Njoro town. The police claimed that a gang of robbers had committed the murder. But most people felt that the killing was retribution for Bonde's vocal stance against the abuses meted out by the local administration and police on the populace in and around Njoro, where he ran an agribusiness management training institute, the Institute for a New Nation, popularly known as The Inn.

The idea to start The Inn had sprung from Brother Josef's objection to the Government's decision in 1995 to invest a huge amount of public funds in a scheme to use the one remaining state-owned farm in the region as a site to adapt a newly introduced exotic breed of cattle to local conditions. To Brother Josef, this was an absurd idea. All around the state farm, local breeds of cattle owned by poor small-scale farmers were dying of diseases that could be easily cured if reliable veterinary services were available. An improvement in these services would have required a fraction of the funds sunk into the scheme to adapt exotic breeds. Moreover, had the planners bothered to ask local residents, they would have been told that their scheme would fail because the exotic cattle would die of the very diseases that were killing the local breeds. And by 1996, it had failed. To Brother Josef, it was a perfect illustration of how out of touch the Government had become with the real problems facing Kenyans. It was clear to him that the badly-needed veterinary services would have to be provided locally. But, first, skills in small-scale veterinary business management needed to be developed. Building those skills was the basic aim of The Inn. But his efforts were frustrated by the local administration.

A student would emerge from The Inn with a diploma in some aspect of primary veterinary care. The Inn would advance him or her a small loan to buy a bicycle and some basic supplies with which to start serving farmers. As required by law, the ex-student would apply to the local administration for a license to operate in the region. But this license would be granted only after bribes had been paid. The local Chief from whose office the application for the license had to originate would do nothing unless "facilitated." Nor would the District Veterinary Officers who had to approve applications, but who viewed the Inn's graduates as direct competitors as suppliers of animal health services. The total bribes often exceeded the amount of the original loan. On many occasions The Inn was forced to loan its graduates more money, steadily eating into its own operating fund.

After months of waiting, bribing, waiting again, bribing again, the license would eventually be granted and an Inn graduate could begin to deliver services to local farmers. Because of the favorable price of milk, farmers were both eager and able to pay full market prices for the services. But the earnings would not escape the notice of the local police prowling the area – prowling not, as their motto proclaimed, *In Service to All*, but rather to extract daily "service charges" from the frustrated graduates struggling to launch and expand their businesses.

The bribes and service charges cut deeply into graduates' profits. Their repayment rates on loans from The Inn were low and irregular as a result. The cost of the program rose well beyond Brother Josef's most pessimistic projection. The Inn was losing money. But even worse in Brother Josef's eyes, so were many of its graduates. Most of them did not last long in their new trades. And the farmers who so badly needed their services were once again forced to travel long distances to Nakuru, Molo, and Elburgon to buy drugs and supplies for themselves, often administering the medicines incorrectly. Many farmers were forced to do without drugs and supplies altogether and watch their valuable animals ail and die.

Brother Josef often complained to his friends about this, but they were powerless to help. In the end, he decided to report the Chief, the Veterinary Officers, and the local police to their superiors in the District and Provincial capitals. To Brother Josef's utter surprise, the offenders were publicly reprimanded by the Rift Valley Provincial Commissioner at a local fund-raising meeting.

The Veterinary Officers were annoyed at Brother Josef. They had almost lost their jobs. Privately, Brother Josef sympathized with them. They were paid starvation wages by the Government, and extortion was sometimes the only way they could make ends meet. He understood their position, but he could not condone it.

The exposed police officers were furious at him. More than once after their public humiliation, they were overheard swearing revenge. The generally held view was that they staged the robbery to have him killed. Some people even said that the police officers were part of the murder gang.

The motivation for forming PNN came from the gradual realization among Brother Josef's friends that even had he lived, he probably would have failed anyway. Local administrators were making The Inn look inefficient when in fact it was a very efficient business. The odds were as highly stacked against him as they were against The Inn's graduates – just as they were against any organization trying to do business in Kenya. The battle he was fighting – the battle that cost him his life – was not just against inept and predatory rural authorities, but also against a much wider and deeper blundering and rapacious system of public administration that was stifling the efforts of millions of Kenyans day in, day out as they desperately tried to make ends meet.

PNN's mission thus became: *To serve the long-term interests of private business throughout Kenya.* The mission sounded simple, almost naïve. But the party leadership soon found that grounded as it was in real people's real problems, the mission allowed PNN to speak to every important domestic and international issue facing the country, and in ways that resonated at all levels and corners of society.

Maaike knew all this. She also knew that PNN was going through a very difficult period. A few months before, members of the party's Executive Committee had discovered that internal security personnel were following each of them. This was an unpleasant discovery but not an unexpected one. They knew that the Stork kept all Opposition leaders under close surveillance. But then they noticed that the security officers seemed to have advance knowledge of exactly where and when the Committee would be holding its meetings. This was privileged information. There had to be a mole among them. Distrust and mutual suspicion invaded the Committee. Accusations of illegal infiltration and sabotage were hurled at the Government through the press. The Government denied everything.

It had all come to a head the previous week. An informant had revealed that PNN's Organizing Secretary, a teacher named Laliro Kwach, had been bought off by Government agents. In exchange for inside information about PNN, Kwach had been given a plot of land in Nairobi's posh Runda Estate. The Government knew everything about them, including bogus "details" about fabricated "foreign masters." A reporter at the Nation broke the "foreign masters" story, complete with concocted million-dollar bank transfers from abroad. PNN was on the brink of collapse.

The only way out was for Kwach to go public about having been bribed, to say that he had been paid to tell lies, and to expose the figures in the Government behind the scheme. He resisted at first. But others on the Committee managed to resurrect his memory and conscience sufficiently for him to see that there was more at stake than his personal reputation, which was in tatters anyhow. It also helped that he had already unloaded the Runda plot on the market, to the tune of several million shillings, and that he could not be charged with a crime because strictly speaking he had not done anything illegal.

A press conference was called during which Kwach announced his resignation from PNN's Executive Committee and dropped the bombshell about the bribe, giving names and dates, and revealing everything that had transpired. It worked. The next day's headline in the Nation read, "Two Cabinet Ministers Named in PNN Bribery Scandal." The Ministers issued sharp denials, which nobody believed. But the damage to PNN's reputation as a clean and independent party was severe. There could be nothing more damaging in Kenyan politics than to be accused of being on the payroll of foreigners. It would take great effort and considerable luck to regain the public's trust.

The Executive Committee was deeply shaken. The Chairman, Victor Nyamaye, took it particularly hard. He and Kwach were close, or so he thought. The man he knew would never have done anything like that. On numerous occasions he had encouraged Kwach to increase the very small income he earned as a teacher by entering into business partnerships of various kinds. But each time, Kwach had declined, saying that he was perfectly happy as he was. And then this! But never before had Kwach faced the prospect of making several million shillings overnight, literally. This was a different game altogether – a wholly new level of pressure, intimidation, and temptation.

For Maaike, the most irritating thing about Sakawa's current involvement with PNN was that it had all begun with her. The party's Treasurer, Fiona Naikuni, was a close friend of Maaike's from their days together at the University of Connecticut. Fiona had encouraged her to become involved with party affairs. But work and household responsibilities had prevented that. Saks was at home the day Fiona visited and made the invitation to Maaike. He generally avoided Maaike's friends, all of whom he considered a little too engrossed in their children's lives, and rather too critical of their husbands. But Fiona was different. Still unmarried and happily so, she had interesting things to say, especially on politics. Rather than make his usual polite but speedy exit, Saks had decided to sit down and chat with them. At the end of her visit, Fiona suggested that if he had the time, there was definitely scope for involvement with PNN. Maaike had shaken her head in wonder and irritation when he immediately accepted.

Saks had plunged headlong into the task of helping to organize various PNN events in Nairobi. His attention to detail and healthy appetite for late-night planning sessions soon became evident. As she lay on the bed and gathered her thoughts, Maaike concluded that he must have been an obvious choice when the position of Organizing Secretary fell vacant.

Maaike was worried about Saks. He was changing in ways that she did not understand. His father's death had knocked him off track. That she understood. She was sure he would recover from the blow. But there was more to it than grieving, she felt. He had always been flighty. Now, in addition to that, he no longer did anything in moderation. There were several outward signs of inner turmoil. He seldom combed his hair. He had allowed his once neat beard to grow long and bushy. While he continued to bathe regularly, he never looked clean. He seemed always to be filled with an irrational sense of urgency, which had invaded all aspects of their life. Even the way he made love had changed, with few preliminaries and no intimate conversation afterwards. Most troubling to Maaike was the change in his relationship with the children. Whereas before she could count on that as a source of stability in the home, now he lurched from shouting impatience and irritation with them one day to contrition-filled gift-showering the next.

"I don't want to waste my life anymore," had been Saks's response to one of her many queries about this new edginess.

"What do you mean? How have you been wasting your life?"

"I haven't done anything with my life. Nothing important, anyway."

He had not been looking at her as he spoke – another new thing – so he did not see her eyes fill with tears before she stood up and walked over to the kitchen sink and turned on the tap to keep herself occupied.

"My brother died at eighteen; my father died at sixty. I am thirty-seven. I need to do something with my life."

He had also become an utter bore. His father's death and the new interest in PNN seemed to have sparked off a political awakening in him. He was writing furiously, churning out page after page of "statements" and "positions" on a range of subjects. Without regard for what she may be doing – cooking, reading, relaxing, watching television – he would descend on her, demand that she give him her full attention, and then read loudly from endless papers and index cards.

Everything he wrote and recited to her made sense.

The previous week, it had been tribalism and the Rift Valley. Yes, tribal allegiances provided richness and depth to Kenyan society while simultaneously underpinning prejudices, shaping animosities, and fueling ideas for which people were ready to fight, kill, and die. Yes, the history of the Rift Valley meant that it would always be a focal point for ethnic confrontation. Yes, if ethnic differences alone were sufficient to breed violence, the country would constantly be at war, whereas it was usually at peace. Yes, the Stork liked to play tribal politics to create division among dissidents, and, yes, the Rift Valley was his favorite playing field.

The week before that, it had been the effects of market liberalization on the poor. Yes, market liberalization was exposing large numbers of people to new pressures that undermined their livelihoods. Yes, much of the new wealth being created under market liberalization was accruing to a favored few individuals around the Stork. Yes, letting the economy run on autopilot was a recipe for disaster.

Yes, yes, yes. This was all true. But coming from Saks, non-stop, in that way, it was torture. It might have been more endurable had he not also assumed a condescending tone toward her. The first time it happened, Maaike ignored it, certain that it was merely her imagination. But when it happened again, she mentioned it to him. He went from denial, to disbelief, and eventually to contrition. He would not let it happen again. But he did, many times, but stopping at the denial stage whenever she objected. To her dismay, the tone worked its way into his usual speaking voice.

Maaike spoke to her parents about it. They suggested that she remind him that she, too, had a PhD from a world-class university. But she knew that would not help. He would just look at her as if she were crazy. "Of course I know you have a PhD," he would say. "I was there when you got it!"

She spoke to her mother-in-law, Rhoda, who grew very upset and offered to talk to Saks. Maaike declined the offer, knowing that it would merely alienate him more. Saks did not like her to speak to anyone about their domestic troubles.

She spoke to her friends. No good.

She thought it through for herself and concluded that the Saks she knew was simply on vacation. He would return. Meanwhile, she would have to find a way to deal with the situation.

Maaike went back downstairs and listened silently to Saks's plans for his new position.

2

Maaike could not have known how near to the mark she was in concluding that Saks had taken leave of his senses. Secretly, he had been working on a book titled *The Truth About the Sollo Murder*. It was a misleading title in that he still knew very little about the murder itself. The real aim of the book was to expose the secession plot. It had become an obsession. He was working on the final chapter.

My family and friends will be very worried when this book is published. They will worry about what might happen to me. Quite frankly, I seldom think about that, but when I do, I find that I do not care. I know this is selfish. I also know that some people's feelings will be hurt by what I have written. I am sorry about that. But I cannot help myself. I had to write it this way. And I must publish it this way. The time to speak out has come.

The Yoruba of Nigeria have a wonderful saying that goes, "The one whose head is used to break the coconut does not share in the eating." They would probably say that we take this saying a little too much to heart in Kenya. Save for one or two exceptions, nobody wants his head used to break coconuts, but everyone wants to participate in the meal. And those who agree to have their heads bashed, too often do it at the wrong times and for the wrong reasons. So we see Bishops, Imams, and all manner of "activists" being beaten up by anti-riot police as they "mobilize" poor, hungry, and idle city youth to disrupt Independence Day celebrations, the Budget Speech, the National Census. Not only is their important demand for more freedom and greater opportunity lost in the ensuing cacophony, they also come away looking self-serving and naïve.

From the look of it, my father's head probably broke quite a few objects before he died. Did his personal sacrifice make a difference? Through its effect on me, it has had quite a bit to do with the path taken by PNN. But what did his self-sacrifice achieve? Was it enough to arrest this country's slide toward tribe-based division? From what we can tell, probably not. He was a brave man, but perhaps he, too, was naïve.

Despite all our efforts to have Semoe Barsone released, he has been found guilty of murdering my father and sentenced to fifty years in prison. He will die in there long before he has served even one-quarter of the sentence. Meanwhile, the real killers roam free and unpunished.

The cattle wars are still raging in the Rift Valley. More soldiers are being sent in by the month. Much more ominously, new clashes have broken out at the Coast. The "indigenous" peoples of that area are supposedly rebelling against exploitation by "foreigners" from up-country, who are now fleeing in thousands. All this after many decades of peaceful coexistence.

Our sources tell us that this new violence is also a ruse – part of the secession plot, which now includes the Coast. They want a sea outlet. The end-game is now a U-shaped country, with the Rift Valley as its western arm, the Coast as its eastern one, and a narrow strip along the border with Tanzania connecting them. And all of this is to be defended by the army – our army.

We are in trouble. But there is still hope. The President's plot will succeed only if he, or his anointed successor in the Loyalist Party, wins the next general election.

So, first, over the next few years, we must ignore his ugly, divisive rhetoric and instead get involved, get together, get organized. And then, come the general election in 2002, we must, each of us, take personal responsibility for this country and vote not from our guts but with our minds. That way, not only will we ensure that the break never occurs, we will also strike the first blow in the long battle against the tribalistic patronage system that is throttling this country. It is that simple. The future is still in our hands.

It was explosive material. Saks knew he would never find a publisher brave enough to take it on. He would have to publish it himself. But he and Maaike did not have the money. Given that he did not want to discuss the book's contents with her, he also could not benefit from her common sense in exploring financing options. He made a quick trip to Songhor to see his mother and ask her for a loan. Seeing the agitated look on her son's face as he made the request, Rhoda agreed without prying into what lay behind his sudden need for money.

Saks revealed the existence of the book the day before its release by Text Book Centre, Bookpoint, and Westlands Sundries. Rhoda was in Nairobi for a medical check-up and was staying with Saks and his family. She and Maaike were sipping tea at the dining table when Saks proudly handed them autographed copies of the book. Maaike took one look at the title, cried out in shock, and threw her copy back at Saks, hitting him in the chest.

"Are you mad?!" she screamed. "Who do you think you are? What do you want to do to us?! You don't care about yourself, but what about us, Saks? What about us? I hate you!" She ran out of the room, out of the house, and into the back yard. Saks did not follow her. He turned to his mother.

"Mama, do you feel the same?"

"Yes, I do, Sakawa. You are a selfish, selfish man. I am very ashamed that I contributed to this situation. You used my money for this, didn't you?"

"Yes, I did. But what's so wrong, Mama?"

"What is wrong? Are you really asking me that question? You disobeyed your father's last wish. You kept this from your own wife. You tricked your mother into lending you money for something you knew she would have resisted. You have endangered all of our lives. Is none of that wrong to you? Are you really that childish?"

Silence.

"You are a disgrace."

"But Mama, if not me, then who? Who is going to do anything about what is happening to us – to this country? I did it because

I could. I could, Mama. Don't you see? Nobody else in the whole world could have done it. Only me. Mama, please understand. Maaike! Maaike! Please come back in. I need for you to understand this. Maaike! Please!"

Maaike came back in and went to stand next to Rhoda. She could not look at Saks, so disgusted was she with him.

"You know, I've never told anybody this, but I could have saved Madi. I could have saved him. Madi could be alive and standing here with us today if I had done what only I could have done. If I had insisted that we use the Kibos route and not the Ahero one, we wouldn't have crashed. I suggested it, but Madi wouldn't listen. I could have insisted. Nobody else in the world could have insisted. Only me. I wanted to. I almost did. But I didn't. It's like Baba said, sometimes you're the only one who can do something. He said we shouldn't do things in isolation, and I haven't. I have been working hard for PNN. But this I could only do myself. I am sorry I had to hide it from you, but if I had said anything, you would have stopped me."

"It is still so selfish, Saks," protested Maaike. "I've listened quietly to everything else you've pushed on me these past months. What makes you think I couldn't have taken this? I'm your wife, Saks! I love you. That means I support your dreams and goals. I will question you and ask you to explain yourself. But I will always, always support you. You should have told me."

Rhoda shook her head. Sakawa was more like his father than she had ever imagined.

"I think I'll start with the tough ones and then do the others," Luka had said to her the day before he disappeared. He was buttering one of the two slices of toast he always had for breakfast with tea, fruit, and juice. He was planning to drive to Nairobi later that morning.

Rhoda did not respond immediately, wanting Luka to look at her. He

*finished buttering the toast, added marmalade, and looked up, but not at
her. Instead he turned his gaze to his left, her right, out toward the view
they both knew well and loved deeply. It had rained the night before. The
air was clear and free of moisture. The small alcove in which they were
sitting had been a late addition to the house, for use on mornings like this,
when Lake Victoria was clearly visible in the distance.*

*"Yes, I think I'll deal with the miller first, and then go to KGGCU,
and then to the bank. I'll see Margaret tomorrow after lunch, or maybe
we'll have lunch together at Nairobi Club. Yup, I think that's better. And
then I'll..."*

*Luka paused to pour tea into his cup. Rhoda watched him. She nodded.
He continued to talk. She listened, watching him. He never met her eyes,
not even as he said goodbye and walked out of their house for the last time.
He should have told her. He should have looked at her.*

"You are so like your father – the part of him I did not value,"
Rhoda said to her son. "He had so many secrets at the end. But I am
not going to let you die, Saks. It is not going to happen again. At
the first sign of trouble, you must promise me that you will leave...
leave Kenya. Promise me, Sakawa."

"I can't do that, Mama, I can't."

"Maaike. Please, tell him that he must."

Maaike shook her head sadly. "I can't, Mama. I can't. You can see
that he does not listen to me either."

Slamming down her hand on the dining table in anger and
frustration, Rhoda left.

3

The Truth About the Sollo Murder was banned within two days of its release. Saks was arrested, charged with sedition, and detained. Rhoda had arranged for two reporters and two photographers to be with Saks around the clock. Pictures and detailed accounts of the arrest appeared in all the major dailies. Rhoda's lawyer, Raju Ahluwalia, challenged the Government to produce evidence refuting the book's claims. The challenge went unanswered. Saks remained in detention. Family, friends, and colleagues continued to agitate for his release, even managing to convince Amnesty International to release a statement condemning his arrest and detention. In the end, the case was dismissed. Saks was released, but only after spending fifteen hellish weeks in prison.

Political detention does different things to different people. Some, like Kenyatta and Mandela, begin it as stormy firebrands but emerge as moderates, looking to embrace mankind with all its faults, ready to forgive their jailers. Others, like Sakawa Sollo, begin it angry and indignant yet without any hatred toward anyone, but emerge livid at the whole world. The whole world. Incensed. Bitter. Violent.

Saks raped Maaike his first night back at home from prison. He did not have to. She was craving him. He could tell. But he raped her all the same, in the bathroom, as she brushed her teeth absent-mindedly, trying to put her finger on what it was about him that had changed. It was over quickly. His rage would not let him last for long. But it was violent. He ripped off the pale blue nightie she had put on specially for him. Before – during what in time Maaike came to view as another life – the nightie would come off after many minutes of kissing, touching, fondling, rubbing. Another life. She stood there naked, embarrassed, confused, covering her breasts with one hand and her pubic area with the other, toothpaste dripping from her mouth.

"Saks!" Maaike cried out in shock and disbelief. "What's wrong?"

Silence. Blood shot eyes. Terrible smile. He grabbed her left forearm with his right hand and twisted it sharply, causing her to cry out again, this time in pain. Her cry seemed to anger him and he shouted at her to be quiet. ·

"Close the door," she pleaded. "The children will hear."

"I don't care if they hear!" he exploded.

"Please close it, Saks. I don't want to wake them up."

Saks kicked back at the door with his left foot. It slammed shut loudly. Maaike jumped. He twisted again. She whimpered, eyes wide open, her embarrassment and concern for the children turning into cold fear. He unbuttoned his trousers with his left hand, still holding her twisted arm with his other hand.

"Turn around," he growled, forcing her to turn to her right. "I don't want to see your face. Bend over. More! Open your legs. Open them!"

He let go of her arm only when he had finished. He left the house almost immediately thereafter, leaving her lying on the bathroom floor, gasping in shock and pain.

The bedside clock read 3.33am when she heard him open the front door, and 3.36 when he climbed into bed, smelling of cigarette smoke and alcohol. He had been at a bar.

"Maaike?" he called out to her. She did not answer. She did not dare move. And then she heard his sobs. Not stopping to ask herself what the tears might be about, she moved across to his side of the bed and embraced his quivering back, kissing his neck, telling him it was OK. He turned, and still sobbing, kissed her back, gently, lovingly, like before. "Oh Maaike, Maaike," he said many times that night as they made love, like before.

She was confused when he would not speak to her in the

morning. He did not utter a single word to her for two weeks. She would try to speak to him, but it was as if she did not exist.

"Saks, what's wrong?" Silence.

"Saks, are you feeling unwell?" Silence.

"Saks, please talk to me." Silence.

"Saks, please at least talk to the children. They've been waiting for you to come back all this time, so they don't understand why you're not talking to them." Silence. But he did begin to speak to the children. At seven and six, the two boys, Malcolm and Jimmy, were old enough to understand that something was badly wrong between their parents, and that the problem stemmed from their father. It took them some days to warm to him. But for Anita, the three-year-old girl, there was no such reservations. The University of Nairobi had fired him while he was in detention, so he was at home most of the time. Father and daughter began to spend many hours together. Maaike saw this as a positive sign. A hopeful sign.

At the end of the second week, Saks met Maaike at the door with a smile. The terrible smile of the bedroom. And blood shot eyes. He had sent the maid to the corner shop with the children. He had been drinking.

"Saks, please no. Please. No," she pleaded as he took hold of her left arm and twisted, causing her to drop the car keys she was holding, along with the bag of groceries she had picked up from Uchumi Supermarket on the way home.

"No!"

Taken by surprise by Maaike's scream Saks let go of her arm. She bolted up the stairs, but he was on her in a flash. She screamed again. He punched her in the stomach, winding her, leaving her gasping for air. He dragged her up the remainder of the stairs and into the bathroom.

He did not return until dinner time the next day. When he walked in the back door, entered the dining room and said hello to her and to each of the children, he looked so disheveled and pathetic that all the things she had been planning to say to him evaporated; all the words she had rehearsed vanished. She and children were already seated at the dining table and readying to start. After washing his hands and face, he took his place next to her. The children wanted to know where he had been since the day before. Why were his knuckles bruised? Had he fallen like Mama? He told them an overly dramatic story about being chased by four dangerous men and having to run very fast to escape them. And so, yes, he did fall, when he hit his foot a huge rock that one of the men had placed in the road to trip him up. But he had leapt up and run even faster. He had tricked the men that he was going one way but had instead gone another way. Everything was fine now.

Maaike listened in silence, afraid to look at him. Afraid of what she would see in his eyes. She could tell that children were only partially convinced by the answer.

"I did not go to work today," she said, keeping her eyes fixed on her plate.

"Really?" replied Saks. She recognized the sound of a smile in that one word and shot him a quick glance. He was smiling. His old smile.

"Yes... I... I had a stomach ache."

Saks nodded slowly. "It's good to rest at home when you're not feeling well," he said softly, reaching over and rubbing her stomach. Seeing the questioning looks on the children's faces, Maaike smiled at him and reached down and covered his hand with hers.

The next day, Saks insisted that she stay in and rest. She was still feeling a little sore, so she let him convince her. But when he would not return her hug as she left for work the day after that, an uneasy feeling began to come over her. That afternoon, she called the house from her office. He answered the phone. But when she identified herself, the phone went dead. It just rang repeatedly when she called back.

Suddenly, Maaike knew what was bothering Saks. He did not want her to work. He was not working, nor was he looking for work. He seemed paralyzed. He wanted company in his paralysis. She was the obvious choice. He thought he could rape and beat her into that role. It was bizarre.

While Saks was in detention, Maaike had been made a Director at Central Pharmaceuticals and Chemicals. There had been no way to give him the good news until the day of his release. She told him in the car on the way home from the Nairobi Provincial Headquarters building where was been set free. It was with his reaction to her news that she had been trying to come to grips as she brushed her teeth the night of the first raping. He had not been happy for her when she had said that she was proud of herself and that her income had almost doubled. Rather, he had seemed almost annoyed. Maaike saw now that Saks was consumed by envy and jealousy. Even if he still had his job at Nairobi University, plus an occasional consultancy, there would be no escaping the fact that she had become the principal income earner in the household.

She saw it all very clearly. Yet she could not believe it of the Saks with whom she had studied late into many a night in California, as an equal. With whom she had trekked halfway across Africa, as an equal. With whom she had made love countless times, as an equal. Which was the real Saks? The one in her mind's eye who she understood completely, or the thuggish stranger she saw in the flesh each day?

They could survive very comfortably on her new salary and allowances. But the higher income came with added responsibilities and less time to spend on the household, and on the children. In a way, there was a very simple solution. Saks could be the homemaker, perhaps devote more time to writing, reading, and an occasional speaking engagement. He was very much in demand as a speaker, especially in the NGO community and in diplomatic circles. With the next general election on the horizon, and with the Stork's grip on power still strong, the "international community" was looking for local voices of dissent. Saks would be perfect. But the new Saks lacked the confidence and motivation to speak out again. His focus was now squarely on her – relating to her not as a helpful home-maker but rather as a tormentor. Something had to change. But she could not bring herself to leave him. Not after everything he had been through. The occasional glimpses of the old Saks gave her hope. But his new capacity for cruelty was beyond her understanding. What had they done to him in prison? When his father was killed, his sister, Soru, had told Maaike what the squatter Barsone had said about his time in prison. The beatings, licking, biting, groping, and everything else. The thought of Saks going through any of that made her tremble.

That evening, Maaike feigned a backache and at dinner an-nounced that she would not go to work the next day if she was still feeling the same. He held her gently that night, rubbing her back for hours. She returned his caresses and knew what she would have to do.

"Let's move to Songhor," she said to him over lunch the next day.

"Eh?" answered Saks, truly taken aback. "You want to move to Panderi?"

"Yes. I'm tired of this Nairobi life," she replied, speaking very carefully, knowing that this was make or break for her family.

"You're tired of Nairobi? But you love Nairobi! You always say it's your favorite city in the whole world. And you've never liked the farm... rural life. What about your job? What about your new job?"

"That was a mistake." She replied, watching him closely, and no-ticing the little smile that slipped into his face for a moment before quickly receding. She could feel him watching her, too. "That was a mistake. That kind of job is not for me. It is too stressful. And anyway, I really am tired of Nairobi. I want a quieter life. Please take us away from here, Saks. Mama also needs the help since Baba died."

"But..."

"You don't need to answer now, Saks. But please think it over."

Saks stood up and raised himself to his full height. Hands in pockets, he paced around the room, his face locked in a frown, all business.

"I will call Mama," he said finally. Maaike nodded, thinking to herself that the old Saks would have said something like, "Let's call Mama, OK?"

Maaike already knew what her mother-in-law would say. She had called Rhoda while Saks was dropping off the boys that morning and told her everything. Everything. Rhoda had cried. Wailed. In shame. In anger. In disbelief. She immediately saw what Maaike was trying to do.

"But what about schooling? You were going to use your new education allowance to send the children to Hillcrest or Banda. There's only Chemelil Primary here. It's a very good school, but nothing like Hillcrest or Banda."

"Yes, that's the hardest part. I will just have to do a lot with them at home."

"No, Maaike, that is not right. The farm is doing well. And it will do even better with you people here. We will be able to afford a good boarding school. .. Turi, Kaptagat, or something like that."

"OK, we can talk more about that. I'd better go. He will want to ring you, I'm sure."

"Maaike?"

"Yes, Mama."

"Thank you."

"There's no other way, Mama. He will kill me if we stay here in Nairobi. I never thought our life together would go this way, but it has. I still can't believe it. Sometimes I look in the mirror and try to tell myself that it isn't real. I know... it's silly. But I really really cannot believe this is happening to me, and that despite everything I still love him. I love the memory of what he used to be to me and the children. I want that back. Something happened to him in prison. He does not talk about it, so I don't know what. But something bad happened. Something inside him is broken. He needs to recover. There is only one way that can happen. The only way he will stop tormenting me and focus on himself is if he feels that I am at his level. That will never happen here in Nairobi. I am now too far ahead of him. He will never catch up. At Panderi we can start again as equals and build for the future together. We can start afresh."

"Thank you Maaike. I will support you. You are saving him."

"I am trying to save my family, Mama... and the children... OK, I must go. Bye, bye for now. I am sure he will ring you."

It was the most difficult decision Maaike had ever made. Many years before, speaking from personal experience, her PhD supervisor, Professor Myra Williams, had said to her, "You know, Maaike, in the end it boils down to our children – for us women, that is. They always seem to come first for us, even for university professors, bank presidents and the like – even for those of us who seem to have given everything for our careers. So when the day comes and you are forced to choose between a path that would make you happier and one that would make your children happier and you choose the latter, try not to be too frustrated or bitter. You may feel very lonely at that moment, but you sure as hell won't be alone."

4

Wilfred Cherono, the Managing Director of Central Pharmaceuticals and Chemicals, looked at Maaike in disbelief as she told him of
her decision to resign and leave Nairobi.

"What happened, Maaike?" he pleaded. "I think you owe me an
explanation. I was advised by everyone not to promote you, but I
just knew you'd be fine. I would have bet a lot on it. I did in fact.
You are a star! What happened?"

"It is complicated, Will. Too complicated to put into words for
you. I just have to do it."

"Is it your husband? Is it Saks?" asked Cherono. When Maaike
did not answer or look at him with her usual confidence, he felt he
knew the answer. That gave him some hope. He had to try to get
her to change her mind. Many other managers and several Board
members had been against appointing a woman to such a senior
position. They feared that she would not be able to devote as much
time and energy to the position as a man. But Cherono had pointed
to her performance record and won them over.

"Please think it over more carefully, Maaike," he continued. "You
have a fantastic future with CPC. Why give it up? Saks will come to
accept it, especially when he sees that he is also benefiting."

It was the last part that got to her. The smug condescension. She
hated it. She had come there to tell him that she was resigning, not
for amateur marriage counseling. She shook her head and stood up.

"I have a question for you, Will."

"Yes?" replied Cherono, pleased that he had managed to get
through to her.

"In fact, I have a few of them. OK, first, what is your wife's job
these days."

"You know the answer to that, Maaike. Monica is the Branch
Manager at Barclays Westlands."

"OK. Second, who dropped off your children at school today?"

"Monica did. The school is on her way to work."

"It's on your way to work, too, Will. OK, third. What is the price of one dozen eggs at Uchumi."

"I don't know. What are you driving at, Maaike?"

"Why don't you know, Will?"

"Monica does the shopping."

"Why is that, Will?"

"Why not? Why should I do the shopping for my home?"

"Why should Monica?!"

"Because she's ... "

"Because she's what, Will? Because she's your wife? Your woman?"

"What's your point, Maaike?" He was irritated.

"My point, Will, is that you have no right to lecture me about what I am giving up, or about my husband's position on my career. I mean, you don't know basic things about your own wife's life, for God's sake! Yes, I had a future with CPC. I know that better than you. And I know why it is that I had that future."

She was shaking now, in anger, her voice a full octave lower than normal – almost a growl.

"Do you want to know what my life has been like, Will? See if this reminds you of anyone else's life. I wake up at five-fifteen every morning to bathe and get dressed. I open the door for the maid at six, then I wake up my two sons and dress them. This is my special time with them. This is when I hear all their funny stories and big plans. My second son, Jimmy, loves music. He loves to sing. He is always composing silly little songs. He likes to sing them for me in the morning. Anyway, this is all to say that I do not like the maid to dress my sons, even though I know she could do it much more quickly than I do. But then I also know that she uses that time to lay the table for breakfast, brew some tea, and eat her own morning meal. By now, Saks might be in the bathroom. I might pop my head in and greet him. I go downstairs to supervise breakfast for the boys. It is now about six-fifty-five. My three-year-old daughter wakes up at seven and calls out for me. I go to her, take her to pee, wash her face, and brush her teeth. I bring her downstairs for breakfast. Unfortunately, I cannot supervise her breakfast because the boys and I need to be out of the house by seven-fifteen, otherwise we will keep the neighbor's children waiting. You see, we drop them off at school each morning. We also must be careful not to get caught in the traffic jam at the Gitanga—James Gichuru junction. When Saks was still teaching at the university, he seldom ate breakfast. But now he sits with the baby and helps her eat. I am happy about that. I arrive here at the office between eight-ten and eight-fifteen. I work all day if I can, but at least once a month, I have to dash off in the middle of the day for one reason or another. One of the children is sick. The maid is sick. Saks needs me to do this or that for him. We have just one reliable car, you see. On Wednesdays, I must pass by Uchumi on my way home and get some fresh milk and bread. Sometimes, I also have to get some vegetables if Uchumi's weekend stocks were not fresh enough to buy a week's supply. The maid is not a very good cook. The children refuse to eat the things she prepares. Saks does not like micro-waved food. He does not like to cook either. We have not been able to afford more household help, so I haven't been able to hire a cook. This is all to say that I must cook when I get home. But first, I check on the children. There is always something out of the ordinary happening that calls for my attention the minute I walk in. But even so, supper is always ready by seven. Homework for the boys is done between seven-forty-five and eight-forty-five. I need to keep track of that and sign the parent confirmation sheets. All three children must be bathed and in bed by nine. I clean up the house for about twenty minutes, catching up as best I can with my husband's day as I do it. I take a bath at about ten and try to be in bed by ten-thirty. I read for thirty minutes to unwind. Usually,

I fall asleep by about eleven. I'm sure that's nothing at all like your day, Will."

Stunned, all Cherono could muster by way of a response was to ask, "Who picks up your children from school and drops them off at home?"

"The neighbors," she replied. "Goodbye, Will. I will ring you next week to discuss my terminal benefits."

WEDNESDAY EVENINGS

"How much longer is this going to go on?"

"I don't know."

"You don't have to be out there by yourself anymore. Everything is moving along as planned, right? Everything is working out, right?"

Silence.

"It's been three years now. We'll both be fifty soon... It wouldn't be so hard if you came more often. We have enough money now. You could come more often... at least once a month."

"I'm still too busy."

"Maybe so, but I spoke with Gerry Carr about that and he said you don't have to work so hard these days. He said you should be able to delegate more. He said your staff complain that you don't let them do their jobs."

Silence.

"The children need you now."

"The boy does not like me."

"No, that's not true. It's not that he doesn't like you. He just doesn't understand why you can't be here all the time. He misses you. That's his way of showing it. I'm really worried about him."

Silence.

"You look good, though," she said, cuddling up closer to him, running her hand downward from his chest.

"Thanks. So do you."

"Thanks... Mmm... look what I found. Did I hear someone shout 'Attention!'?"

*   *   *

Is that it?

Should he say, "The truth is that after the first year, there was really no need for me to stay on in Redding for the real estate business. Everything was in place. It was just a matter of waiting for the boom to come. I could have moved to Washington. But the distance seemed to help with my relationship with your mother. We became friends again. But looking back, I think I sensed that something was still missing. I think I see it now. If I had been able to see it then, I would not have kept you all waiting. I would have come. But I could not see it."

Was that it?

The evening after Maaike asked him to consider a move to Songhor, Saks went to Metropub in Nairobi West for a drink. He left their maisonette in Kilimani at about five-thirty and drove straight to Metropub. As he drove down Argwings-Kodhek Road past Yaya Center and on toward Hurlingham, he noticed two new housing developments that had been completed while he was in detention. The sense of lost time and lost opportunity that he had been feeling of late intensified for a moment and then passed on, leaving a dull ache in the middle of his chest.

The ache never left him. Nor did the fear. He was always afraid.

"Suck it," Reddy Kilowatt had commanded, his voice thickening in anticipation of pleasure. Kilowatt was standing in front of Saks, his dirty prison overalls bunched at his ankles, his penis hardening into a throbbing erection. Saks was sitting down on the one stool in cell 57 – the cell he shared with Kilowatt and two other men, KK Brown and Mister Dee, who were sitting behind him, playing a game of draughts with bottle tops on a board scratched into the cell's grimy cement floor.

"You had better suck it, Soulman," chuckled KK, using the nickname he had coined for Saks. "Kilowatt won you for himself. General China would have killed you."

"Quiet!" Kilowatt snapped at KK, his voice quivering slightly. "Suck it, Soulman."

It was Saks's first day in Kamiti Prison. General China had pounced on him in the shower room, groping for his penis, licking the back of his neck, moaning breathlessly. Fuming but also terrified, Saks had flung General China off, knocking him to the floor. General China had sprung up, his hands balled into fists, his bloodshot eyes wide open and tearing in anger. The other men in the shower backed away. General China was dangerous.

"You think you can refuse the General, eh? Eh? I will have you then I will kill you."

The General felled Saks with a sharp uppercut to the chin followed by a karate kick to the belly. He stomped down hard on Saks's head and then descended on him, already hardening in readiness. He curled his hands around Saks's neck and squeezed.

"Open!" hissed the General, tightening his grip. "Open!"

The impact from the General's landing on his back had winded Saks. Before he'd refilled his lungs with air, the General's hands had closed around his neck. Saks felt himself begin to faint. He was going to die. He opened.

General China began to pant. Only one of his hands was on Saks's neck now but his fingers were pressing very hard against Saks's Adam's apple. With his other hand, the General was trying to guide himself in. Panting, pushing hard, he was almost there.

"Please, please!" Saks croaked out, causing one of the watchers to laugh.

"No!" gasped Saks, and as if galvanized by the laugh, he somehow wriggled free and rolled out from under the General.

The General was too aroused to be fully angry. He threw himself back on to Saks, who was still on the wet floor, struggling for air. This time, General China kept both hands around Saks's neck until he felt his victim begin to go limp. Panting, moaning, pushing, ready again.

Reddy Kilowatt walked into the shower room.

Kilowatt had noticed Saks earlier in the day. He had liked the look of him – the freshness and innocence in his eyes, the shape of his mouth. He wanted Saks for himself. With two quick looks, he ordered KK Brown and Mister Dee to step forward from the watching group and rescue Saks. They pulled General China off Saks. The General was already too far gone. His semen spurted out on to Saks's back and legs. Sighs of disappointment rose from the other watching men, three of whom nevertheless quickly brought themselves to groaning climaxes.

"He's mine!" protested General China. "Please let the General have him for one day. Please, just one day." But even as he pleaded, the General knew that Reddy Kilowatt – a murderer who was serving a life sentence in Kamiti – had nothing to gain from generosity. This was a man who through men like KK Brown and Mister Dee controlled all aspects of prisoner life at Kamiti. A man who even the wardens feared and went to great lengths to please. General China knew that Reddy Kilowatt would never agree.

Saks was lying on his back, staring up at his rescuers, trying to collect himself, choking back tears.

"I should have just killed you!" snarled General China, spitting down at Saks as he walked out.

Reddy Kilowatt arranged for Saks to be reassigned from cell 81 to cell 57 right away. Saks swapped cells with Yellowman, who, fearful of what might happen to him outside Kilowatt's circle of protection, begged and pleaded to be allowed to stay in cell 57. Kilowatt refused and had KK Brown and Mister Dee throw the terrified Yellowman out.

That evening, after supper, as Saks was still trying to drive from his mind the image of floating cockroaches in the thin bean stew served for dinner, Kilowatt initiated him in cell 57's nightly ritual.

"Suck it."

First Saks ... Soulman. Wash off.

An hour later KK Brown. Wash off.

An hour after that, Mister Dee. Wash off.

Every night. For fifteen weeks.

Saks shook his head in disbelief. He knew that the nightly ritual had spared him from AIDS and the other venereal diseases circulating around Kamiti. But how much of a blessing was that, he wondered. How much? He slammed his fist against the steering wheel in anger. How could it have happened to him? How? Not to him. Not every night for fifteen weeks. But it had. It had. There had been no escape. There still was no escape. It was always there. The ache. The fear. The shame.

Saks drove on slowly, mulling over Maaike's proposition. He chose to take Mbagathi Way to Nairobi West, which took him past Kenyatta Hospital, Sunview Estate, Nyayo High Rise flats, and down to Langata Road. Traffic was already heavy, but not as bad as it would have been on Uhuru Highway, had he chosen to take the Nyayo Stadium route. By the time he pulled up in front of Metropub, he was pretty sure he had made up his mind.

Saks normally preferred not to arrive at Metropub during the day. At night, the dirt and grime on the walls of the adjacent shops, the dust and litter on the sidewalk and road, the grubby clothes worn by the street children – at night, all of this disappeared. But during the day, everything was fully visible. It turned his stomach. But he needed a drink. More than that, he needed the easy companionship of friendly men. It was a Wednesday. The group would be large.

Jimmy Rateng Okoth was already there, deep in conversation with someone. Like Saks, he was an ex-tenant at Kamiti Prison – a fellow ex-detainee. The crime for which he had been held for three years was to publish a pamphlet detailing the Government's involvement in the ethnic clashes.

"Freedom!" Rateng called out to Saks in Kiswahili, revealing a mouth with two teeth at most, the others having been dislodged in Kamiti.

"Truth!" responded Saks, also in Kiswahili, as he had learned to do in prison. They shook hands as they had done in prison – with their left hands, each one's palm closing around the other's forearm.

"I'm hungry, friend. Won't you give me something to eat?" Rateng' implored.

"*Nyako!*" Saks called out to the waitress. From her sluggish response, he saw that she had been dozing. "Rateng' is hungry! Give him something." The waitress brought over a warm Tusker and opened it. Rateng' nodded his thanks to Saks and continued his conversation with the person sitting in front of him – a person visible only to him.

As Saks sat down at the usual sidewalk table, his back to the wall, looking out on the street, he reached into his trouser pocket to see how much money Maaike had put in there for him that morning. Three thousand. Enough for a few rounds at Metropub, and then maybe one or two more later on at Club Dolce. He ordered a cold Pilsner.

2

Wednesday evenings were weekly highpoints for Patrick Okullu. He looked forward to them from Thursday mornings to Wednesday afternoons. On Wednesday evenings, he saw his friends when their many problems seemed to weigh only lightly on them. So his own troubles loomed less large in his mind. And on Wednesday evenings, he saw his mistress, Juliet Adhiambo. In her company he could forget altogether even these seemingly less imposing woes. Without Wednesday evenings, he could not face his life.

Patrick liked to spend at least six hours with Juliet before going home. And it took at least two hours to get into the right mood to see her. So he tended to arrive at Metropub fairly early and leave fairly early. That day, he was there by six and found Saks talking to the new waitress, a light-skinned Tanzanian with an almost perfect figure but sour face. Unless she learns how to smile, this one won't last, he thought to himself. We come here for pleasure not pressure.

Saks saw Patrick walking up and smiled brightly at him. Patrick smiled back, marveling to himself how different Saks had become since his release from detention. He was a changed man. He talked more. He laughed more. They seldom saw Maaike these days, but Saks himself was a nicer man to be around. To Patrick, the reason for the change was obvious. While Saks had suffered before – his brother's death, his father's murder, and so on – he had never lost anything into which he had chosen to pour his soul. So his heart had remained closed, never quite tuned into the hardship distributed around their little group – the hardship spread around the country. Saks could never be relied upon to contribute to collective efforts, to show up at fund-raising meetings, to house a stranded relative or friend from up-country for a month or two. It was always his wife this, his wife that, his children this, his children that. As if none of them had wives or children! At least Saks's wife worked and made good money. At least his children were healthy.

Patrick's wife, Amanda, sat around the house all day, gossiping with her endless string of lazy friends, whose husbands also slogged all day. These days, she would not even take the children to school. She had complained and complained until he hired a driver. So these days she did not emerge from the bedroom until after ten o'clock. And she had become totally frigid. All the things he liked to do were no longer permissible. Somehow dirty. After years of doing them. One by one, they were removed from the bedroom scene.

"I am forty-six, Patrick. I cannot do that anymore."

"Why not, Amanda?!"

"I just can't!"

Now it was done one way – the standard way – in the dark, once or twice a month. She was on another diet. This one was working, but much too quickly. She had lost fifteen kilos in eight weeks. Her once smooth and tight skin hung off her like a cockerel's. The sight of her body made him sick. But even so, deep in his heart, he understood what she was going through.

Two years earlier, Carol, their fourth and youngest child, had been hit by a speeding motorcycle while out for a walk with their then housemaid. Carol was five years old at the time. Her little body had almost disintegrated from the impact. She lost one leg and almost all her blood. Had she not been as strong a child as she was, she would have died on the spot. In the car that took her to the hospital, she lost consciousness, for good. They kept her at Nairobi Hospital for three months.

When Carol finally came home, her special bed would not fit through the front door without being turned sideways. Patrick had to pick up what remained of his once too-big-for-her-age daughter, carry her through the door, hold her while her bed was being wrestled into the house, take her into her new room – the old guest room for which they no longer had any use because Amanda already did not want visitors and their sympathy – and lay her down carefully on the bed. He noticed how bad Carol smelled. Blood from her slow-healing leg wound. Shit and urine. But he also noticed that as he held her in his arms, her body softened, became less tense and rigid. She knew him. That hurt more. He said her name twice, looking closely at her. Her droopy eyes began to tear.

"Amanda! Look! She knows it's me! She knows where she is! She knows! We must hold her and talk to her."

"That is nonsense, Patrick! Look at her. That is not my daughter. That is not her! She's better off dead!"

"Don't say that. Why give up?" Patrick had asked that day and time and again since then. "She is still alive. Doesn't that God you're forever praying to say that all life is precious?"

It made no difference. As far as he knew, Amanda never went into Carol's room. And she insisted that the door leading to that section of the house be kept shut at all times. But Patrick understood. It was when Carol came home that Amanda began to lose her sex drive and jump from diet to diet. Every day after work, it took all his strength and will power to bring himself to walk into Carol's room, pick her up, and hold her for an hour, reading and talking quietly to her.

Every day except Wednesday.

He smiled at Saks and sat down next to him.

3

JJ Onyango arrived in a subdued mood. Work had gone well that day. Business was good overall. He and two former university classmates had recently formed an insurance brokerage firm, Aminisha Ltd. Despite the difficulties the Stork and his cronies were creating for the economy, the demand for insurance was growing steadily, and not just in Nairobi. It seemed that more and more firms and households were keen to protect themselves from risks linked to the fraught political environment. Aminisha was riding the wave of commissions and fees earned on sold policies. Business was very good.

But at home the last few days had been difficult. About six months before, the security guard employed by the owner of the block of flats where he and his family lived had approached him for a loan of five hundred shillings. The fellow's name was Michael. Apparently, Michael needed the money to buy medicine for his wife, Janet, who was ill with malaria. He had promised to repay the cash in a few weeks.

JJ knew that Michael's monthly salary was no more than three thousand shillings. To minimize the potential loss, he decided to give Michael two hundred instead. Two weeks later, when JJ and his family returned from church, Michael was waiting with the two hundred shillings. Surprised and not a little embarrassed, JJ told him to keep it for as long as he needed it. Michael accepted the offer, explaining that Janet's condition had deteriorated. He had been unable to pay for any additional treatment. He was now reverting to prayer.

JJ and his wife, Connie, were appalled by the story and asked Michael to bring Janet to their house so they could take her to their doctor. The next day, their doctor confirmed that Janet was very sick and would die if not treated quickly. The doctor was certain that she had tuberculosis and that her constant headache, nausea, fatigue, diarrhea, stomach ache and mouth sores pointed to other severe ailments. Sensing JJ's uncertainty, the doctor noted that treatment would be expensive and advised JJ to consider the matter carefully. JJ agreed but meanwhile offered to cover the costs of diagnostic tests and any drugs the doctor felt Janet needed right away.

They spent the rest of the day in labs, x-ray units, and pharmacies. The tests and medicines cost five thousand five hundred shillings – almost twice Michael's monthly salary.

At home that night, JJ and Connie began to grasp how, in the space of a few hours, Janet's life had become their personal responsibility. The next day, the doctor's worst fears were confirmed. Janet was suffering from advanced tuberculosis and required immediate hospitalization. JJ arranged to have her admitted into the Mbagathi TB unit.

Janet seemed to recover over the next few weeks. Michael's spirits lifted visibly. Much to Connie's amusement, he started to refer to JJ as "boss." While the new title may have been good for JJ's ego, it implied a dependence they did not want to encourage.

The window in one of the bedrooms in JJ's flat looked out on to the driveway, at the end of which was the gate and the guard-room where Michael spent his days while on duty. The latch to this window was loose and often fell off and down into the driveway. It was difficult for Michael not to notice when this happened. One day, about a month after JJ and Connie had helped him, Michael informed JJ that he had asked the landlord to send a workman to fix the latch. It was a nice gesture. JJ had not asked him to do it. But for some reason, as Michael described the arrangements he had made to have the latch repaired, JJ found himself saying that the window was fine as it was and did not need fixing. Michael was visibly hurt; it had been his way of giving something back for everything JJ and Connie had done for him. JJ knew he should have accepted the gift graciously. But in hindsight, he saw that, subconsciously, he had been looking for a way to send Michael the message that he should no longer consider the Onyango family to be a part of his support group. JJ did not want anything from Michael, and he wanted Michael to know that he should not expect any more help from him. Michael seemed to get the message and began to keep his distance.

One day, about two months on, Michael did not report to work as usual. The following day, he arrived at JJ's door and, clearly agitated, almost demanded that JJ give him some money so he could take Janet to his rural home in Seme, near Kisumu. She was no longer responding to treatment and her condition was deteriorating rapidly. He was sure that she was on the verge of death. Rather than have her die in Nairobi and then have to incur the expense of transporting her corpse across the country for burial, or worse, for a Luo like him, be forced to bury her in Nairobi, Michael had decided to take Janet home to die. It would be much cheaper and less complicated.

Michael's response to JJ's first offer of one thousand shillings was that it was not enough. Surprised at the man's audacity, but still overwhelmed by his story, JJ doubled the offer, which Michael accepted and then left with barely a word of thanks.

For many weeks, neither JJ nor Connie saw Michael. They wondered what had become of him. And then one day, one of his Michael's co-workers conveyed the sad news that Janet had died soon after arriving at Michael's rural home. Even sadder was the news that the one-year-old daughter Janet had left behind had also died. Apparently, Michael's first child had also died soon after his birth in 1995. Michael's family had vanished without a trace.

JJ and Connie knew that they could have done much more for Michael and Janet. They had suspected that Janet had AIDS, but they were not sure. Even so, they might have tried to save her one more time by having her admitted into a hospital at their expense.

But on the spur of the moment, without too much thought, they had chosen to do as Michael requested and helped him take her away from help and to certain death. It was his decision to make, but they had not tried to convince him otherwise.

The fate of Michael's family was probably sealed long before JJ and Connie ever met them. But this experience raised questions for them that they had yet to answer. How do you choose the boundary of your family in a society with as little room for error as this? What are the rules that distinguish how you should behave toward family, friend, and stranger when your choice can mean the difference between life and death?

JJ greeted Saks and Patrick as warmly as he could.

"You look tired, JJ," noted Patrick. "*Nyako*, give him something to eat."

4

"Quiet please!" called out Jacob Odero as he walked up.

"The men are drinking!" replied the three men already there.

"I said quiet please!"

"The men are drinking heavily!"

Laughter, long smiles, and shaking heads as always. Odero was a character. He sat down next to Saks, making sure to leave at least two chairs between him and Patrick whose habit of picking up, examining, and often returning pieces of chicken and beef from the communal tray disgusted him to no end.

It had been a good day for Odero, though he had woken up with an anxiety headache. He had an appointment with his account manager at Barclays Bank. The fellow was new in the position, so they had yet to develop a relationship. La Fontaine, Odero's restaurant on Muindi Mbingu Street, was on its knees, badly in debt. He had not serviced the overdraft for four months. The only reason the bank had not moved in on him was because La Fontaine was once *the* restaurant on Muindi Mbingu. That was before the 1992 election when the Government printed mountains of cash to finance its campaign. The shilling halved in value overnight, effectively doubling the prices of most of La Fontaine's supplies. The restaurant never recovered from that blow. Everything became a struggle. Odero took a double blow because he had been speculating on dollars. The shilling's plummet caught him with one hundred thousand dollars tied up in a shilling-denominated fixed deposit account. He could not reconvert to dollars as planned at anything but a huge loss. But he had debts to repay in dollars. So he had to cash in.

"I was fucked by the Stork," he had said at the time, and many times since then.

Kindly come to our offices to discuss a repayment schedule for your seriously overdrawn current account number 1916347.

That was all the man had said in his letter. Really? After eighteen years of excellent patronage?

What was he going to do? La Fontaine's cash flow was measly. Tourists were no longer spending much time and money in Nairobi's central business district. Business lunches were growing rarer with each passing day. He could not raise prices – not with Stephanie's Teashop around the corner charging next to nothing for everything and constantly full of customers. Why were so many people satisfied with such low quality? He could not understand it. He needed to buy time. He knew he was going to lose everything to the bank before the end of the year. He needed three more months to divert the little cash that was coming in and re-invest it elsewhere in the names of his wife and children.

At breakfast that day, Odero's wife stared at him in shock as he poured himself a large glass of milk and gulped it down. He shocked her further by asking for a large bowl of cornflakes with extra milk. He downed that. He then ate six slices of cheese.

The meeting at Barclays was at ten-thirty. By ten, Odero was letting off quiet but stinky ones at three-minute intervals. He produced several good ones during the fifteen minutes he was kept waiting in the reception area. The look on the stuck-up secretary's face went from open contempt, to surprise, to disgust, to desperation. She almost pushed him into her boss's office. Ten-forty-five. They were coming every thirty seconds.

"Mr. Odero," said the unsmiling manager in opening, not bothering to extend his hand in greeting. "Sit down here please," he continued, pointing to a chair at a small round meeting table.

"What's your first name again?" asked Odero.

"Denis," replied the manager curtly, clearly irritated but also puzzled. "Did this fellow really just fart?" he seemed to be asking himself.

"OK, Denis. What can I do for you?" Another one... a long one.

"Eh?" asked Denis, barely breathing.

"I asked what I could I do for you." Another one.

"Yes, well," gasp. "Eh, well. It's the overdraft on your account. It is badly in arrears." Another. Gasp. Denis stood up and walked across the room to his desk. Odero got up and took the seat in front of the desk. "No, no. No need to move. Please..."

"OK," said Odero, sitting down, letting it all come freely.

"Your account," gasp. "Can we work out a payment schedule?"

"I need three months, Denis. We are turning things around."

"Yes, turning them around. That's excellent. Three months is fine with me."

"Could I have that in writing please, Denis?" A deep one.

"In writing?"

"Yes, Denis, you know how it is."

"OK, I will send you the letter tomorrow."

"Actually, I'd rather have it now, if you don't mind. I will be traveling to Nyakach tomorrow." Another one.

"Mary!" Denis squeaked into the intercom. "Come in please."

The letter was dictated, typed, and printed in four minutes flat.

Odero walked out of the bank at ten-fifty-seven with the letter in hand. He barely made it to La Fontaine before the explosive event his flatulence had been heralding took place.

It had been a good day.

"Yes, yes, the men are drinking!"

5

It was usually only after a Wednesday evening session at Metropub that the internal turmoil brought on by George Obel's monthly weekend sojourns home to Rarieda lifted from his imagination. Every trip back home seemed to be a journey not only forward over space but also backward in time. No matter how often he went, he could never control the initial shock he felt at how primitive and backward his rural homeland remained, and at how so many people living there seemed to be stuck in a long-lost past. The internal turmoil sprung from the obvious fact that neither his village nor any of the other identical ones scattered around the shores of Lake Victoria were caught in a time warp. This was 1999. This was the real thing. Luoland was lagging. Lives three were hard.

His seventy-two-year-old mother was still pissing and shitting in a long-drop. Still storing drinking water in a clay pot that stood in the corner of her mud hut. Still cooking her meals outside on a pot balanced on three rocks above an open fire made from twigs gathered for her from nearby thickets by young children. Still eating her meals sitting in a semi-dark room lit by a single candle to which swarms of mosquitos were drawn. Still being hit by malaria every other month.

Every Wednesday night, at some point JJ could be counted on to lay the blame for all of this at the feet of the Government – both the Stork's and the one before.

"You know why Luos oppose this Government?" JJ would start. "It's because this Government is anti-Luo. You feel bad about your mother. I feel bad about mine. But they never had a chance. This is 1999. Where are the roads, the powerlines, the bulk waterworks, the hospitals, the schools that would have given them a chance? Where are they? This is 1999, man! The road density per person in Siaya District is barely higher than Turkana District's! And everyone knows that there has been no serious public investment in Turkana since Independence. We are the same! But nobody says anything! All the big investments using donor money go elsewhere. The other day some guy in Treasury told me to my face that Kenya does not borrow for Luos. To my face! Can you imagine! And, I swear, he wasn't joking one bit!"

Obel agreed. The bias against investment in Luoland was clear and infuriating. Yet he also knew that there was more to it than that.

His eighty-year-old father was still refusing to let him and his siblings lift their mother out of her pitiful condition. Still insisting that, as a matter of principle and fairness, he could not allow one of his three wives to live in comfort while the others were left behind. Still ignoring the argument from Obel and his siblings that their mother should not suffer because their stepbrothers and stepsisters lacked the unity and enterprise needed to properly support their own mother. But the old man would not budge. "This is my home! What is so wrong with it? If your mother wants more, she can go and live with you!"

His mother never complained. "This is my life. This is my home."

It was agonizing to see and hear. The hardship. The stubborn courage. Not just there. Everywhere.

A cousin who had become a recluse and alcoholic after having to perform an anesthesia-free lumpectomy on his mother's swollen breast because there was no money to take her to hospital.

Another cousin whose children kept dying a few months after birth, and thus who was being beaten by her husband, but who was more terrified of life as an unattached woman without a house and home of her own than of life as a battered wife.

The local secondary school that had collapsed again because too few parents could pay the fees that would have topped up the teachers' salaries and kept them in place.

The armed robbery of the one public transportation vehicle that served the area, the decision by the owner to concentrate on other routes, and the return of tortuous treks to and from the nearest market center.

The paraplegic who had cultivated two acres of cotton on his own – crawling back and forth across the plot on his belly – so that he could help send his brother's daughter to Lwak Girls Secondary School.

The mentally disabled seven-year-old who had pulled her father, mother, and twin brothers from their hut, which carbon monoxide from a half-lit charcoal stove had rendered a death hole.

The AIDS that was hitting just about every homestead, one after the other. What were they going to do with all those orphaned children?

It was overwhelming if you opened your eyes and heart to it.

Each time Obel left Rarieda to return to Nairobi, he vowed to do something to help – something more direct than usual; something more meaningful and tangible. The drive back to Nairobi on Sunday afternoons was always filled with silent planning along those lines. But then back in his house in Woodley, as he watched the evening news on TV and caught up with the weekend's events around the country, the burning from the raw spots left in his mind by the facts of life in Rarieda would begin to abate. Come Monday morning, daily routine would set in, further assuaging the mental abrasions. Occasionally during the working day, a distressing image from Rarieda would come vividly into view. But he could seldom pause to examine it. Tuesday and Wednesday would be much the same, the past weekend's anguish gradually receding into the corners of his mind. Come Wednesday evening when he climbed out of his car, joined the group, and curled his hand like this around a cold White Cap, he would be almost fully rebalanced, his thoughts turning to the up-coming weekend. Maybe dinner at Haandi on Friday?

Perhaps a family trip to Lake Naivasha on Saturday, or an outing to Village Market on Sunday?

"Obel, come and sit here," called out JJ. "I want to talk to you about that car you are trying to sell."

6

Lawrence Ogot and Peter Owino arrived at seven-fifteen. They had been together all day. Ogot worked with the Nairobi City Commission. Owino was a trader who had been trying to unload twenty million shillings worth of gold smuggled into the country from DR Congo via Uganda. Owino's problem was that it had been too much gold to convert directly into cash through normal channels. There were spies and thieves all over the place, especially in the banks. They would have converged on him within hours. Ogot had helped him find a buyer who would not ask too many questions. It had been a good day. It had been a good week.

This was Owino's biggest break yet. Not even the windfalls that came his way from deals cut during the 1997 elections came close. And the take was all his. Only Ogot remained to be paid, and he was not greedy.

Owino had gone to DR Congo himself. He had spent six months there being kicked around by that fat Ugandan Brigadier Bageya and his troops. An errand boy. A go-between with the Congolese miners because he spoke fluent French and Kiswahili. And he had a face that showed no emotion. A foolish errand boy. That was all the Ugandans had thought of him. But he was not as foolish as they thought! They were all dead and he had the gold.

He was standing in the mine foreman's office when the break came.

"Go and tell Nzahabwanamungu that we are hungry – hungry for food, and hungry for gold," Brigadier Bageya had barked out at Owino, a beef sausage in his chunky left hand, a gently foaming bottle of Bell lager in his right. "Look," he continued, gesturing in a circle with the sausage, "There are no more trees remaining. No more mahogany, no more ebony. It has all gone to Belgium, France, and Italy. They use it for musical instruments – violins, guitars, pianos... all kinds of instruments. One violin costs twenty thousand dollars. Did you know that? Eh? Did you? Eh? You should know these things! Tell Nzahabwanamungu my boys are now restless. You tell him it is time for the gold. And tell him that we need more pigs. More sausages. And wine – red wine! Go! Go quickly!"

So Owino had gone, but slowly, at his own pace. He was tired. Tired of this work. Tired of being away from home. Tired of little deals that consumed all his time and energy. Tired of hanging around, waiting for other people to decide his fate.

He was thirty-nine years old. Married fifteen years. Four children. One son, three daughters, in that order. All the girls were fine. The boy worried him. He was always so quiet, so sullen.

"You must help me with Bobby," his wife, Margaret, had said to him the last time he was home. "He does not listen to me." They lived in Kariobangi, which was falling increasingly into the grip of organized crime, with the police at the heart of it all. A neighbor's sixteen-year-old son had been gunned down in broad daylight by an on-duty policeman, apparently because he had failed to deliver his end of a drug deal. Margaret wanted them to move away from there. But where to, he would ask. Where else could they find a three-bedroom house for eight thousand shillings per month? Why couldn't he just find a normal job, she would counter. Why did they have to live like this, never knowing where the next month's rent would come from? Why? She was tired of it. He was tired of it as well. All he needed was a little luck. Better luck.

He had been on the verge so many times. One conversation away from the big one. One phone call. One meeting. One person. He had been certain the iron sheets deal would be the one. He had done everything right. But the core takings from the deal had gone to the Stork's nephew. Sixty-three million! He had been given just thirty thousand – the rate for a minor go-between. But, shit, without him, nothing would have happened! How would they have been able to ship the stuff from Thika to Mombasa to Mogadishu, get it out of that port untouched, to Dar es Salaam, to Mwanza, and on to Kisangani? How?! How would they have been able to convince the Somali warlords to go along with the ploy to make it look like a shipment bound for Yemen? How?! The Stork and his people were so greedy. So ungrateful. They made him sick.

They made him sick – his failures. But they did not make him bitter. And it showed. Owino had an open face – the kind of face normally found either on a man at the height of his powers, or on one yet to be thrown about by the world. He was sick and tired of failing, but it did not show on his face. And so men who were afraid and suspicious of other men trusted him with information. And so he found himself in the thick of mega-deals that shaped lives, countries, and histories. And so he found himself working for Brigadier Bageya of the Uganda People's Defense Force – a man officially charged with keeping the peace in Kivu, but unofficially looting non-stop, sausages and beers in hand.

And so Owino found himself sitting across from Francois Nzahabwanamungu, foreman at Brigadier Bageya's personal mine – which the Brigadier had named Dorcas Mine, after his late mother. And so he found himself sipping a cup of sweet tea, reading a three-year-old *Economist* magazine, waiting for Nzahabwanamungu's response to the Brigadier's directive about wine, sausages, and gold when Tony Kategaya, the leader of Dorcas Mine's Team 3, burst into the office.

Hands shaking with excitement, Kategaya placed a gleaming rock on the table.

"It is five meters wide and eight meters deep," Kategaya had blurted out in a mixture of French and Kiswahili.

"How long?" asked Nzahabwanamungu.

"At least three hundred meters, maybe even four or five. I don't know for sure. But it is very long."

"OK."

"So, Monsieur Pierre," began Nzahabwanamungu, after dismissing the excited team leader, looking straight at Owino with eyes that said: It is now or never. "What do you want to do about this?" It was quite simple. That evening, they poisoned Brigadier Bageya and his three Lieutenants with arsenic from the refinery. They laced the wine and sausages. On seeing their leaders fall, the troops dispersed into the forest, afraid that they, too, would perish, or worse, be accused of murder. They reappeared one by one and in small groups, hungry and thirsty, looking for new leaders. They found Nzahabwanamungu and Owino in charge. They followed, joining Dorcas Mine as Team 5.

The five teams worked eighteen-hour shifts for twenty-eight days. They brought out mound upon mound of gold-speckled rock, which was quickly refined into coarse but unquestionably authentic bars of the valued metal. To each his fair share. Every man left Kivu with enough gold to make a multi-millionaire of him in any East African currency.

The day he returned to Nairobi, Owino went straight to Ogot's office. He found Ogot's desk empty.

"He is coming," said one of Ogot's three officemates, pointing to Ogot's chair. Owino knew that while the coat hanging on the chair was intended to signal Ogot's impending return, it was not a reliable indicator of such an eventuality. Like hundreds of other similarly displayed coats in City Hall, Ogot's was a decoy intended to lend credence to the statement, "He is coming." Owino knew that the coat never moved.

So Owino waited. He waited all day, unwilling to walk around Nairobi with his gold, which was sitting in a small but heavy bag he was trying to carry as nonchalantly as possible.

Ogot returned a few minutes before five o'clock, just to check if he had received any important messages or visitors during working hours.

"*Omera*, what is this?" Ogot exclaimed on finding Owino sitting in front of his desk. "You are here?" They shook hands vigorously, smiling widely. They were old friends from St. Mary's Yala. "*Aiee! But you are so thin!*"

"And you are so fat!" laughed Owino, always amazed at his friend's ability to live large on his puny civil servant's salary. In coming to Ogot like this, it was on that ability – on the skills and knowledge behind it – that Owino was counting.

The two men could not have been more different. Owino had spent the two decades since they left St. Mary's jumping from one occupation to another. By contrast, after leaving secondary school, Ogot spent nine months in a technical college in Kitale and emerged with a diploma in accounting. An uncle then helped him land a job as a clerk at the then Nairobi City Council. He moved from one job to another within the Council, learning everything there was to learn about the city. As a Luo, he soon found that he had little chance of being promoted into a leadership position. At first, he chafed at the injustice, as one after another inferior character from a more favored tribe was promoted over him. But in time he realized that his longevity and obscurity in the Council gave him unexpected but fully logical advantages. He knew who was doing what, where, and with whom. And, most important, nobody feared him. He was too lowly and unimportant to be feared. For him, the breaks, when they came, were small, almost imperceptible. But they came in a steady stream – week after week, month after month, year after year.

"Ogot, go with this man... what's your name again? Yes, go with Mr. Sadhrudin to Industrial Area. He will explain." That order – which had been issued that very morning – had come from the Town Clerk, Ogot's current immediate supervisor. It turned out to be an assignment to pick up a load of paint for flats the Town Clerk was building in South C. That was where Ogot had been most of the day.

This Sadhrudin knew the system. Or at least he thought he did. He had assumed Ogot was also to get a cut. "How many for you, Ogot?" he asked as they climbed into the waiting car.

Ogot knew the system, too. He had not expected it to work for him this time. He did not hesitate.

"One hundred."

Sadhrudin shook his head in anger and whirled on him. "No! Twenty-five and that's it!?

Ogot smiled brilliantly and crooned, "Oh Sadhru, don't be upset. Let us say fifty and leave it there, OK?"

Sadhrudin shook-nodded his agreement-disagreement but did not say anything.

Ogot did the calculation quickly in his head. Fifty cans of emulsion paint. White. They would sell quickly. Twelve hundred shillings a can. Sixty thousand shillings. Not a bad day's work.

Ogot did not push. Ever. He just waited. Soon his problem became finding ways to hide his wealth. He knew the value of obscurity in that environment. He knew that he had to move his family out of Nairobi. He could not keep them near him and continue to allow them to live in near squalor at the edge of Kibera slum when he had growing property holdings and millions of shillings deposited in bank accounts all across the country. But where could he move them?

Ogot's dealings in Nairobi during the mid-1980s had alerted him to the Stork's long-term strategy to shift public resources out of Central Province and into Rift Valley Province. This, Ogot had guessed correctly, would impact all resources, especially funds for education. Ogot had also guessed correctly that the intensifying competition for places in top-rated Government-supported secondary schools and public universities would be resolved based on tribal and thus regional considerations. Seats in top secondary schools would be set aside for candidates from primary schools located in areas favored by the Stork. The same would hold for university applicants from secondary schools. He knew that many children from non-favored tribes schooling in the favored areas would benefit by default.

There is value to obscurity, Ogot would remind himself from time to time. People do not notice you. People do not think you think. How could they think he thought when they gave him this kind of explosive message to convey? It was a hand-written petition to Dr. Alfred Siromene from seventy-five of his tribesmen in City Hall, including Ogot's immediate superior.

"Ogot, take this to the office of Dr. Alfred Siromene. 3rd Floor Chester House." That was six years ago.

The envelope was sealed and signed at the seal. But Ogot opened it and read the petition. Of course he did! What did they think? He found another identical envelope in the stack he kept for use in such situations, inserted the letter, sealed it, and expertly re-signed his boss's signature.

"Dear Dr. Siromene," the letter began. "We are your brothers and sisters in the City Council. We need your help. We are poor but our children must not be poor also. They need good education. They must be doctors and lawyers. Give us good schools in our areas. Help our children gain admissions into universities."

When Ogot dropped off the letter at Siromene's private office, the secretary opened the envelope immediately and then looked up and eyed him closely.

"Who gave this to you?" she demanded suspiciously.

Ogot told her he had been sent by one of Siromene's cousins in

City Hall. She nodded OK and placed the petition in Siromene's in-tray.

So Ogot moved his family to Nakuru, which was near enough to Nairobi to make weekend visits feasible. Nakuru was also large enough to ensure continued obscurity for his family while allowing him to provide them with a decent standard of living. And, most crucially, despite the Stork's efforts to develop Eldoret into the new capital of the Rift Valley, Nakuru was still the true heart of the Valley and thus an assured target and beneficiary of the planned reallocation of the country's public resources to the Valley.

Ogot's strategy paid off. He already had a daughter doing well at Alliance Girls and a son doing well at Alliance Boys. The third and fourth children were on similar tracks at Nakuru Primary. Barring disasters, they would each win admission into their first-choice programs at the University of Nairobi.

On the day Owino found him away from his desk all day, Ogot had finished with Sadhrudin at about three o'clock in the afternoon. He had spent the rest of the afternoon at the Treasury trying to ascertain the full degree of truth in a rumor that the Government was about to unilaterally change the way in which civil servants' pensions were paid. The current practice was to pay retirees their dues in one lump sum. But with massive World Bank-enforced retrenchments in the offing, and thus thousands of early retirements in prospect, that approach was fiscally untenable. The proposal under consideration would stagger payments over a period of ten years after retirement. But everybody could see that this would reward nobody but the Treasury. The shilling could not hold its value over one year let alone ten. For Ogot it was more than a rumor. Again, as always, the information had been handed to him in a sealed envelope.

"Take this to seventh floor Treasury. Chief Planning Officer."

A memo in the envelope confirmed that the new policy would

be implemented the very next month, beginning with City Commission employees.

By the end of the day, by the time he returned to his office, Ogot knew what he would have to do.

"Yes, *omera*, I'm fat," laughed Ogot. "I will need it. I am retiring next week. Retirement means hunger in this Kenya of ours."

"Retiring? But you are only forty! Why?"

"Things are happening, my friend. Things. Come, let's go," he said, taking Owino by the hand and walking with him like that out of the building and to the taxi park outside the Six Eighty Hotel. Ogot could see that his friend was in no mood to take a bus or matatu.

Unloading twenty million shillings worth of gold was no easy matter. But within one week, Ogot had identified an Ethiopian dealer with links to wealthy families in Yemen and Oman. The Ethiopian's commission would deplete Owino's hard won cash by two million shillings. Owino balked.

"It is this or nothing, my friend," Ogot counseled him. "You must accept. There is no other way. These Arabs are the only ones with that kind of money but no questions. You must accept."

When they walked up to Metropub that Wednesday evening, Owino had a sheet of paper in the inside pocket of his jacket with twenty entries in two neat columns. Each one represented a bank account containing nine hundred thousand shillings, or its US dollar equivalent. The deposits had been made mostly in banks in different Kenyan towns, along with others in the Bahamas, Malta, and Wales.

Ogot watched his friend closely throughout the evening. In the past, Owino would celebrate even the smallest of achievements with intense bragging and several days of heavy drinking. How will you react this time, my friend, wondered Ogot. He was pleased with what he saw. Owino sat quietly and mostly listened. He paid for one round and was one of the first to leave. As Owino got up to leave, he looked at Ogot and said, "Tomorrow?" Ogot nodded. They would agree then on Ogot's cut.

7

"This guy's a woman," said Sam Opata, pointing to a picture in the World News section of the Standard.

"Who?" asked Patrick, ready for an entertaining answer.

"This one, Kim II Sung," replied Sam, waving the paper around to make sure he had everyone's attention.

"Kim II Sung is dead," said Patrick, shaking his head but smiling, encouraging Sam to continue.

"OK, OK. I mean the son. The daughter..."

"You mean Kim Jong II?"

"Yes, that's the one, Kim Jong Il. He's a woman."

"What do you mean he's a woman? The guy's a guy. Isn't Kim a man's name in Korean?"

"That's the point! Don't you see?! Look at him closely. Look at this picture. He's a woman. I mean, where was he all those years? Eh? Wouldn't Kim Il Sung have bragged about his son? Then he dies and this character appears out of nowhere. No facial hair, hips like an old lady, then that bloody walk of his... small little steps like a scared girl. And he holds his face like a woman. You know, all soft".

"What about boobs? Where are they?"

"They're small! Maybe he... she has one of those training bras, to keep them flat... you know..."

"Yah man, I know what you mean. My daughter has them these days. He may be right. *Aiee!*"

"Nonsense! Bullshit!"

"He's a woman. You'll see. You'll see. Anyway, guess what happened to me on Friday night?" Once Sam had everyone's attention, he milked it for as long as he could. He was the public relations officer at the International Institute for Agricultural Science and Technology in Kabete. It was an ideal occupation for him. He liked to talk. He did not wait for a response.

"You know that new bar on Langata Road called The Big Barn?" Sam continued.

"The one owned by that *mzungu*... the South African with big money... what's his name again... Retief van den Brink, or something like that? That one?"

"Yes, that one. I was on my way home to Ongata Rongai and I thought why not stop in to take a look and have a drink. Well, I drive up to the gate and find it locked. I remember thinking it was odd. It's six o'clock, people are leaving work, the place is a bar, the gate should be open, right? I hoot and a guard comes. My car was in the garage, so I had borrowed one of the Institute's cars with red plates. I saw him look at the front plate and sort of nod as if he recognized it. He did not even look at me but just opened the gate. As I drove in, I sort of saluted him to say thanks... you know... for fun. But the guy looked shocked and began to wave his arms about. I thought that was strange, but I just assumed he was motioning to someone else. I drove on and parked my car. There were already many other cars there. Why was the gate closed, then, I wondered. Anyway, as I opened the door to get out, I found the guard standing there. He looked very angry. I asked him what he wanted. He said, 'You cannot stay here.' I said, 'What?' He said, 'You must go. You cannot come into this place. You are not allowed.' 'What do you mean I am not allowed?' I asked. 'No Africans can come into this place,' he said. 'What do you mean no Africans can come into here? Who said that?' I was very angry, so I was shouting. He said, 'The boss said that. No Africans are allowed to come in.' The guy was shaking, probably afraid of losing his job. But I did not care. I was so angry! There was no way I was going to leave without getting into the place. So I closed the car door, locked it, and began to walk toward the bar, which is pretty nice, actually. It's built like one of those barns in an American movie – you know, big wooden beams, high ceiling with no ceiling boards, no interior walls, winding stairs up to a loft sort of area. A very big bar that stretches almost the entire length of the place. I tell you, some of these *wazungu* know how to do things. Anyway, before I had taken even two steps, this guard grabbed my arm. The poor guy. I hit him hard on the chin. He fell. But I knew he would not give up, so I moved quickly and got into the place, just as I heard the guard blowing his whistle. There were *wazungu* everywhere... mostly Kenya cowboys... you know, those khaki shorts and shirts, long socks, pipes, cigars. Like I said, the place is nice. It smelled good, too. Gin and tonic... cigars... But the looks I was getting were something! I have not been stared at like that for a long time. I tried not to look at them and walked toward the bar. By then, the guard I punched was at the door, along with two others. They did not come in right away. I got to the nearest end of the bar and ordered a Tusker. I still remember the barman's name: Simon. It was on a name tag. He looked confused. So I said it again, very slowly like this: 'Simon, may I please have a Tusker." He began to serve me but then stopped. Van den Brink was walking up. The guy is huge, man. He looked angry. I was afraid he was going to hit me. I turned away and began to order again. But before I could finish, van den Brink said very loudly, 'We don't want any wogs here! Get out!' Everyone in the room was watching. I was scared. But I said to myself, stay calm, you're already in here. They won't throw you out. Hah! Before I could say *ng'we*, van den Brink called in the guards and told them to throw me out. Those three guys picked me up like a suitcase and carried me out to my car. I was so shocked I did not even resist. And the one I had hit before got his revenge properly, right here in my back. One of them said, in English, 'Fucking wog, don't come back here again.' Can you imagine?! So that's what happened to me, my brothers. Right here in Nairobi. Kenya. Africa."

"*Aiee, bwana*, what are you going to do? You can't just leave it like that."

"I've written letters to both the Nation and the Standard. But I think they are too long. They won't be published."

"Call a reporter to do a story, then. I know someone who would be very willing to write one."

"Maybe ... Actually, that's a good idea."

"You know, the same thing happened to a friend of mine in Kampala. The same, same thing. There's a bar there called the Pink Avocado, also owned by white South Africans. Those characters are bad, man. They think they can step all over us just because we buy their juice and cornflakes. It's pathetic. Sorry, Sammy, pole sana."

"I tell you," said Sam appreciatively. "I know they're not all like that. I work with some really nice ones. Good people who feel bad about things... you know. But this sort of thing makes even the decent ones harder to get along with... harder to trust. And then, as if I hadn't suffered enough for one week, look at this. Today a marabou stork shat on my shoulder in ABC Place. That stuff stinks, man!"

8

Edward Ochola had been unable to eat meat since the funeral of his sister, Christine Akoth. The problem had actually begun when he went to the City Mortuary to pick up her body before the ten-hour journey to their home in Alego. She had died of blood-loss induced shock, apparently after a botched abortion, most likely somewhere in Eastleigh, where her body had been found dumped in a ditch. The police had arrived on foot and commandeered a *matatu* to transport the body across town to the City Mortuary. Christine had lain there for one week before anyone in the family noticed her silence; she had been keeping to herself for some months. It took another week to locate her, two more to get her into the ground.

On the Friday morning before the funeral, Edward and twenty other relatives gathered outside the Mortuary, along with hundreds of others there to claim corpses to be transported for burial in rural homelands across the country.

"We should just pay them what they want and let them bring her out," suggested Tony Ojai, Edward's eldest brother, who was the one who had identified Christine's body the fortnight before. "It will not be easy to do it ourselves," he added. He was still unable to sleep properly from the experience.

"No," insisted Michael Opiyo, an uncle on their mother's side. "Three thousand shillings for what? That is enough to fuel my Datsun from Nairobi all the way to Alego and back to Kisumu. No way! We will do it ourselves."

Tony shook his head. He wanted no part of it. "Take this, you will need it," he said, handing Edward his handkerchief.

"Ochola, come with me," ordered Opiyo. Turning to the women in the group who had come to dress Akoth, he added, "We will bring her to the dressing room."

"Her name is Christine Akoth. Can you tell us where she is?"

Edward and his uncle were standing in the Mortuary's reception area. His uncle was talking to the thin oily-faced attendant.

"Yes. She could be in that one, or that one," replied the attendant, pointing to two stained doors behind his desk. "When you find her, call us. We will help you move her."

Opiyo strode confidently to one of the doors and pushed it open. He was met with a smell so strong and foul he gagged, stopped dead, and backed up sharply, bumping into Edward who had been following as closely as possible.

Recovering quickly, Opiyo opened the door again and walked in. "You take the other one," he instructed Edward as he disappeared into the room.

"Go on," chuckled the orderly, seeing Edward hesitate, "Just open it and enter... like your friend."

Edward took out Tony's handkerchief and held it to his mouth and nose. Trying his best to keep from having to breathe too often, he opened the door and stepped into the room.

One twenty-five-watt light bulb shone its weak light into the room from the farthest end. It took a few seconds for Edward's eyes to adjust. Soon he could trace the outlines of heaps of blackish-brownish sacks arranged in rows that traversed the full length of the room. His foot struck something sticking out from one of the heaps to his immediate left. The object rolled from the heap with a strange sucking-popping sound. Puzzled, Edward leaned over and reached down to pick it up, his other hand still holding the handkerchief to his face. Just as his fingers closed on the object, his eyes, closer to the ground now and thus better able to focus on the heaps around him, told him what he was about to pick up. The object had been a foot once attached to the pile of corpses arranged head to foot, head to foot. With his head at that height, he was staring straight into the lifeless faces of men and women long dead. His fingers sunk into rotten flesh. He jerked up with a shout and ran for the door. There was no handle.

"Open!" he screamed pounding on the door with this sticky hand. The orderly let him bang for a few minutes before opening. Edward rushed out of the room to find a bathroom, where he spent fifteen minutes trying to wash off the smell of rotten flesh. He did not succeed.

It took two hours and three different rooms, but in the end Opiyo found Akoth and brought her out. "No way will I pay these people to do their jobs! No way!"

Later at home, even after he had washed the rotten smell from his hands, Edward was unable to forget the odor or feel of the rotting flesh, which he came to associate with all meat. Even the most thoroughly cooked meat made him feel ill. He could no longer bring himself to supervise the roasting of the Wednesday group's goat and chicken meat. It used to give him great pleasure to watch little old Okech cut up the selected portions, slap them on to the grill, turn them over and over with his bare hands, and serve them sizzling and crackling on the large communal tray the group preferred over individual plates. Not any more.

As he sipped his beer and watched the others eat, Edward realized how tired he was these days. Everything was a struggle. There was so little pleasure outside groups like this. At home, there were mainly problems, mostly not of his own making. An unemployed brother. Another pregnant but unmarried sister. Many unemployed cousins. One *harambee* after another to raise money for school fees, hospital fees, weddings, funerals. A constant battle to avoid the increasingly common plunge from the middle class into the mass of working poor. Dust everywhere during the dry seasons. Mud everywhere when it rained. He was tired of it.

"My wife won a green card," he said into the lull in conversation caused by the arrival of the food.

"A green card? To where? The US?" This from Sam Opata who rarely ate more than a few pieces of meat and had already called for soap and water to brought over.

"Yes, to the US."

"Congrats, man! You're lucky! When are you going?"

"I don't know. We might not go."

"Eh? Are you mad? Why not?"

"I don't know. It's a big step..."

"Nonsense! It's a very easy decision. Don't complicate things, Eddie. Get that green card and go. If you fear that you will miss Kenya, then come back for holidays."

"Life in America is not easy. The green card is just an entry card. We will have to find jobs."

"Of course it is not easy in America. Why should it be? But at least you can try this, try that, make mistakes, and still survive. Anyway, Kenyans who get green cards always find jobs and do well over there. So will you."

When his wife, Maureen, had opened the letter from the US Immigration and Naturalization service and read the news, she had almost flung herself from the balcony of their Umoja Estate flat in excitement. She had forced him up from the sofa and into a five-minute dance around the tiny house, their stunned but increasingly excited children looking on.

"We're going to America! We're going to America! We're going to America..."

The house changed immediately – the feel of it. Maureen lost the dissatisfied frown that had gradually worked its way into her face over the nine years of their marriage. She was even more tired of their life in Kenya than was he. She became more open to sex, which loosened Edward's tongue in the morning, bringing more frequent smiles and laughter to their children. They were all excited.

Edward knew in his heart that they would go. They had to. There was no coherent argument not to. He just had to find a way to tell his mother and father. That was the problem. He knew it would break their hearts, especially after losing Akoth so horribly. His parents needed him.

"I can't leave my parents... I am the eldest son. I don't want to abandon them. How will I help them from America?"

"You know, Ed," it was Sam speaking. He was very thoughtful and eloquent. Everyone always listened carefully when he spoke. "You are right to worry about them. But I think you shouldn't do it in a way that clouds your thinking. Your parents are typical of many in that generation. Mine are gone now, but they were the same. That generation in Luoland is caught between worlds. If the stories of their lives are ever told, I think mostly those stories would be about how they were pioneers."

"What do you mean, pioneers?" That from JJ.

"I mean they were pioneer explorers of a space between two very different worlds. I am over-simplifying, but I think the overall story is true."

"I like that image of my parents as pioneers." This from Patrick. "I love it, actually. They were special people. But I don't quite get you, Sam. What do you mean?"

"Well, one world would be the world of their own parents," Sam continued. "In that world, wealth was based mainly on land. Control of that land was the birthright of sons, generation after generation. The things you did in life were few – farming, herding, fishing, trading, hunting, whatever. You did them well. You did them deeply. But they were few. The other world is the world of their children – that is, us... you and me. In our world, wealth comes from a much wider range of human activities. Mostly it comes from access to skills and financial capital that must be built up over many years by both men and women – sons and daughters. I know this is an exaggeration, but I think it holds. How people navigate the space in between matters. For example, Saks, I am thinking of your parents. For whatever reason – maybe due to your family history – they managed to make the leap from their parents' world to ours very early. You had a great platform to do things. But for the reasons JJ always mentions, there are not too many parents like them in Luoland."

Saks nodded but said nothing. His thinking about his father's legacy was still muddled. And increasingly he saw that he had squandered so many of his advantages. He could not yet put it all into words.

The waiter Okech walked up with a fresh tray of roasted meat. "Bring some more *ugali, mboga, and kachumbari*," called out Ogot. He also motioned to the Tanzanian waitress to add another round of drinks. This conversation was a good one. It would go on for a while. He liked the idea of leaping. That was what he had been trying to do over the past few decades in the Nairobi City Commission. He was almost there. He thought of Owino sitting next to him. Tomorrow they would meet to agree on his share of the twenty million. He would not push Owino too hard. The man deserved his chance to make a good leap. He had worked hard for it. Two million had gone to the Ethiopian. That left eighteen. He would take two like the Ethiopian. That seemed fair. Sixteen million would be a good leap.

"You are so right, Sam. So right..." As he listened to Sam, Patrick had removed his notebook from his briefcase. Referring to the notes he had been scribbling down, his brow furrowed in concentration, he continued, "You know what I see when I look at the lives of my parents and others who did not make the leap – or haven't yet made it? I see how they worked like donkeys for years and years but suffered in their final years, as if everything they had done meant nothing. I see how in their old age they had more land than they could ever use, yet they were poor and unable to cover basic day-to-day needs. I see how they were caught out because they followed the rules of their parents' world for too long. I see how it was only when they were old and suffering that they understood that the financial wealth that might have brought comfort to their final years should have been built decades before. So, yes, I agree that they were pioneers, but they did not really know what they needed to be doing. They needed to have understood money long ago. I think the whole Luo community still hasn't understood it."

"I'm not sure that what applies for Luos as individuals also applies for Luos as a group," said Sam, pleased that his idea had been embraced and expanded. "But I must say I prefer that kind of thinking about the Luo community to the "Luos-have-not-been-supported-enough-by-the-Government" arguments. I like it when we give ourselves more agency. That is, when we are the ones choosing. Agreed, our choices in Luoland are more constrained than, say, those in Kiambu or Bomet. But they are ours to make."

Ogot wanted to respond to this.

"I don't think it's an either-or thing," he began. "There are issues at both individual and tribe level. They are related. We need to deal with both at the same time. But I think I'm with Sam when he says that choices matter. I agree that most of our parents didn't really appreciate how important it was to let go of some of the biggest parts of their own parents' worlds. They never thought of it like that. But they were pioneers all the same. They opened space for us, whether it was like Saks's parents or like mine, who were peasant farmers to the end. By the way, I don't think that all the things they held on to were bad. Some were good! In fact, many were! Their pockets may have been empty, but their culture was rich and their spirits were full. That brings me to the Luo community. Shit, I love it that we are the way we are. In so many ways, we are still like our grandparents. I love it. Sometimes I almost love the idea that we are ridiculed and badmouthed so much. They laugh at how we enjoy ourselves and then they copy us and act like they invented what they copied. It makes me sick, yet I love it. To hell with them. We shouldn't lose who we are."

"No, we shouldn't," agreed Jacob. He was certain that some of La Fontaine's problems were linked to his being one of the few Luos in Nairobi's restaurant business. Some people simply would not do business with him, no matter what he did or said. "But to hold on to who we are, we need to have money. Anywhere in the world, culture costs money to sustain and preserve."

"Wow, what a contradiction!" exclaimed JJ. "What a paradox! To hold on to tradition, you need to modernize!"

George Obel wanted to speak. The conversation had rekindled the almost fully suppressed inner turmoil brought on the previous weekend's trip home to Rarieda. He didn't mind the resurgence of the discomfort. Something in his mind was moving in a different way than usual.

"I want to come back to our parents. Those of us who still have parents caught between our world and our grandparents' world do what we can for them. But for me it never feels like it is enough. The gaps facing that generation are huge. Like Patrick said, their accumulating should have happened a long time ago. And we must be honest and admit that out there in Luoland there still isn't enough accumulation happening. Most people are still living hand to mouth. Things are changing but not fast enough. I hear what you say about agency and all that, Sam. But we need fast and big change. And that can only come if more public money finds its way into Luoland. JJ is absolutely right about that. Private money always follows public investment. In the absence of public investment, private capital goes to sleep or runs away."

Edward nodded. It was true. The gaps to be filled were immense. Whatever he and his working siblings sent home was never enough. His mother and father were generous and principled people, with a strong sense of community and collective responsibility. Anything they received was shared with scores of needy people in the clan, leaving them with little for themselves. But more than his money, he knew his parents needed his time. They just wanted to see him. Talk to him. Hear news of his children. His work. His friends. Based as he was in Nairobi, he already did not see enough of them. What would a move to the US mean?

Edward shook his head and picked up his glass. He looked across at Sakawa who was smiling at himself, obviously pleased about something. "Saks," he called out, "You are too quiet. What are you smiling about? What are you plotting?"

"I have decided that I am going to move my family to Songhor."

6

THE MEN DO NOT EAT WINGS

"What has happened'?" the man asked... "What did he do?" His wife was struggling to speak. Their son had done something.

"He..." she began again, but then broke down and wept into his ear for almost a minute. He resisted the temptation to complain about the phone charges...

"What did he do?" he asked again.

"He... he molested a girl at school."

"Eh?! He raped someone?"

"No. He molested her. It's just as bad. My boy... molested... a girl. " She broke again.

This time he interrupted her. "Who is the girl?"

"She's someone at school, older than him...twelfth grade, I think. Apparently, she's not the best of girls. But that doesn't change it."

"What have you done?"

"There is nothing I can do! It's a police case. The school is involved... He's going to be expelled... he's going to go to jail." She began to cry again.

"Don't be stupid!"

"Don't call me stupid! He molested someone! The law says he will go to jail!"

"Have you hired a lawyer yet?"

"No, I..."

"Then you are STUPID! I'm coming now." He slammed down the phone, fuming.

"*Tell me everything,*" he said to the boy the next morning. *He had caught the last flight out of Redding to San Francisco the afternoon before and then the last one from San Francisco to Washington DC, mercifully non-stop.*

He had been surprised to find the boy waiting for him at the airport. The fellow seemed to have grown at least two inches since their last meeting, just four months before. And he was fuller in the shoulders and thighs. "*What a beautiful son I have,*" *he said to himself as they shook hands and then hugged awkwardly, the boy grinning so widely that his father could not hold his serious countenance for more than a second or two. They stood there grinning at each other for many seconds.*

"*Huh?*"

"*Tell me what happened... the truth.*"

"*OK,*" *said the boy, beginning to wring his hands nervously and breathe deeply. They were sitting at the kitchen table at home... at the mother's house. They were alone. The mother was at work. The father reached out and put his two hands over the boy's and looked directly into his son's eyes. He rarely did this. So now it had the desired effect. The boy calmed down.*

"*OK... she came to a soccer game. She's always hanging around the team. Just about everybody has screwed... has been with her. We had a...*"

"*Hold on. Is she white?*"

"*Mixed... white and Guatemalan or something. She looks white.*"

"*How many other blacks are on the team?*" *He had yet to see the boy play soccer. The mother said he was very good.*

"*I'm the only one.*"

Pause.

"*Go on.*"

"*We had a game at Georgetown Prep. We won... I played well... scored twice...*"

"Where was your mother?"

"She went with sis on a school trip to the Shenandoahs. Ryan's mom was going to give me a ride, but when this girl started her thing, I told Ryan to tell his mom that I'd find my own way home. She had her dad's car. We... we started there. But then she wanted to get a hotel room. I said OK, but I have no money. She said, no problem. She drove to a weird motel off Commonwealth Avenue in Alexandria. They knew her at the front desk. Mr. and Mrs. Jones, she said. They gave her a key. It was crazy. Anyway, we got to the room and there were no condoms in the dispenser next to the bed. So I said no way. No condoms, no sex. She got mad and said, I paid thirty dollars for this room. You'd better give me some of that black dick or I'll say you raped me. I thought she was joking so I said, for rape you have to have some sperm ... some semen. No semen, no rape. But she was not joking. I guess nobody had ever told her no. She got real mad then and said she'd say I molested her. I realized this was trouble so I told her to just... to get lost and I left. I had to get a taxi. The police came for me that night. I couldn't reach mom right away, so I had to spend the night in jail. Bad news."

"Why didn't you call me?"

"I don't have your number memorized. And I thought... I thought it might be better if mom told you."

A long silence.

"OK. That's fine. Does your mother know this story?"

"She won't listen to me. She won't talk to me. She seems to believe that whore."

"She is disappointed. The idea that you could have taken advantage of a woman is very difficult for her to accept."

"But I didn't do anything! I didn't take advantage of anyone!"

"OK, OK... Does your sister know this story?"

"Not yet."

"Tell her, and ask her to talk to your mother. I will also try. But we have a bigger problem. You are in trouble."

The boy jumped a little at the change in tone.

"Your entire life is at risk. All your dreams may be finished if we do not handle this properly. But do not worry. We will handle it properly. You must also do your part. First of all, no more foul language. Remember that I am your father and I do not like that kind of thing. Secondly, what is this girl's name?

"Jacquie... Jacquie Morris."

"From now, she must be Miss Morris".

*   *   *

"The most we can hope for is a suspended sentence with probation, and only if your son pleads guilty. Maybe six months, more likely one year," said Marion Singer, a highly recommended lawyer acquainted with one of the other parents at Bishop Ireton High School. They were sitting in her luxurious office on the seventh floor of a building overlooking the Potomac River in Rosslyn.

"No. That is not acceptable. I want complete exoneration. A clean record. Nothing less."

"That is not possible," replied the lawyer, rolling her eyes slightly upward as if preparing to explain a life-lesson to a still-naive child.

"It is. You must destroy Miss Morris."

"I cannot do that, sir. Your son molested her. According to both Virginia law and Federal law, he is liable for his actions."

"He did not molest that woman. He told you so."

"Yes, he said so, but no jury in Virginia is going to believe him. I'm sorry but that is that."

"What do we owe you, Ms. Singer?"

"Huh?"

"What do we owe you for your services up to this moment?"

"Twelve hundred dollars."

"Here you are, in cash. You are fired!"

*   *   *

"Gerry. I need some help."

"Shoot" said Gerry Carr, his boss back in Redding. They were speaking by phone.

He explained everything, slowly and methodically, as if giving one of his weekly progress reports.

"So I need a new lawyer. A black one. I don't know one here. And nor does... nor does the boy's mother." His voice trailed off. He was suddenly exhausted. He sighed audibly and said, "I was wondering if you knew someone who could point me in the right direction."

Carr was quiet for some moments.

"Hello? Gerry?"

"I'm here. Just thinking. OK, this is my reaction. First, I'm really sorry about this, Sam. Like you, I believe the boy's story. I also think you're right that the only way out is to destroy the girl's credibility. But I think you're wrong about needing a black lawyer. Over there in Alexandria, Virginia, the Judge is probably going to be white and suspicious of black youth. So will the jury. You need a white lawyer. I have a friend who fits your needs better than probably anyone. He's a real asshole, but he's very good, He's not cheap, but I have a feeling that won't matter.

*   *   *

"Had you ever been to that motel before the said May 17, Miss Morris?"

"Yes."

"How many times?"

"I can't remember."

"You cannot remember? Why is that Miss Morris?

"I just can't."

"Did you go there the week before, on May 10, with Mike Marino?"

"He paid."

"Yes or no, Miss Morris."

"Yes."

"Did you go there two weeks before that with one Jimmy Garis?"

"Yes."

"How about two weeks ago, with the same Jimmy Garis?"

"Yes."

"So you went – and you still go – to that motel quite often, Miss Morris. Tell me, Miss Morris, do you always use the same room?"

"Yes."

"Why is that?"

"No reason. I just do."

"Do the 55 notches scratched into the headboard have anything to do with that?"

Giggle.

*　　*　　*

"I move that the case against my client be dismissed for lack of evidence. I move also that all references to the alleged crime be removed from State and Federal records.

"Granted in full. The case is dismissed."

*　　*　　*

"Is that it?"

Humming to himself, the man splashed cold water on his face and looked at his reflection in the mirror above the sink. He seldom looked at himself in this way. He stepped back and turned a bit to get a sidelong view. He had lost weight; it showed on his face. He took off his shirt and found that there, too, he was narrower, firmer. He stepped out of his trousers and turned to the full-length mirror. His paunch was barely visible. He took off his underwear and stood there naked looking at himself. And quite suddenly, an image of his wife leapt into his mind and found an immediate physical expression. He laughed out loud. Eight years and now thousands of miles apart, and still she had this power over him. He laughed again, put his clothes back on, walked back to the living room of the hotel suite and picked up the phone.

Should he say, "I do not know what really happened in that motel room. There was a time when I thought I did, but not anymore. Whatever happened happened. But I do know that without me and what I represent – the things your mother never understood and probably never taught you –without these, you would have been sent to jail and would not be where you are today. I want to know that you know that."

Was that it?

When Rhoda called him to share the shocking news of Luka's murder, Boro Tindi, Opposition Member of Parliament for Kisumu East, had been preparing to travel to Bonn to give a speech at a conference on political reforms in Africa. He was looking forward to the trip. He had not been to Europe since the mid-1980s. His wife, Leah, would travel with him. She and the wife of his old friend, Professor Willem von Spee of the University of Bonn, had already developed a full programme of activities for the week after the conference.

He had been allowed to choose a topic and theme for the speech. It had been an easy choice. He wanted to use the speech to place the current tense political climate in Kenya in historical context. He felt the speech was coming along nicely.

A fondness for consensual politics has been embedded in Kenyans' collective imagination for a long time. Its roots can be traced to the Lancaster House Conference – the series of meetings in 1960, 1962, and 1963 during which Kenya's constitutional framework and independence were negotiated. That four-year period yielded three milestones that continue to define our politics. First, the interim constitution issued by Colonial Secretary McLeod in 1960 following deep disagreements among the British Government, the White Settlers, and the Africans. Second, the negotiated framework for self-government in 1962. Third, the 1963 conference in London that finalized constitutional arrangements for Kenya's independence as a dominion, with entrenched provisions for citizenship, fundamental rights, and a bicameral legislature. Over those four years, two things happened. First, a deeply held partiality for open public debate set into the psyche of the new political elite. Second, a deferential patience with elected leaders took hold of ordinary Kenyans.

Our current President understands this taste for consensual political outcomes better than anyone. He weaponizes it constantly, deliberately, subtly, to shape the conduct and outcome of debate after debate, crisis after crisis. Democratization. Market liberalization. Privatization. Public sector retrenchments. He deals with them in the same way. At base, his approach is simple. It is a pure numbers game: count the likely winners, count the likely losers, shift the rules to ensure that the winners are people like you, or people you like. The trouble with this strategy is that the winners are never fully clear, yet the losers are always obvious. The winners often do not even know that they have won, whereas the losers are invariably fully aware that they had fared poorly. The President's skill as a politician lies in showing the winners that they have won, that he is fully responsible for their victories, and that further gains hinge on their helping him fully throttle the losers.

The collective cost has been dear. We now have a paradoxical situation marked by extremes. At one extreme is a crop of adventitious leaders devoid of real roots or followings, but with total loyalty to the President. At the other extreme are radicals baying for change, many of them having spent time in detention for their beliefs and actions. And yet both groups – the loyalists and the radicals – are similar in their belief in consensual politics. Each one wants to convince Kenyans that their particular extremist path is the one to follow. Each group truly believes it would win a fair election. Two groups of extremists who think they can unite the country. It is quite a paradox.

That was as far as he had reached when Rhoda called. He had cancelled the trip to Bonn. But even as he prepared to bury Luka, the idea he had begun to frame lingered on in his mind.

Boro had been a winner many times and a loser almost as often. He had won whenever the Government needed an eloquent and moderate Luo within its ranks. He had lost whenever the Stork's political calculations favored more radical Luo leaders. Or, as was more often the case, he had lost when those radical Luo leaders meted out their own brand of retribution against perceived Government collaborators in Luoland.

Ironically, following a major falling out with the Stork, Boro was currently enjoying a period of acceptance by the radicals. He had served as a Cabinet Minister in the Stork's Government through much of the 1980s. The Stork valued his natural charisma, eloquence, and grand ideas for national development. He spoke glowingly of Boro at public gatherings and had him represent Kenya at many high-profile meetings abroad. Predictably, Boro soon was viewed as a threat by power brokers closer to the Stork than was he. Bit by bit, through character assassination, disparaging innuendo, and outright lies, they turned the Stork against him until one day in 1987 he found himself unceremoniously dumped from the Cabinet. Later that year, with the Stork's full endorsement, these forces ensured that he lost his parliamentary seat in the general election. It was a difficult period. But well aware that in politics things could change quickly, and knowing that the Luo radicals would not welcome any conciliatory overtures from him, he remained loyal to the Stork, and to the ruling Loyalist Party.

It stayed that way for several years – right up until the eve of the 1997 general election when, once again, the Stork publicly humiliated him by flouting proper nomination procedures and unilaterally anointing one of Boro's rivals as the Loyalist Party's candidate for the Kisumu East parliamentary seat. The LP leadership did not even have the decency to inform Boro in person. He was on his way to address an LP campaign rally only to be informed that there had been a radio announcement of the decision to dump him.

Incensed, Boro defected from the LP to the Western Alliance Party, which drew most of its support from Luos. Not only did he win the hotly-contested nomination race within WAP, he obliterated the Stork's hand-picked LP candidate in the election. Better still, Boro had moved so quickly, and used the press so skillfully, that his version of the episode was the only one made public. In short, Boro told the country that he had been publicly loyal to the Stork for decades. That he had dissipated a small fortune doing the LP's bidding, both in Luoland and elsewhere in the country. That he had even sacrificed friendships and family relationships in the process. All for nothing? He deserved better. There was no way he would go quietly. For once, the Stork and the LP were rendered speechless and never presented an alternative interpretation of what happened.

But at sixty-eight years of age, Boro wondered if it had all been worthwhile – the thirty years of public life. He understood and valued the role that consensual politics played in Kenya, especially when viewed alongside the periodic violent implosions in neighboring countries. He always held his tongue when other Africans ridiculed Kenyans as being too willing to suffer in silence; too timid to rise up against poor government. "We prefer to meet, talk, and vote," he would respond quietly. But Boro had grown weary of the current version of consensual politics in which change for the better had become so slow yet that for the worse seemed so rapid.

His cousin, Engineer Wanga Roche, the MP for Bondo, had invited him to lunch three weeks before and told him that he planned to run for the Presidency under PNN. He had already secured the support of PNN's Executive Committee. Before going public with his ambition, he wanted to be sure he could count on Boro's intellectual and financial support. The news had taken Boro by surprise. Wanga was only fifty years old. Boro had always imagined that when a Luo Presidential candidate emerged, that person would come from his generation, not Wanga's. But his cousin was dead serious. He intended to run in 2002, and he planned to win. Boro pledged his full support. There was no way he wouldn't. Things had to change.

Change for the worse. His brother, Luka Sollo, the most apolitical person he had ever known, had just been killed, and politics seemed to have played a part in his death. Another brother, Samson Okello, who had lived in the US for thirty-plus years, was about to make as huge a political blunder as could be possible for a non-politician. Boro still knew very little about Luka's murder. But that murder almost made more sense to him than this business with Okello.

* * *

Boro knocked firmly on the door of room 623 at the Nairobi Intercontinental. He was alone, having left his driver and bodyguard waiting in the lobby. He did not want them with him for this. He was not sure about Okello's state of mind, nor was he sure how he himself would behave.

Okello opened the door almost immediately and stood there, waiting, beaming at first and then beginning to sob. Instinctively, he had looked over Boro's shoulder, expecting to see their brother Luka's calm face. But Luka was dead.

The two brothers hugged and then stood looking at each other for many seconds, holding hands, tears falling, humming. They looked alike. Both dark-skinned, both heavy in the shoulders and thighs, both just over six feet tall. Both had the easy smiles and quiet, observant eyes of their father, Ang'awa. They closed those eyes and prayed, beginning with the Lord's Prayer and two Hail Marys. Boro used his prayer to begin to prepare Okello.

"Dear Lord," Boro began in Dholuo, "We thank you for bringing us here together, even though it is at a difficult time. You have taken away your son, our brother, Luka Sollo, to his holy resting place beside you. We can never hope to understand your glory, or hope to grasp the meaning in the terrible way in which you took him back. But our faith in you remains strong and we remain your loyal servants on this earth. We ask for strength and for glimpses, however brief, of your grace and wisdom. This we pray through Christ our Lord, Amen."

"Amen," said Okello, crossing himself, his body beginning to tremble deep inside – a trembling that would last for many weeks.

They sat down across from each other at the small meeting table. Boro asked about Okello's flight from the US and then quickly went over the preparations for the funeral, which was scheduled for that Saturday, three days hence.

"How are the children?" asked Boro in the end.

"They are fine. Oak just left for France. She got a job with Bankers Trust. I think I wrote to you about Cedar's new job at Johns Hopkins. He is happy."

"And Sage?"

"She's also OK. I just talked to her. She's OK. She says hello and sends her condolences. She wanted to come but... She says she ordered flowers. Were they delivered?

"Yes, we got them yesterday. Please thank her for us."

"She sent some money as well. I will give it you later."

An uneasy silence set in. The two brothers spoke often by phone, but they had not seen each other for two years. There was a distance between them. But it was a familiar gap – one that in the past would disappear within days of Okello's arrival in Kenya. But this time, it was different.

"I will be staying on after the funeral," said Okello eventually. "Jackson wants to get things in place right away."

"Yes, I know," said Boro, watching his brother closely. "You are to be part of this new Economic Reform Team for Kenya."

"Yes. I am looking forward to it."

"But why you? Why would you be asked to be on that Team? You have not lived here for years. You have never even worked here. Honestly, what do you know about Kenya's economy? What do you know about the Kenya Government?"

Okello had telephoned Boro three weeks earlier, two days before Luka 's murder. It had been very late at night. Boro had been fast asleep, dreaming of Ongile Rabuor, a boyhood friend he had not seen for many years. Luka was also in the dream. He was not in view, but Boro could feel his presence. It was as if Luka was hiding. The phone began to ring just as he and Ongile began to talk. Ongile called out to Luka to answer the phone. But the phone kept on ringing. Ongile motioned to Boro to wait and ran out of the room. Boro waited, assuming that Ongile had gone to pick up the phone, or to find Luka. But the phone kept on ringing and ringing. Suddenly realizing that the ringing phone was the one by his bed, Boro awoke with a start. Disturbed. Puzzled. Why was Luka hiding? Why did he not pick up the phone?

Boro remained sufficiently disoriented throughout the ensuing conversation with Okello that the next day it took some effort to convince himself that his brother's news was real. Boro also feared he had been too harsh with Okello. Too direct.

"I am calling because I have been asked to join the new Economic Reform Team for Kenya," Okello had announced, once they had exchanged greetings.

"Eh?"

"I said I have been asked to join the Economic Reform Team for Kenya … as the … "

"You are coming back to Kenya?"

"Yes."

"To do what?"

"l said I have been asked to … "

"Yes, I heard that. What are you going to do?"

"I am going to be the Deputy Permanent Secretary in the Treasury."

"Ha!" laughed Boro. "You are not serious! You are going to be the Deputy PS Treasury? You?"

What did he know about Kenya?

Okello hesitated before answering. He had hoped that by now, his elder brother would be more accepting of his decision to take up the job. But Boro's incredulous and irritated tone was the same as it had been during the telephone conversation three weeks before. Then, as now, Boro's raised voice and cutting words had angered him. Yes, Boro was his elder brother, but that did not give him the right to speak to him as he was a naïve teenager. But now, as he had done then, Okello swallowed his pride. Smiling widely to make sure that his voice carried no anger, Okello said, "You are right. I do not know very much about Kenya's economy. I also do not know much about the Government. But I know a lot about public administration. And since I have never worked in Kenya, I will be able to be impartial. I will not fall prey to corruption because I have been working outside the system. I am a US citizen but a Kenyan by birth. I will be trusted by other Kenyans."

Boro burst into laughter. "You are joking!"

"What do you mean?" protested Okello, still in control of himself. "I am not joking at all! I am very serious!"

"Look," said Boro. "You had better understand that you are on that team for only one reason, and that is that you are a Luo – a harmless one that nobody knows. A Luo with no following and no power. That is the way the President plays the game."

Unable to hold it any longer, Okello exploded in anger.

"Why does everything have to come down to Luos and tribes for you?! It's always Luos this, Luos that. You accuse the President of being a tribalist, but if he is, then you are no different. Stuart Jackson is heading the ERT. He is white! How do you explain that?"

"Okello, it is so obvious! Jackson is a *kaburu*... a Kenya Cowboy. Jackson understands that politics in the Kenya of today is all about tribes. You ask him. You'll see. He was asked to lead the ERT because he is a *kaburu*. Kenya's white tribe. He is being used. He is liked and trusted by his fellow whites at the World Bank, and in London, Paris, Stockholm, wherever. That is very useful to the President. He needs World Bank money right now. Remember that up until last year, Jackson was in the Opposition. By agreeing to be part of this ERT thing, he has been compromised. He is being used to soften the donors and split the Opposition. Do the President's people know that you are my brother... and Luka's brother?"

"Of course they do. I told them."

"What did they say?" asked Boro in disbelief. It was even more absurd than he had imagined.

"They said they respect you and that they had nothing to do with Luka's death so they saw no problem. In fact, they said it would help them make their case that they had nothing to do with the killing."

"And you agreed to that?"

"Why not? Is there any proof that the Government was involved?"

"Not as yet, but... "

"Then why are you assuming that it was?" asked Okello, losing his patience and interrupting Boro mid-sentence.

"You could not begin to understand, my brother," said Boro. He had been hoping to convince Okello to reconsider his decision to join the ERT. It looked so bad. Luos were laughing at them again. He could push harder, but he did not want to alienate Okello. It was time to end the conversation. "Let me leave you to rest," he continued. "I am glad you will be here with us for some time. It has been many years since we had a chance to meet and talk regularly. Maybe that will be the one good thing that comes from Luka's death."

"Yes, it is good to be here."

"Sleep well. I will send my driver to help you in the morning," said Boro as he opened the door to leave.

"There's no need for that, Boro. I have already been assigned a driver and car. Let's talk in the morning."

*   *   *

Okello did ask Jackson.

"You were hired because you are competent and can obviously do the job," replied Jackson. "The headhunters identified you from a pool of over two hundred very strong candidates. Your record in public administration in a fast-developing part of the United States is exemplary. Your letters of recommendation were excellent. You performed extremely well during the interview. You were by far the best candidate. We were especially impressed when you said that for many years you had been looking for a way to come back to Kenya and help the country get out of the mess it is in. Do not let the doubters infect your mmd. Just do your job well and everything will be fine."

Okello was satisfied. He had been hired on merit.

During the lavish State House ceremony to launch the ERT, the President himself struck the first odd note. It was the week after Luka's funeral.

"You see," the President began in Kiswahili, after delivering his prepared speech in English. "This group of people looks like Kenya, does it not? You see? Here is ... em ... *Bwana* Jackson, a white Kenyan who was recently a leading figure in the Opposition but has now joined hands with us to revitalize our economy."

The ERT members were lined up in front of him. Walking down the row, the President continued.

"Here is *Bwana* Kariuki, from Central Province. Here is *Bwana* Ikaria, from Eastern. Here is *Bwana* Okello, from Luo-Nyanza... the brother of our late friend Luka Sollo... and the brother of my good friend Boro Tindi, the MP for Kisumu East. Here is *Bwana* Amiti, from Kisii-Nyanza. Here is *Bwana* Noor, from North Eastern. Here is *Bwana* Balala, from Coast. Here is *Bwana* Shiganga, from Western. You see my friends, the ERT is like Kenya. Diverse. Strong. Competent. I thank the World Bank for its support for this Kenya-led initiative, and I especially thank Mr. Stuart Jackson for showing that even people with different political views can work together for the good of the country."

"Why is he describing us based only on our regional affiliations?" Okello asked himself. "Why mention Luka and Boro? Why say nothing at all about what we will be doing in the ERT?"

Then came Sakawa's book. When Saks was detained, Okello's first instinct was to resign. But then Boro telephoned and demanded that he do so.

"You must resign!"

"Why?"

"What do you mean, why? They killed your brother; they have detained your nephew! What else do they have to do?"

"Boro, do not lecture me about how I should react to Luka's death and Sakawa's detention. I am doing this for people like them. I am doing this for Kenya... not for the President. If things are going to change in this country, they have to change from inside the Government first. What will I prove by resigning?"

" You are wrong. You do not understand these people. Those big ideas of yours are just nonsense to them. If you stay in there, they will lose any respect that they may still have for you."

"No, Boro, you are the one who is wrong. I am not going to give up. I am not going to resign."

The sound of Boro's disgust and dismay stayed with Okello for a long time. He trusted and admired Boro very deeply. Surely someone like that could not be totally wrong...

Then came the big trip of the entire ERT to the World Bank's headquarters in Washington DC. The aim was to reach an agreement that unlocked the next tranche of World Bank budget support to Kenya's budget. But discussions were strained from the outset. The Bank expected immediate action on key policy measures – more and quicker retrenchments of civil servants, greater transparency in public procurement, arrest and prosecution of corrupt officials. But the President had instructed Jackson to stall. Torn between loyalty to his boss and fear of appearing weak, Jackson chose the former and stalled. The Bank responded by indicating that it would delay the release of the next tranche of funds until the conditions were met. The talks were abandoned prematurely.

The night before the dejected ERT members left Washington for Nairobi, they attended a dinner party hosted by the Kenya Association in Washington. Instead of the anticipated cordial gathering of fellow citizens and friends, the occasion turned into a Kenya Government-bashing session led by several self-exiles. The infuriated but timorous Kenya Ambassador to the US – in whose care the ERT had been throughout the visit to Washington – led them out of the venue to a chorus of boos and hisses.

What are you doing with these people, Okello asked himself all the way back to Nairobi. They had no mandate at all. Before, he would have been on the other side, demanding that the Government do better. Now, he was part of the problem. And to make it worse, half the time he didn't even know what they were doing. They were too quick, too sly. They would come in and ask him to sign something that looked harmless enough. And then two weeks later he would find that he had handed them another tool to loot and ruin yet another public agency. Then he would be too ashamed to say anything, and they knew it. He saw that he was no longer part of the solution, and that perhaps he never was.

The final straw was the confrontation with Alfred Siromene. As Deputy Permanent Secretary in the Treasury, Okello had informed his boss, the Permanent Secretary, that the Office of the President had overspent its travel budget by over two hundred percent. Without a major realignment of the overall budget, there was no way to honor a request from State House for twelve million dollars to cover the cost of the President's up-coming trip to the Commonwealth Heads of Government Meeting in Canberra. Moreover, there was something very fishy about the request. Such trips normally cost four million dollars. Why did they need an extra eight million? On the eve of the trip, with the Permanent Secretary having suddenly and mysteriously been sent on mission to Geneva, Okello was summoned to State House by Siromene.

"You stupid Luo!" began Siromene, even before Okello had sat down. They were in Siromene's primary office. "Who do you think you are? You think we brought you here to tell us what to do? We do as we want! You understand?! I want that twelve million dollars credited to the State House travel budget line by tomorrow noon!"

Siromene stood there, waiting for an answer. He was not the kind of man to walk away from a confrontation until he had extracted full surrender. But nor, by then, was Okello willing to back down. He was fed up.

"Yes, I am a Luo, and I am proud to be Luo," Okello began, standing up to leave. "But, no, I am not stupid. You make the transfer yourself."

Okello started to move toward the door, but Siromene blocked his path. He had more to say.

"You are stupid! You are weak!" snarled Siromene, his face contorted in hatred and contempt. "What do you think you are doing here? Eh? Eh? Why are you here? Why are you still here? What kind of a person are you? What kind of a man? Why are you not with your brother and sister-in-law in the courts begging the judges to order the release of your nephew? You are just like your other brother. Stupid! You people think you are so special. But you, you are also stupid. Another stupid Luo. You are even too stupid to kill! Go to hell! Go back to America!"

"I intend to," said Okello as he pushed past Siromene toward the door. "As I said, make the transfer yourself."

One part of Okello wanted to return the insults. But he had seen enough of Siromene's methods to know that the man was capable of anything. The man had all but admitted to having Luka killed. Consciously clenching his teeth to stop himself from saying anything further, he walked out the door, and out of State House.

He returned to his office in Treasury Building, sat at his desk, and hand-wrote his resignation letter to Stuart Jackson. He left the letter with Jackson's secretary on his way out.

Back in his suite at the Intercontinental – the suite that had been his home for one year and four months – Okello hung up his jacket, removed his shoes, and lay down on the bed. He knew he had done the right thing and felt totally at ease. Boro had been right all along. Okello would have to find a way to tell him... to apologize.

For now, Okello wanted to talk to his children. It was one-thirty in the afternoon in Nairobi. Oak would be at her desk at Bankers Trust in Paris. Cedar would be waking up in Washington DC. He dialed the number of the long-distance service provider, listened for a moment and then dialed Oak's number.

"Hello. Oak. This is your father. Fine, fine. Could you set up a conference call with Cede? Is this a good time? OK. I am waiting."

She called back in a few minutes. Cedar was already on the line.

Okello: Hello, Cede.
Cedar: Hi, dad.
Oak: Hello, Oak, right?
Okello: But I already greeted you.
Oak: No, you didn't. You said, "Hello. Oak." Not, "Hello, Oak." There's a difference.
Okello: OK, OK. Hello, Oak, my dear daughter.
Oak: Hello, daddy. How are things over there in Kenya?
Okello: Fine, fine. I resigned today.
Oak/Cedar: What?! You resigned?! Why?!
Okello: I had to.

Cedar: But what about everything you said about helping change the Government from the inside, fighting corruption?

Oak: Were you fired?

Okello: No, I was not fired, Oak. I resigned. There is a difference, you know.

Oak: Touché! OK, you resigned. But why?

Cedar: Why? What happened?

Okello: I changed my mind.

Oak: You changed your mind about what?

Okello: About everything. About myself.

Cedar: Dad, you're not making any sense. You don't just change your mind like that, out of the blue. You don't just walk away from a job like that. What happened?

Okello: Some men know how to eat wings.

Oak/Cedar: What? What was that? What do you mean, "Some men know how to eat wings?"

Okello: It is too complicated.

Oak: Oh thanks, daddy. Is this why you wanted to talk to us – so you could have someone to condescend to?

Okello: No, no. It's just that I am still trying to understand it myself.

Oak: Fine. Then let's talk about it. That's why you called, right? You wanted someone to talk to, right?

Okello: Yes. That's right. Is Cede still there?

Cedar: Yes, I'm here. I'm thinking about this wings thing. Is it a Luo thing?

Okello: I suppose so.

Cedar: Is it chicken wings?

Okello: Yes, if you take it literally.

Cedar: So it means that chicken wings are for women, the rest of the chicken is for men, but sometimes men choose wings? Is that it? Is that what it means, dad?

Oak: No, that isn't it. I mean it is, but then it's more... deeper... I think.

Cedar: Is that it, dad? Dad? Are you still there?

Okello: I am here. I need to use the WC. You two carry on. I am coming.

2

Okello had rushed back to Nairobi after Luka's funeral and plunged headlong into his new job as Deputy PS Treasury. Not until late September, almost eight months into the position did he feel that he had the measure of the job and thus comfortable enough to leave his desk and Nairobi for a weekend. He chose to travel home to Uhanga.

He took the Friday evening fight to Kisumu, was met at the airport by Boro's driver, and arrived in Uhanga well after nine in the evening. Boro was already there, as were several of their cousins and uncles. It had been almost three years since Okello's last visit to Uhanga, so he was the center of attention, the focus of many a joke. They talked and drank well into the night. The conversation could not help but settle for a while on Sakawa's detention the previous week following the publication of his book. Nobody confronted Okello over his continued presence on the Government's Economic Reform Team – not even Boro with whom he had not spoken properly since their disagreement over whether Okello should resign from the ERT. But then nor did anyone hold back in conveying anger and disgust at the Stork and the Government. By then, Okello was already feeling gloomy about the ERT's prospects for achieving the promised changes in Kenya's economic policy and public sector management. Had any of the men taken him on directly, Okello would not have offered much resistance. He retired to bed long before the others.

It was a good weekend to go home. A major fund-raising meeting was planned for the Saturday. The local community was planning to approach an external donor for financial and technical support for a community-operated water supply and sanitation system. A series of fund-raising rallies had yielded three hundred and twenty-five thousand shillings as the community's contribution to the initiative.

However, the previous Treasurer of the coordinating committee had embezzled twenty thousand shillings before being found out and replaced. The fund-raising event was intended to replace the lost twenty thousand.

Uhanga lies at the mouth of the wide rain shadow that begins on the northern shore of Kenya's portion of Lake Victoria and stretches north eastward toward Lake Turkana, interrupted only by a small, wet, and thus densely populated trapezoid cornered by Yala and Mumias to the south and by Eldoret and Kitale to the north. Both the long and short rains are unreliable in Uhanga, often arriving much earlier or later than expected, and seldom lasting long enough to yield good grain harvests. That year, the short rains were late. They should have begun much earlier in September. A hot, humid wind signaled that they were imminent. But meanwhile, the parched landscape lay thirsty for the first drops of water to fall from the sky. Cropland had long since been cleared and ploughed in preparation. Cans of saved seed were ready for sowing. If only the rains would come.

It seemed that every poor rainy season brought about a discernible spurt in the already steady flow of Uhanga's men away from lives as farmers and herders toward lives as laborers in towns across the country. The migrants' meager incomes could not support wives and children in the towns. So those women and children stayed behind. Save for tiny remittances that arrived with varying frequency, the women fended for themselves. The men's small earnings also meant that they could afford only infrequent journeys back home to Uhanga. The visits were invariably short and unsatisfying. Nevertheless, very often they yielded pregnancies for the women, and soon welcome but taxing new mouths to feed.

These left-behind women were the force behind the water project.

They wanted their men back home. They wanted easier lives for themselves and their children. They knew that water was key to meeting both objectives. If, went one argument, they had more reliable water supplies for their crops and animals, then the land would yield more to sell, and their men would not be forced to leave in search of cash. And if, went another, the women and children left behind had cleaner and more regular water supplies in their households, then they would be relieved of the back-breaking burden of collecting unhygienic water from ponds and ditches shared with livestock.

The women had organized themselves into groups according to the locations of their original, pre-marriage homes. This led to five groups: the women from Gem, Nyi Gem; the women from Sakwa, Nyi Sakwa; and Nyi Alego, Nyi Loka, and Nyi Uyoma. These groups had conducted mini-fund raisers as pre-conditions for membership in an umbrella group, the Uhanga Women's Self-Help and Savings Group, which from its acronym, UWSSG, came to be referred to as "Yusig." The three hundred and five thousand shillings on hand was the product of the efforts of Yusig and its constituent groups.

An engineer estimated the total cost of the project to be one million seven-hundred thousand shillings. Yusig's leaders knew that raising that amount of money was beyond them. They did not have the required network of contacts. They approached the Honorable Boro Tindi and asked him to serve as the Patron for the project. The women loved Boro for his easy smile, common sense, and sharp wit. They also recognized that having grown up in Uhanga, Boro had a firm grasp of local conditions. As MP for Kisumu East, he had immense stature and strong pulling power but no vested interests in local politics. Boro agreed without hesitation, wishing, as he did, that women in his own constituency were as highly motivated and organized.

Like Luka, Boro had shifted his rural homestead from Uhanga to the sugar belt. In his case, the shift took him to a farm near Kibos, a small trading post twenty kilometers east of Kisumu, near the border between Nandi and Kisumu Districts. But unlike Luka, Boro intended to be buried alongside his ancestors in Uhanga. So he liked to support self-help efforts in Uhanga such as the next day's meeting, at which he would be the Guest of Honor.

As with all Yusig-organized events, preparations for the meeting had been meticulous. The women had designed, printed, addressed, and mailed the invitation cards to hundreds of clan members and friends scattered across the country. They hired a team of secondary school boys to cut and transport wood for construction and cooking. They hired the same boys to collect papyrus reeds from the lakeshore. They sewed these reeds into the large mats that would sit atop wooden beams, forming a tight canopy against sun or rain. They bought and prepared the food that would be served to guests in five nearby houses organized according to the five Yusig sub-groups. They rented a public address system. They welcomed guests with well-rehearsed songs and dances, and spontaneous ululation.

In the past, Uhanga's men might have raised questions about their lack of involvement in Yusig and thus also in the planning for the meeting. But enough of them could clearly see the tangible benefits accruing to their homes from Yusig's many activities, alongside the intangible gains to their spouses from the companionship and mutual assistance cultivated within and across Yusig's sub-groups. Only a few men stayed away by choice.

By eleven o'clock, all the invited guests had arrived. Yusig's constituent sub-groups were fully represented. Excitement and anticipation filled the air. As usual, the meeting began with a prayer. But this time, it was a tortuous one, delivered by the local pastor, Reverend Justus Oliech, who had begun to fancy himself as Uhanga's answer to the American evangelist Billy Joe Farmington, from whose awe-inspiring revival gathering in Nakuru he had returned the previous week. The Reverend had yet to master the art of holding the attention of a large gathering. The endless and flatly-delivered prayer sucked all the initial enthusiasm out of the air.

"This will not do," muttered Nora Owirro to herself. Nora was Yusig's Organizing Secretary. She was also filling in temporarily as the Treasurer. "This will not do at all. We have worked too hard to let this man ruin it all with his pathetic praying."

"What is not what?!" yelped Nora, in English, as the pastor let out his fifth ending "Amen!"

"What is not what?!" she repeated, springing to her feet and waving the fuming pastor toward his seat, determined to reinject some positive energy into the meeting.

Nora spoke perfect English, and everyone knew it. So whenever she interrupted a meeting with this sort of half-rubbish statement, she invariably got a laugh.

"What!" the crowd laughed back.

"Not what!"

"Not!"

"Amen!"

"Amen!"

"Praise Him!"

"Let His name be praised."

"Hallelujah!"

"Hallelujah!"

"What is not what!"

"What!"

Laughter and clapping.

Nora sat down, pleased with herself. The mood was right again.

Pamela Oluoch, Yusig's Chairwoman, stood up to open the meeting. But then to everyone's shock, before she had said a word, she burst into tears. To make matters worse, she did not make a move to sit down but just stood there crying. When her sister, the choirmaster, led the choir into a solemn dirge, everybody understood what was happening.

Two months before, Pamela had lost a third son to AIDS. The first two sons had been married and were therefore nursed by their wives. This third one had been single and still living at home. Pamela had been forced to nurse him to the end. She had nursed many terminally ill relatives. But they had all been women. Caring for a male child – a grown man – had almost broken her. Her husband had been unable to handle the pain and anxiety and had left everything to her. Everything. The tears of shame and self-pity. The violent outbursts when terror overwhelmed him. The erections as he awoke. The embarrassed smiles. The saliva. The urine. The shit. The shit. The shit. The knowledge that he was going. The silent farewell with just his eyes, the rest of his body locked in an unending spasm. The end. Two months and she had never cried. And now, in front of all these people, out it came.

"Please come and sit down," someone came and pleaded with her. It was her husband.

"No," Pamela gulped, unable to stop the tears. "This is my meeting." She stood there and cried bitter, wracking tears for many minutes, with the choir helping her along, her husband and friends, too.

"God bless you!" several people called out as Pamela finally stopped, wiped her eyes, collected herself, and began to speak.

She spoke briefly about Yusig's past achievements, and then at length about its plans for the future, once the water problem had been solved. A maternity wing at the local health clinic, so that women could give birth in clean and safe conditions. Zero-grazed cattle, so that the children could have more milk to drink. An electric generator at the church-cum-primary school, so that groups like theirs could hold evening meetings. Then she invited Nora to give the Treasurer and Organizing Secretary reports.

"This is nit wit!"

"Wit!"

Then came the obligatory address by the local sub-chief. As usual, the sub-chief announced that any youths who engaged in disorderly conduct that evening would be jailed overnight. That evening, as usual, his warning was ignored. And as usual, the sub-chief did nothing about it. Everybody knew that as long as they did not harm anyone, he would leave them alone.

The choir sang two moving songs, one a well-known hymn about the Virgin Mary, the other a comical and somewhat un-Christian recreation of Boro's widely reported hilarious speech in Parliament in defense of polygamy.

"It takes much time and effort for a man to learn how to love and care for a wife," Boro had argued in closing. "Just like a carpenter never stops once he has learned to build the perfect stool or table, a man's ability to love and care for a wife must be shared with others."

The Kisumu-based singer and harpist, Okoth Sibuor, and his three-piece band had been invited. They played two popular tunes, which were eagerly consumed. And then Okoth announced a new composition.

"This one is named, 'Paths'," said Okoth in his gruff voice. "This is our first performance."

One sharp down-stroke of his bow on the harp string and they were off, the drummer establishing the cadence, the metal percussionist shaping it, Okoth's unmistakable deep, growling voice – soon to be joined by the higher, softer ones of his companions – punching out the memorable lyrics.

What is this life I call my own,
What do I fear lo lose?
What boundary to scan and draw,

From somewhere up above?

My wives, my sons, my daughters,
My lands, my huts, my things.
My paths, my works, my private masks,
All mingled, mangled there.

Only reflected my face can I see,
Only accepted my place do I know.
Just paths criss-crossing, one.

My wives, my sons, my daughters,
My carvings on life's rock.
To them there seems no single doubt,
I'm mingled, mangled love.

Mingle-mangled, mangle-mingled,
Love and life, love-life.
No boundaries to draw and scan,
No tears of pain, just joy.

I place my hand on my father's axe,
I cut away the past.
Just paths criss-crossing, one.

What life is this to call my own,
To grasp so tight and close?
To fear a change in path, work, mask,
To seldom pause to mark.

How did I come to this here point?
When did I start to shiver?

Why do I choose this life each time?
What triumph might be mine?

I curl my hands around my father's hoe,
I dig toward the future.
Just paths criss-crossing, one.

What is this life?
What life is this?
What is this life?
What life is this?

Just paths criss-crossing, one.
Just paths criss-crossing, one.
Just paths criss-crossing, one.

The crowd exploded into applause, repeatedly chanting, "Just paths criss-crossing, one!" Okoth Sibuor and his two partners, obviously relieved and thrilled at the reaction, beamed, bowed, and bowed again. Boro produced five thousand shillings and requested that they perform the song again, which they did, more slowly, adding a dipping, lilting syncopation that brought even the old men and women to their feet, their creaking shoulders, knees, and ankles groaning in the sweet agony of release. Younger men and women looked at each other longingly. "Did you hear that?" their eyes asked. "Did you?"

The Chairwoman introduced Yusig's Patron and the meeting's Guest of Honor, the Honorable Boro Tindi, MP for Kisumu East, respected son of Uhanga.

"There, there!"

"Say it, Tindi!"

"The cat said scat!"

"Speak, we are listening!"

"Scat!"

"Quiet!"

Okello was sitting with a group of cousins toward the rear of the gathering. He marveled as Boro metamorphosed before their eyes. Seated, Boro's ill-fitting suit made him look uncomfortable and constipated. But when he stood up, danced a jig, intoned, "What is this life? What life is this?" and closed his eyes and shook his head as the crowd completed the refrain, Boro looked like he did on his entry into politics at thirty-eight. Like a man who was going places.

"Mano thum mamit manadi, yawa!" he began, confirming his deep enjoyment of the new song, shaking his head in wonder.

He thanked Yusig for the work they were doing to uplift the community. He said how proud and honored he was to have been asked to serve as Patron. He promised to do everything in his power to ensure the success of the project.

"Piss, miss, and then hiss!"

"Hiss!"

"Quiet! Quiet!"

Boro was optimistic about the amount of money they might raise that day. He could tell that Okoth Sibuor's music had opened hearts. Now he needed a way to both open minds and pull them together. Only then would the money flow.

Ever since Luka's murder, Boro had often found himself thinking of their father, Senior Chief Mathew Ang'awa Osewe. And now with Sakawa's detention and Okello's stubborn refusal to see the mistake he was making by continuing to serve on the ERT, the image of Ang'awa seemed to be with him constantly.

What would you think of us, Babu? Would you be proud? Always, always strive for excellence and refinement. That's what you used to say all the time. If you look at it, you would say, if you really look at it, life is so vulgar, so crude, so base. Without elegance and finesse, life would be unbearable. But with refinement of even the smallest thing, everything changes. The vulgarity, crudity, and baseness do not disappear; they just cease to be overpowering. But you must be excellent to achieve refinement. Boro had learned himself that you must love to find excellence.

So, looking out at the expectant crowd waiting for him to show them a way forward, Boro sang the story of Nwanji the warrior. He sang it slowly, in Dholuo, with great love, his voice gathering strength with each note.

On his entry into politics thirty years before, Boro would sing many of his speeches. His first election campaign had been against the brilliant but stiff Nathan Ojuok. After a rally during which Ojuok tediously lectured the crowd and Boro sang to it, the race had become a no-contest. These days, while Boro was almost always singing at home, he seldom sang in public. But today, with his father's image filling his mind's eye, and with Okoth Sibuor's band providing lively background music, Boro sang and sang.

In this version of the story, Boro emphasized Nwanji's leadership qualities, his love for the clan, and, most of all his fierce pride.

"Pride is a complicated idea," Boro said at the end of the story, noting that many faces still had expectant looks on them. He still needed to hammer home the point somehow. "In these times, when money seems to rule our lives, there are many proud people. There are many people who are proud in a bad way. There are many people who are conceited. There are many people who think too highly of themselves. They are vain about their appearance, their advantages, their achievements. Such vain and arrogant pride always falls. It always separates people. There is nothing wrong with taking pleasure and satisfaction in something you have done. I am sure the women of Yusig are happy and content with all that they have achieved. But some people take it too far. That kind of pride was not the pride of Nwanji son of Silual. His was a different kind of pride – a pride that drew from his mettle. His was the pride you see in a fine bull, as it demands the best from itself and those in its path. That kind of pride is good. That is the kind of pride we should be trying to teach our children. I see it in Yusig. I saw it many years ago in my late father, Chief Mathew Ang'awa Osewe. I see it in my nephew Sakawa Sollo, who at this very moment is sitting in Kamiti Prison because he showed some mettle. And when I look around me today, I see it in many eyes. I can feel it moving around among us. Come up now! Step forward and show that pride!"

The contributions totaled an astonishing seventy-five thousand six hundred and sixty-seven shillings, with Boro, Okello, and other town-dwellers contributing a little over sixty-five thousand. The ten thousand and sixty-seven shillings contributed by the local community almost doubled their previous highest one-day collective outlay.

The meeting ended with another lengthy prayer from Pastor Oliech, but even that could not dampen the collective recognition that something important had been achieved.

It was time to eat.

Boro, Okello, and fourteen cousins living in Nairobi were lunch guests of Nyi Sakwa, the Yusig sub-group led by Nora Owirro, in whose house the meal would be served.

"Welcome, welcome," Nora said as her husband, Jecton Owirro, led the guests into their house. She had left the meeting right before the fund-raising session to rejoin the eight other women from Sakwa she had left behind preparing the meal.

Jecton and Nora Owirro were exceptions in Uhanga. They were doing well despite Jecton's absence. Soon after leaving Uhanga for Nakuru, Jecton had found work as a forklift driver for Kenya Breweries. As a semi-skilled technician, his salary was high enough – and he was careful enough with that salary – to be able to build a permanent brick house in Uhanga for Nora and their three children. Nora's job as a teacher in Uhanga Primary School added both income and stability to the household.

The Owirro house had been lovingly prepared for the sixteen visitors. All the chairs and tables were spread with bright green and pink crocheted covers. Purple and red bougainvillea cuttings hung from curtain boxes or stood in water-filled soda, wine, and oil bottles placed here and there. Place settings of various styles lay neatly on the dining tables.

Once the guests had taken their seats at the tables, a young woman carrying a crate of assorted sodas went around the room opening each person's selection – Coke, Fanta, Sprite, Stoney Tangawizi. Okello was parched and requested water. The young lady smiled and shook her head. She knew how difficult it would be to find and present water of a sufficiently high standard of hygiene to satisfy anybody who did not live in Uhanga, especially on a day like this. The seven cartons of bottled water bought in anticipation of such a request had been exhausted within the first two hours of the day's proceedings. The young woman explained this to Okello and offered him a Sprite, which he accepted, beginning to better appreciate the true extent of his ancestral homeland's water problem.

Three more young women entered, each carrying kettles of warm water in one hand and shallow basins in the other. In the basins were half-bars of hand soap. All hands and some faces were washed, throats cleared. Laughter. Bobbing Adams apples. Jiggling breasts. Naughty jokes. Smiles from the hosting Yusig sub-group members watching from their vantage points half-inside, half-outside the doorways.

The food was brought in. It was steaming hot, having spent only a few minutes in bowls and dishes en route from pots sitting on charcoal stoves and wood-burning hearths outside. White *ugali*, brown *ugali*. Plain rice, *pilau* rice. White *chapatis*, brown *chapatis*. Fried fish, stewed fish. Fried chicken, stewed chicken. Fried beef, stewed beef. Fried innards, stewed innards. Cabbage. Kale. Peas and carrots. A short prayer from Owirro. "Welcome!"

Okello plunged into the *ugali* and fried fish. Even as his right hand shaped the first ball of *ugali*, he could tell it would be perfect. Its color and texture confirmed that it had been made with unsifted maize meal, which, though he seldom ate it, was his favorite. The *ugali's* slightly smoky smell revealed that it had been cooked slowly but completely on a charcoal stove. The fried fish was also perfect – crispy on the outside but soft on the inside. He was soon done with it. He was in the mood for dry meat and reached for the nearest dish of fried chicken. One piece remained. He pierced it with his still unused fork. But just as he pushed the piece of chicken off the fork and on to his plate, it was snatched away and another piece deposited in its place. He looked up to find Nora standing behind him. The original piece of chicken was on a plate in her hand. She was smiling at him. She turned to go.

"I wanted that piece," Okello said, stopping her with his still clean left hand.

"Eat that one," she replied, surprised but still smiling, "It is bigger."

"No. I wanted fried chicken. This one is stewed.'

"Oh, I see. Then let me bring you some fried chicken."

"No. That one is fine. I like it."

"No. This one is not for here. It should not have been served to you."

"It is OK. I like that piece."

"No. I will bring you another one." Nora was growing embarrassed.

This was bad behavior from Okello. Other guests were now watching them. Nora's husband Jecton was sitting across from Okello, looking irritated and embarrassed. He would have to say something if it did not end quickly.

Nora caught her husband's look and made to leave again. But again Okello stopped her.

"Nora, please," he said, "Don't bother. I will eat that one." He stood up and reached for the plate.

"No!" Nora insisted, annoyed and upset. Okello was spoiling everything by drawing attention to her. "Don't you see this is a wing? The men do not eat wings!"

Stunned and stung, Okello let go of the plate and sat down. Nora disappeared into the kitchen. Within seconds, she was back with a new plate on which she had placed two large thighs and a breast. She removed the plate with the piece of stewed chicken, which had also been a breast.

"There," she said, looking directly at her husband. "Isn't that better?"

Jecton smiled at her, nodding his approval.

Okello nodded as well but said nothing. He did not like thighs and breasts and seldom ate them. Thighs were tasteless. Breasts were dry. He crammed them down without pleasure. He was the last to finish.

After the guests left, Nora and her team of helpers cleared the tables and then brought in their own food – fresh *ugali*, but leftovers of everything else. Some rice, a few *chapatis*, some fish, some beef, some cabbage, some kale, a few chicken thighs and breasts, many chicken wings, and lots of gravy. They ate slowly and with great enjoyment. Swigging gravy directly from their plates. Nibbling delicately at the wings. Diligently using their lips and tongues to tease out the sweet, soft meat nestled in between the fine bones, laughing repeatedly about Nora's encounter with odd Okello.

3

Oak: I think it means... well... I mean... some men don't know how to eat wings, right? I mean ... it takes a lot of self-belief to eat wings when the rest of the world is saying you should be munching on thighs and drumsticks and so on ... right?

Cedar: Yeah... yeah... I think that's right. I guess it's about what happens in the world of men ... the world of inherited privilege... You may really want the wings, but then there's this little voice inside your head that has been there for as long as you can remember, telling you to keep on picking up the drumsticks and thighs. And you regret it... But then... you can't... I mean you shouldn't concentrate too much on the wings... The harder and drier parts matter, too... right?

Oak: Yeah... I suppose you have to know when to pick up the wings and when not to...

Okello: Hello. I am back.

Cedar: Hi dad. We think we figured it out, but we want your version first.

Okello: I am moving to Washington.

Oak: What? When did you decide that?

Okello: I don't know. Just now.

Cedar: Dad! What's wrong with you? We're talking about one thing and you start on something else.

Okello: It isn't something else. It's the same thing.

Oak: What does mom think of this? Does she even know?

Cedar: How is it the same thing?

Okello: No, your mother does not know yet.

Cedar: What does your coming to DC have to do with men eating wings... men not eating wings ... or whatever?

Okello: Do you ever play that harp I gave you?

Cedar: Oh dad!

Okello: Do you?

Oak: He plays it sometimes, when he's feeling really low or really good. Right, Cede?

Cedar: Yeah.

Okello: I have not played a harp for many years. There is a song I heard a while ago. I would like to play it on that harp.

Cedar: Really? How does it go?

Okello: It is complicated... it goes something like this. "*Mae ngima mane? Mae ngima manadi, yawa?*" That is the chorus. Then there is a part that goes, "*Monda, yawuota, nyiga. Puothena, utena, gíga te.*"

Oak: What does it mean?

Okello: The first part, which was a sort of chorus, means, "What is this life? What life is this?" The other part means, "My wives, my sons, my daughters. My land, my houses, my things."

Cedar: It's pretty flat, and low, too.

Okello: They sang it that way. It was deep-deep.

Oak: What's deep-deep?

Cedar: What about that thing you're doing with your voice, in the middle of each bar?

Okello: That is mine. The harp would be doing something like that, too.

Cedar: Pretty neat, dad.

Oak: When are you going to DC?

Okello: I don't know. Soon. Very soon. I think I will try to leave this weekend for Redding. And then to DC after that.

Oak: Oh God! I'd forgotten all about your job back in Redding? You're on leave, right? You have to go back, right?

Okello: I am not going back to the Department. I want to do something different. And anyway, I do not need to work.

Cedar: Oak, did you hear what I just heard? Did Mr. Work-Makes-A-Person just say what I heard him say?

Oak: Yup, I think you heard right. He has definitely lost his mind out there in Africa. He has gone totally nuts!

Okello: Heh, heh. You children are fools! Not even big fools, just little ones. Little, little fools!

Cedar: Dad?

Okello: Yes.

Cedar: Where are you going to stay when you come to DC?

Okello: I am not sure. I cannot stop thinking about that harp. I want to play it. I want to play some music. It is very odd. I need to talk to your mother.

Cedar: Please stay with me for a while when you come, dad. Please dad. I have plenty of room.

Oak: Be warned, daddy. He farts all the time. All the time. But he cooks, too. Not a bad deal overall.

Okello: That will be nice, Cedar. Very nice. Thank you.

Cedar: Alright! Then maybe you'll give me some straight answers to my questions.

Okello: Heh, heh. There are no straight answers to such questions, my son. There are no straight answers at all.

7

IT SCARED HIM

I

The marabou stork circled the huge rubbish heap twice before landing, its head and neck – which had been retracted during flight – popping up and out as its feet settled confidently on the pile. The stork was certain the heap had not been there the day before. Every day seemed to bring a new one. While the stork preferred to feed on fish and small animals, the ever-increasing mounds of carrion and refuse kept it fully satisfied.

To the stork's intense irritation, a vulture and two crows swooped in and took positions on the outer edges of the heap. But the irritation did not last for long. The three new arrivals clearly did not intend to encroach on the portion of the heap the stork had claimed for himself.

The stork settled into a relaxed foraging rhythm. Soon, its hunger wiped away by carefully selected morsels, the stork flew off toward its nest, from where it could digest the meal in peace and safety, its beady eyes watching the goings-on down below.

Blue button, then star. No. What was it? Red, then star? No! Why all these stupid buttons?! Why couldn't they just have a simple system like before?

The President stood up, rounded his desk, crossed the room in four huge strides, jerked open the door.

"Get Staff!" he barked at his startled aide-de-camp, who, as always, was standing right outside the door. "Quickly!"

He slammed the door shut, spun around, and headed toward the new painting. It was not as good as the others. He did not like the little specks of yellow and orange mixed in with the red. They spoiled it for him. What was the point of going to all that trouble if the stupid artist was going to ruin the red? The fool!

There was a sharp knock on the door. It startled him for a moment. Disoriented him. For a few seconds he did not know where he was. This had been happening a lot of late – the sudden disorientation. It was totally unpredictable. It scared him. But no one seemed to have noticed yet. He glanced down at his watch, but without his reading glasses all he saw was a blurry watch face. Irritated, but slowly regaining his bearings, he looked up at the calendar. Friday, October 13, 2000. The day before had brought another big street protest.

"Nairobi-based Kikuyus and Luos. Nothing to worry about, sir. The rest of the country is with you." So said Doc.

Maybe, mused the President, maybe. But Doc's political instincts were not always as good as his business sense. The man had taken to writing everything down – as if that would make a difference. Why leave that kind of trail behind? But that was a small problem. These protesters were more worrying. They just kept coming back.

What did they want? But even as he asked himself the question, he knew the answer. They wanted power. They wanted a new leader.

"Hah! Let them come and try this," he said out loud, "Let them come. They will see how hard it is to lead this country. Let them come and try to govern over this kind of diversity. Everybody wanting something from you. Everybody wanting you to solve their problems. Nobody you can trust. Let them come. They will see."

Another knock on the door. A little louder.

"Come in!" he called out, now fully oriented and centered.

Josiah Tiiro, State House Chief of Staff, stepped in, closed the door, and stood waiting for the signal that he could enter further. It did not come. This would be a short one.

"I want to see Security, the AG, the PC, CID, Police, and you... and Doc... at eleven-thirty tonight. Arrange it"

*   *   *

"Who is behind these marches?" the President demanded, glaring down at the six men seated around the table. "Who is paying for them? CID! You must know."

Patrick Rone, newly appointed to the Directorship of the Central Intelligence Department, was feeling extremely uncomfortable. Fifteen minutes into the meeting, the President had yet to take his seat at the table and was instead pacing around the room, round and round the table. It was Rone's first summoning to one of the President's dreaded late night security meetings. Rone's predecessor had never liked the meetings – always nervous and unsure of himself when informed that his presence would be required. Rone was beginning to see why. The seats were too low for the table, which only added to his sense of being small, inadequate, and out of his depth – sensations rendered more acute by the President's towering figure pacing around the room. Rone's assumption that he needed to convey that he was giving his full attention to the President by keeping his eyes trained on the man meant that he was constantly turning his head and torso this way and that. Now that Rone himself was the center of attention, the President came and stood directly behind him.

Rone dared not turn around, sensing that it would be better to take a moment to regain his composure. He shuffled busily through some papers he had brought with him, buying himself some time while he shaped a credible answer. He could feel the eyes of the other six seated men boring into him. None of them was going to help him. All six had been close advisors to the President for at least ten years. The Head of the Presidential Security Unit, Joshua Mutai. The Attorney General, Austin Mwapi. The Nairobi Provincial Commissioner, Suleiman Abdul. The Police Commissioner, Jonathan Muli. The State House Chief of Staff, Josiah Tiiro, who, eighteen months before, had survived an effort to have him relieved of his duties and appointed Ambassador to Australia. The State House Physician, Alfred Siromene. They all feared and hated Rone, of that he was sure. As demanded by the President, the CID made it its business to learn everything there was to learn about men like them.

There was in each of their files.

The Head of the Presidential Security Unit was fucking his personal assistant, whose wife was threatening to tell the Chief of Staff, who was a homophobe and would surely have the Head fired. The Attorney General owed Standard Chartered Bank seventy million shillings but was unable to meet the interest payments as was on the verge of having his family home seized to cover the debt. The Provincial Commissioner had tested positive for HIV/AIDS but was keeping it from his wife and family. The Police Commissioner's son had raped and impregnated a neighbor's housemaid but had soon thereafter been sent away to a boarding school in Uganda. The Chief of Staff was embezzling millions from Tana River Development Authority, which was being run from State House. Siromene had recently balked at a fifty percent increase in the price charged by Geoffrey Smalley the contract killer, who was now threatening to provide a newspaper reporter with documented evidence of Siromene's direct involvement in a number of political eliminations.

Rone knew it all. And all six of them knew that he knew. None of them was going to raise a finger to help him answer the President. Luckily, Rone did not need their help. The problem was that the President would not like the true answer.

Rone's men had been trailing the protest leaders for many months. The student leader, Okoth Omore. The lawyer, James Wanyoike. Reverend Thomas Aquinas Mbowa. Professor Gina Ngoye. PNN's entire Executive Committee. And many more. CID officers followed these people everywhere, broke into their homes, harassed their spouses, and intimidated their employees and friends. The pressure had brought many successes. Some of the activists had been bullied into silence or inactivity. But the expected collapse of the protest movement had not come. The previous week, disguised as a lame painter, Rone himself had infiltrated a secret recruiting meeting in Komarock estate. He had been stunned to find not the hordes of unkempt youth and street children among whom he had imagined he would be easily overlooked, but rather scores of well-dressed professionals from all walks of life. Each one was listening intently to the invited speaker, PNN's Secretary General, Faith Magere. Rone had felt out of place in his faded overall and grimy cap, but keeping his mouth shut, he had not attracted undue attention. The speech by Magere had been brief but sophisticated.

The political situation in Kenya has been so tense of late that many people fear the worst. At least seven demonstrators were killed last week, and almost every day brings new stories of violence and destroyed property as Government security forces clash with private citizens. These are criminal acts that must be strongly and loudly condemned.

But even at this difficult time, I find myself hopeful for the future and

*encouraged by what I see. In my opinion, the many confrontations we have
witnessed share a common root. The issue – particularly as we gear up for
the 2002 election – is whether our political system will be governed by the
tribalistic patronage of the Stork and those around him or by the voice of
the people.*

*The process of economic change currently underway in Kenya is driving
this contest. With rapid and complex developments in technology and in
the larger society, Kenya is one of the countries at the crest of the wave of
economic liberalization sweeping the globe. We are at the heart of it all –
right at the center of the world. Some Kenyans view these facts and these
changes optimistically, confident that they will bring wealth to all and
allow us to fulfill our democratic ambitions. Others are less sure, and fear
losing their own liberties in a world overshadowed by distant institutions
and economic powers. But all Kenyans are acutely aware that the Government can lend a decisive hand to the forces of change.*

*Economic liberalization is clearly generating new wealth. But in
Kenya's tribalistic top-heavy system, this new wealth is not shared by all
citizens. Those whose hands were already on the levers of power are acutely
aware that the Government can influence who benefits from new economic
opportunities. They are loath to relinquish their privileged positions.*

*The Stork's Government thus is an engine of tribe-based domination
instead of an agent of popular will. The Stork's Government is more interested in maintaining old forms of influence and patronage for a minority
than in expanding opportunity for the majority. This, I believe, is the root
of our current troubles.*

*The more I think about all this, the more people I speak with, the more
convinced I am that there exists in Kenya today a grand coalition of voters
who have more to gain from equality than from tribalism and Presidential
favor. And this is the core issue.*

*If the 2002 election is free and fair, it will be a referendum on liberty
versus power. It will be a referendum on the character of our future. That is
precisely what the Stork's Government fears most. That is the reason why*

the Stork's Government has long refused to discuss changing our Constitution to give opposition groups a fair chance of capturing the Presidency and the Legislature.

For those of us in the Opposition, the crux of the problem is that no single party is strong enough to win a general election on its own. A coalition of parties could prevail, but the Constitution will not allow a coalition Government. We need to find a solution to that. And we will. Given the Government's fierce and deadly grip on power, the battle might appear to be lost. But I see a glimmer of hope in Kenyan history – in our long struggle for political independence from Britain. A key legacy of this struggle is the understanding that political engagement is a right of all citizens and an appropriate response to community and national crisis.

Try as it might, the Government just cannot beat down this spirit. Paradoxically, the Stork has helped sustain that spirit over the years by frequently appealing to our nationalist ideals to score political points, especially against foreigners. This spirit underlies the good leadership being shown by so many of our colleagues who have repeatedly risked their lives by agitating for change. More important, this spirit underlies the determination of ordinary Kenyans to choose liberty over tribalistic patronage.

I believe the Stork is scared. I am confident that liberty and reason will prevail over tribalistic raw power. Our collective memory says this is inevitable. That is why I believe that the Kenya our children and grandchildren inherit will not only be a peaceful Kenya, but also a Kenya in which their life-chances will have more to do with their own personalities and their parents' investments in them than with somebody else's tribe-based access to, and abuse of, power.

"We are in trouble," Rone said to his deputy the next day. "Democratic principles are taking hold everywhere. People are tired."

But how could he possibly say that now?

Rone looked up briefly from his papers. His eyes fell on Siromene who, as always, was watching the President, who had moved from behind Rone and was now standing behind the Attorney General, who was studiously picking his nose, rolling up the snot between his thumb and forefinger, and flicking it away. Pick, roll, flick. Pick, roll, flick. Disgusting, thought Rone. But nobody else seemed to be bothered by it.

"Sir," said Rone, beginning his answer to the President's question. "We believe it is the Germans. They are doing it through the Gunter Clausen Foundation – that NGO with offices in Westlands. We must lodge a formal complaint with the German Embassy and deport the Foundation's Country Representative. We must also freeze the Foundation's bank account. That will help for some time. But our guess is that other donors will fill the gap. We must hit the protesters and their leaders harder. They must not be allowed to regroup. We must crush them. The general election is less than two years away."

8

BOY-CHILD

The harpist was euphoric, as were the drummer and metal percussionist. They had just given their best-ever performance.

It was early morning. Their work had begun the evening before at the homestead from which they were preparing to depart. The previous year, their host, the headmaster of Uhanga Primary and Secondary Schools had married a second wife, who had recently given birth to a son. The party was therefore partly to celebrate the new arrival. But more than that, it was to project the headmaster as a man worthy of support in his bid to be named the area Chief.

At first, there had been no energy in the celebrations. The headmaster and his plump second wife had placed themselves under the front awning of his hut. The baby was lying in his mother's lap. There were plenty of guests. But like their hosts, the guests looked bored and sleepy.

The headmaster's lean first wife was busy organizing food and shepherding arriving guests toward her husband, co-wife, and stepchild. She performed these duties happily. The homestead was more hers than anyone else's. She was secure. She had few worries. Her four children were all in school but still available to help with her crops and livestock. She and her children had plenty of milk to drink. This new woman would occupy the man and keep him from intruding into the life she had been building for herself. She often needed sex. More than that, she needed to be held. The former she got easily, from young unattached men. The latter was harder to come by. She was still soft and alive on the inside, but a bit too thin and hard on the outside for anyone to want to hold for more than the short time it usually took to satisfy her temporarily. There was little she could do about that, so she gave it little thought. What she missed most were the conversations she and her husband used to have... before the other woman came. That gap was harder to fill. The only other man with a mind like that was his father. So quick. So attentive to detail. But he was gone now. There was little she could do about this either. But it gnawed at her. She really missed the conversations. She, too, sensed the lack of spark in the evening.

The trio of musicians began the evening's entertainment with a popular dance tune, which none of them liked too much. It was too simple. Three of the guests got up to dance but they were clearly just going through the motions. The harpist stood up, leaving his colleagues playing but still seated behind him. He began to walk around the circle of guests, inviting more of them to join the three dancers. A few complied. He stopped in front of the host and his wife and incorporated two praise-filled verses into the song. They smiled and clapped stiffly, remaining seated. He was on the verge of moving on when he noticed an odd movement of the baby's hand. He stopped and watched it more closely. There was no mistaking it. The baby was keeping time to the music with its hand, flapping it back and forth, almost imperceptibly. It was following an odd rhythm. It did not seem to be based on the drumbeat, as would have been normal. Rather, it seemed to be following the harp. But then not quite. It was just off-beat there as well, focused on some point in the middle of the outward stroke. The harpist changed the pace of his strokes, drawing them out. Within half a stroke, the tiny hand flap was back with him. The harpist wished he could see the child's face, but a blanket covered it.

The drummer and metal percussionist had been with the harpist for two years. They had joined him because of his reputation as an innovative composer. But in that time, he had not produced a single new tune, seeming to be content with small adjustments to old ones. Now as they listened to the odd rhythms coming from the old harp, they knew that their wait was over. Carrying all three stools, the two men crossed the circle and joined their leader.

The harpist sat down on his stool and instructed his colleagues to follow his cue. For a long while, he experimented with different ways to best catch the rhythm being set by the baby's flapping hand. Speeding up his strokes, slowing them down, always watching the flaps. He knew he was close. But it remained just beyond reach.

The drummer could also play the harp. He saw that the harpist was close to finding the rhythm but looking in the wrong place. The drummer hesitated. The harpist did not normally welcome technical suggestions from his colleagues. The drummer feared a reprimand. But this was too important. He would risk it.

"Try two strokes in one," suggested the drummer quietly.

The harpist saw it right away, but still not all of it. He still needed some help. He nodded encouragingly at the drummer and handed over the harp, taking up the drum himself.

It had to be on the outward stroke. Begin gently, pause slightly, then finish hard. A normal inward stroke. Gently out, pause, finish hard, back in normally. Gently, pause, hard, normally.

The drummer handed back the harp and retrieved his drum. The harpist smiled gratefully. That was it.

The three musicians began to stare intently into each other's eyes, searching the space between them for the best combination of the three instruments. The pause and the end of the normal in-stroke were the ideal boundaries of the most effective drumbeat. The best metallic riff was a slow but delicate one centered on the hard segment of the out-stroke. They were concentrating so intensely that they did not immediately notice that everyone was up and dancing.

It was an overwhelming sound. They played through the night, composing one new song after another, pausing only once to eat and relieve their bladders.

The morning light found the three musicians at a loss. They had discovered music that they knew would make them famous. Their consciences would not allow them to depart without acknowledging the source of their inspiration. They wanted to leave some kind of compensation.

But the source of their inspiration was a child. An infant. Nobody would believe them. Their hosts would almost surely accuse them of trying to bewitch the child.

The harpist sensed that the child might one day be a great musician. He could think of no more appropriate gift than his own harp.

"But we will need it," protested the drummer.

"I will find another one," replied the harpist, growing surer of the correctness of his decision with each passing moment.

Their hosts had gone to sleep right before dawn. They would probably wake up after many hours. The musicians could not wait for that long. Their next engagement was two days' walk away. They needed to leave. They asked that the headmaster be awoken. He emerged groggy and sour-tempered.

"What do you want? I paid you all your money," the headmaster snapped at them.

"Yes, that is correct," replied the harpist, realizing that he would have to be careful. His group traveled widely and met all kinds of people. He had seen this kind of person many times. This kind of man – one who had tasted the white man's life – this kind of man often shunned the old ways, and sometimes did not know how to accept a gift. He would have to praise him first.

"It was a great honor to play in this your home yesterday. It is not often that we are able to play for a man the people are saying will be the next Chief."

The headmaster's face softened. He wanted very badly to be named Chief.

"We thank you for allowing us to play for your new wife and new son. To show our appreciation to you and your wife, and as a symbol of our best wishes for your beautiful son, we would like to present you with this harp. We hope that it will serve as a small reminder of an enjoyable celebration. We also hope that the boy-child will one day find enjoyment from playing it."

The headmaster eyed the harp and bow with inner distaste but outward neutrality. Music was the last occupation he would encourage any of his sons to enter. They were going to be scientists, teachers, businessmen, lawyers, politicians. Responsible, God-fearing men. Leaders in the community. That was why he had returned to start the school – his own school, for his own children and grandchildren.

The harpist was right to wonder if the headmaster would value the gift. But he was wrong to imagine that the man might reject it. While the headmaster aspired to a white man's future for his children, he himself had been born and raised a Luo, and he had chosen to live a Luo life. That origin, breeding, and long trail of decisions would not allow him to turn away a gift of any sort, nor would it let him dishonor the wishes of the grantor.

"Thank you, brother, thank you very much. God bless you. My son will play this instrument."

Acknowledgements

Several friends and colleagues helped me bring the first edition of this book to completion. I remain deeply grateful to each of them: Gem Argwings-Kodhek, Geoffrey Orwenyo, Jeremy Byemanzi, John Lynam, Jolly Basemera, Maria Mulindi, Naome Nampumuza, Nate Holt, Nicodemus Musinguzi, Paul Sserumaga, Richard Oyare, Sarah Nalubwama. For both the first edition and this second one, my wife, Cheryl Richardson, was by my side – listening, challenging, constantly encouraging. Without her and our three children, Theo Opata, Elan Ndenga, and Clara Agono, neither book would have been written. They have my undying love and gratitude. A special thanks goes to Clara Agono for the cover design and internal illustrations. My late father, William Odongo Omamo, loved the first edition. Sadly, he did not live to see this second one. He might have liked it as well. His model of manhood still looms large in my mind as a guiding light. My 92-year-old mother, Joyce Achola Omamo, constantly urges me to write (and live) with purpose and integrity. I hope this book lives up to that standard. Both she and my late father will never stop inspiring me.

Printed in the USA
CPSIA information can be obtained
at www.ICGtesting.com
LVHW071317011023
759824LV00004B/20